# ANGEL
# DANCE

## *A Classic Lesbian Thriller*

## by M.F. Beal

The Crossing Press
Freedom, California 95019

**Library of Congress Cataloging-in-Publication Data**

Beal, M. F.  (Mary F.) , 1937–
    Angel dance : a thriller / by M.F. Beal. --1st ed.
      p.  cm.
    ISBN 0-89594-417-0
    I. Title.
PS3552.E134A82  1990
813' .54--dc20                             90-40974
                                                CIP

The drug program was part of a much larger CIA program to study possible means for controlling human behavior. Other studies explored the effects of radiation, electro-shock, psychology, psychiatry, sociology and harassment substances.

—NELSON A. ROCKEFELLER, Chairman
Commission on CIA Activities
Within the United States.
*June 1974*

There are (according to the medievals) nine orders of angels, each order has 6666 legions, and each legion 6666 individuals (which makes 399,920,004 angels). Of these, according to Revelations, Satan drew one-third with him (133,306,668); but some doctors hold that those which fell amounted only to the number of one order (44,435,566).—Pelbartus de Temesvar (c. 1490), Aureum Rosarium, s.v. 'Daemones', ii, §18 (fol. 120). [Lea, Materials, i, 73.] But there are disagreements: thus Alphonso de Spina, Fortalicium Fidei, 1. v, fol. 274a, argues that the nine orders of angels amount to 19,998 legions; the number of demons in 133 'computa' and 306,668 demons (accding to dist. XIV, cap. ii).

But the common opinion of the doctors is that as many fell as would constitute an order, and commonly the number of fallen angels is given as 6666 legions, for there are as many legions in each order as there are individuals in each legion. Therefore the true sum of the fallen demons is 44 computa and 435,556 demons.—[cf. Lea, op. cit., I, 99.] Lea cannot find in Ducange an explanation of 'computa' but for reasons I find mysterious argues it's 1 million. 'The only conclusion to be drawn from all this is that the number of demons is 44,435,556. It is impossible however to reconcile the two statements.' Ib. 99-100.

—C. WAYNE COLVER

# 1

The first time I saw Angel Stone in the flesh was at George's Downstairs and she had her fist cocked with determined inefficient aim at the chin of a man I dimly recalled from . . . ? As I watched, she thrust out and up in a slow punch which softened, reaching, and I remember thinking: it's hard to hit a man the first time. Then blood pattered, the man lurched back—I recognized him as Michael Tarleton, Angel's sometime husband— and George moved his Kojak face between, hissing, *Easy now, easy* . . . A pair of panting animals, drunk most likely, weaving like circus bears under the gray outwash of two elderly light fixtures.

A fight between wife and husband—not something you even think about these days, especially at George's, where drinking is the only recreation in the big low-ceil- inged room under a Bleecker Street boutique. There were once a couple of tables and because of that people came to shoot pool and drink beer, even some of the Charlton Street folk who were running through their first successes. George read *The Village Voice* and con- gratulated them when their letter, column, book, con- tract, came to public note: "Just remember I knew you when." As the place became popular, people came to stand and drink hard, watching the pool players. Final-

3

ly they only watched each other so George took out the games: he knew what the customers wanted. Pretty soon his Downstairs was a safe place to fight a little for people suffering their first failure at success; George ran a few tabs. So you could go any Friday or Saturday and watch heterosexuals work out; a good family man, George discouraged gays.

This was a Thursday in May: Angel's book had been out just over six months. The split between her and Tarleton was rumored for March, although it wasn't until April that she threw a shoe at a nosy photographer and our mutual friend Lenore called me at the newspaper to arrange our meeting at George's. Then the mutual's reneg this afternoon:

"Kat, something's come up, I can't make it."

"What's going on, Lenore?"

"We've got a witness on a police brutality case; I just can't let it go by. But Angel knows you're looking for work. She'll be there at ten."

Now the clock over the cherrywood bar said ten two. George's bullchest bent towards Angel's ear and he said something I couldn't hear, teeth pulled long and yellow between ridged lips as I reached Angel, placed my hand on her arm. Tarleton's body bowed away from the drip of blood; a red-haired woman held a wad of tissue while Angel's eyes were rimmed white and she stared like I was holding a knife at her throat. "Kat," I said. "Katerina Guerrera. Lenore told you." George shrugged back to the bar, watching, hands on hips, as we walked away my arm under hers, elbow bent, her knees jello every third or fourth step until outside, when I let her sink onto the worn marble stair while I tried to sort out just what was going on.

The night stretched stars like Woolworth engagement

sets between shades-drawn parlors of electricians, hoods, college professors; and the dark windows of the meat market across the street were phallic with sausages and provelones. This was the first time I ever had reason to be suspicious of mutual friend Lenore, although I had known she was burning out when she insisted we confer while leafletting: "It's more important than anything we could say to each other," were her words.

Then when she spent four thousand of her committee's winter budget on publicity for a relatively low profile college tour (billing a victim of CIA-financed torture) and nearly five hundred on longdistance promotion . . . well, it was one of those cries for help, as they say. On the other hand—maybe with this other thing, this Angel Stone, she acted correctly, knowing herself close to the edge, knowing she must pass Angel on or be dragged closer . . . dealing with Ms. Stone you had to say to yourself at some point, "¡Cuidado! This is a very famous person."

Angel's eyes watched. "I can go now, if you give me a . . . hand," she said, so I steered her toward the corner taxi stand, sensing she was trying; she'd squared her shoulders and though her knees went now and then, she was breathing deep, working. In the cab she caught my eyes again. "This is a hell of a job interview, isn't it." She giggled and gave an East Village address. "My apartment. If you'll come up."

I nodded. Her face was puffy, not at all the sleekjawed cameo of the dust jacket hiding *Moonrape*'s indigo buckram. Her eyes held well and she seemed out of the shock of the fight, but the classic bow of lips through which white scar ridged turned soft and indefinite, some fear leaking upward from her lungs.

"What did George say to you?"

She shook her head, scattering fine colorless hair, then lolled back on the seat top. At first I thought her resting, then realized she had passed out.

I stayed in her two-and-a-half over a bialy factory until she went to sleep in a rec equipment goosedown ripstopnylon sleeping bag behind boxes of books and manuscript stacked three high, contents noted: ANGOR WAT—SUTTEE; MOONGODDESS; FEM. ICONOGRAPHY. That surprised me a little; I mean I never really thought about *Moonrape* as such a *researched* book, (*off our backs* said simply, "Read this book . . . "). The *Times* review conceded "sound political anthropology . . . a reasoned argument . . . " which was enough to earn *it* an editorial in *Plexus*: "Feminism Co-opted?" Everyone had opinions about *Moonrape*; it was easy to forget what a big change it made.

She explained why everything was boxed. "I just moved, had to have a new place . . . The reason I asked Lenore if we knew anyone is I've gotten threatening letters . . . " So she tried to find them, moving stacks of magazines, papers, manuscripts, letters, notes. Later she began to cry spontaneously, as if a particularly painful thought had pricked. She was lyric with drink and also sodden, begging once for some of the Scotch under the sink then asking why she wanted . . . A million thoughts swirled my stomach on edge; burned out—yes that was me. The day-by-day of working on a four-sheet community weekly: I had once too often lifted the phone to wheedle cajole threaten an edition onto the streets Friday at five p.m. to catch the energy of the work-weekend. And why? When you were successful in reporting the news, it drew the Feds fast as meat brings flies. Wasn't even what I trained for . . . So what *had* I trained for? . . . When gentle snores from behind walls of boxes announced the "controversial feminist academic" had acheived delta sleep, it was almost three forty-five and I flipped a coin to see whether I should speed through a second straight day or catch the subway uptown to my birthplace, Seventieth and Amsterdam.

I was born Maria Katerina Lorca Guerrera Alcazar, of Cuban-born Cecilia—the daughter of a physician who believed women should be taught to read, who was as a result a primary grades teacher when it became necessary for her to emigrate to New York, where she met Homer, a Spanish refugee of '38, who was a first-year student during that war. He is an automobile mechanic now and my mother works for the city as a teacher's aide on a Head Start program. I'm twenty-nine years old.

After public school I was selected by examination to Performing Arts in the field of dance. Later, I received a New York State Regent's scholarship and an NDEA loan to attend CCNY, where I majored in physical education, minored in theater. My sports are archery/tennis. After graduation, I joined a newly-organized street theater group working a summer parks project. That winter I got a job in my father's shop and earned $6.80 an hour as an apprentice mechanic, while our group submitted a proposal to eighteen foundations on *Community Dialogue.* We got nine-five from National Endowment, bought a bus my father and I put into traveling condition, and went on the road. But we just couldn't make it pay. We campused and no one would sponsor us so we had to play a part of campus we could split from fast, which meant no props. One of our best bits was Indian Clubs, but we lost so many we had some heavy discussions why the students, sleek in middle-class teeth, weren't supporting us, since they obviously loved us—and decided we were not giving them something they valued. So a few of us split off to teach Chinese style boxing. In four years we lived in seven U.S. cities, each time hoping to stay long enough to see some of our students installed in a storefront dozo, discovering people were willing to pay enough for us to live on to learn the art of unarmed self-defense. There were, of course, the moments when *revolution* and *criminal* got pretty close, once spiderwebbing violent at a shopping-center Bank of America. No injuries, but no surprise when four of us got pulled on weapons charges. The weapons were a crossbow, two hunting bows—fifty pound pull—half a dozen twelve-dollar throwing knives, and an M-1 with the sear pin filed. The government had us cold-cocked; nobody had relatives who could afford the Supreme Court and the community was starving, shooting up in doorways, making more babies, boozing burglarizing serving in Vietnam. Two of our people got five to eight; one was killed in a prison riot that never even made network news; some of the rest tried Venceremos. Everybody knew nobody knew what they were doing or why, but you found something and did it; that was the price of survival. We watched Freddie Prinz on the tv and called him The Hungarian, and when we found a war chant, we sang it.

> Los bottaron
> De Vietnam
> Los tenemos
> Ahora en Cuba
> Dales, Cuba
> Dales duro

Panama
Dales duro
Venezuela
Dales duro
Puerto Rico
Dales duro

Slowly, we became impatient with the male left "who will sup even with the devil to gain their ends." Right now there was no doubt in my mind: *Angel Stone had written a powerful book about women,* would most likely do ten times the good for the world I ever did. But looking over the shoulder of a dozen or so of her pages was an older mentality, a glance backward at the middle class which authored her, whose initials were W.A.S.P. Thus, if I took her offer of a job I'd be announcing retirement from fifty years of Guerrera Alcazar commitments just as the family had again succeeded in educating one of its members. If you laugh I will kill you; the old man didn't quit till he was half-dead of high blood pressure and drinking coffee and declaiming in front of the Guernica in the front room, listing the day's totalitarianisms: the man who has spoken to him as if he is a halfwit, the shoddy cars he has put back together once again, the Government. My mother is still fighting.

When I let myself in, the clock by my bed announced five thirty-seven. I set the alarm for nine: if I got up then I could do what I had to do so the paper would come out Saturday morning at the latest. I forgot about Angel Stone and fell to dreaming of horses' bulging nostrils and dismembered bulls and naked lightbulbs.

I did not waken fully until the second ring of the doorbell, which told me I was alone in the flat. The clock said eight fifty-eight, as I looked it clicked and began to shrill and the doorbell stopped. I reached without thinking, shut the alarm, then realized what I had done. So I got up and put on a bathrobe and went to answer the door.

There were two of them. One was a tall skinny anglo dressed sportinggoods salesman-style, the other thirtyish, Puerto Rican, looking like he had the sunny side of a duplex in New Jersey. He was the one who knew who I was and introduced himself as Manteca while his friend played Ignatz. They showed me the photographs and I said I never knew Rudd had a sister named Nancy and they asked did I know any of the people and I said no. I recognized two. We were standing in the hall and it was time for good housewives to take the laundry down but no one would look into my eyes and I began to get angry. To Manteca I said in our mutual tongue *What a shame in a great country like this there are no decent jobs available and you have to do this to support your family.* First he looked uncomfortable and then he looked ugly. The anglo's face changed and I realized he understood what I said. They went away, leaving a calling card with the toll-free phone of their office in raised letters. I went back to bed.

Sleeping, I dreamed. Manteca goes home, angry because I haven't accepted his offer of two-fifty a month to keep an eye on Angel Stone and when he gives his wife a love-pat on the ass she, who has had trouble all day with the youngest child (who is just like his father), she turns and tells him, an FBI agent, to go find something else to do if he doesn't have anything better. He hits her on the jaw. She turns into a mountain lion and sinks her teeth into his shoulder. The door opens, anglo arrives as Gary Cooper and rolls a cigarette in one hand while he gestures with the other and makes a speech: "Women used to wear aprons. They used to be soft and warm. That's the trouble with the country, y'know." A huge tear slides down his nose.

A little before five, a call from the office: Liz asking for a six p.m. meeting.

"Oh, yeah? What's up?"

"You're on the agenda."

I thought okay, culture vs. politics, and when the receiver began to buzz realized I hadn't hung it up. I took a shower. I went into the kitchen and said hello to my mother—coming in with a sack of groceries. She said, Hunh, she could see I was going out, did I plan to be back in time for dinner? "I've got a meeting at six, then I have to see about a job." She gave me her most skeptical look, meaning: *what kind of job are you going to get from an evening interview?* and then: "There are no other jobs available?" "This woman works during the day, Mama. A teacher." She let go. I took the subway downtown and was only five minutes late for the meeting.

Ellie was cleaning the layout table but everybody else was crumpled into chairs except Val, who was filing. We all nodded or said hi but nobody overdid it and the room was very quiet when I sat down on the edge of my desk. I felt dry and numb and nothing mattered. Jeanette said a man had been waiting when she got home to her apartment the night before, the boyfriend of a former roommate, that she agreed to go and have a cup of coffee with him and it wasn't until he started asking a lot of questions that she got suspicious and asked him what he was doing these days and he said he was working for the Justice Department. Dorothy said she thought part of the ethics of group self-defense was *not* to take risks for other people and *not* to advocate anything you would not do yourself.

"I had a visit this morning: two Feds."

Val let the file drawer click. "I think we should move our subscription list."

Ellie continued to wipe the layout board. "Maybe they're just checking to see if we over-react. They're fishing, they're trying to suck off our energy."

"You don't think we should pull the list?"

"I think we should use the least amount of energy necessary to deal with these creeps."

"Well, I think I'd feel better if I talked with our attorney." Jeanette bit her lip and a pearl of blood appeared. "I mean, this guy came on like a friend. Are they allowed to do that?"

"At least with male agents you have a start. It's women agents I worry about. At this point we understand not all women are our sisters."

"Potential sisters, however."

"Yes."

It went like that for about fifteen minutes and they decided to talk to the attorney, tighten up, and get paranoid. That brought us to item two, which was me.

Val: "Some time ago you mentioned you were wanted on a felony warrant in Illinois. That still the straight goods?"

Kat: "Yes. Statute of limitation for the state is five years on that charge. Or, this Thanksgiving. I'll have something to celebrate."

Dorothy: "I think they would like to use that as a pretext to bust us, Kat."

Kat: "I agree."

Val: "I have to criticize myself for enjoying your out-front political style. I pushed you to be macho because it made me feel safe. I could privately agree with you while you were in the line position without danger to myself."

And so on. I remember saying something like "Look, you don't have to apologize to or for me. My own criticism is I've been bringing my anger into this program. Please—you're fine, we are all fine. Let me take three months. Meanwhile I'll clear out my desk, should have done it months ago."

A melting moment when everybody tried to look everybody else in the eye and found they could. Then we went down to the White Rose on the corner and stood at the bar with the old Irish bucket-men and the younger Puerto Rican pimps and had a beer while we tried to get into a conversation with one of the prostitutes. She almost went for it but her pimp got restive and hustled her out on the street even though she bitched it was too early. But she left laughing: "I need to join the union!"

Then I called Angel Stone. Pa Bell's *disconnect* tape: she had moved again. I rode uptown to make sure and the door opened not to boxes and books but to plastic blowup furniture and tape deck. The new tenant whom the doorplate announced as I. G. Farb invited me in to talk, but I could see what he needed was a nice singles' bar. I told him maybe later and split.

Monday I was first at the office to pack up. A reporter called to say he was doing a piece on the demise of the revolution, did I have a comment? I thanked him for the publicity, hung up. Then I sat down at the old office upright and began to put together a resume. I was wondering whether or not to tell the truth when there was a knock. I shouted "Come in" and looked up to find Michael Tarleton, sobered, chagrined, peering apologetically around my door. Maybe it was the black beret he wore on his shortish reddish afro making him act a little incongruous; anyway he stared with almost hooded brown irises dilating to take in the paraphernalia of a women's press: walls papered with slogans and exhortations by females he'd probably never heard of. As he saw me his hand moved toward his nose, and he smiled.

I smiled back. "Looks okay to me. Could have sworn she broke it, though."

He shifted a pile of back issues from a chair and sat. "Not quite. But my assailant has bruised the hell out of it. Couldn't breathe without catching flies for three days." He smiled again. His teeth looked like he'd just come from the dentist and he was wearing a French pullover of sky blue. "So I was lucky, you see . . . once again." He lit up a Marlboro and I lit a Kool and I liked him. I guess I liked him as much as I could like anyone of a different sex, race, and class. He said, "You probably wonder why I'm here."

I was waiting; I already had three theories. One, he didn't know where Angel was and thought I did; two, he knew where she was and wanted to know whether I did; three, he wanted me to find her because he knew neither of us did. So while I waited for him to offer me a rental car plus expenses to serve notice of divorce proceedings, I wouldn't have been surprised if he had put on the make. Instead, he took a long drag from his cigarette and began to tell me the story of his life.

"I met her right after finishing my first documentary. Someone told me she'd done a piece on Asian antiquities which related to the cults of the Great Mother, and it fit in with something I was trying to put together on the Daughters of the American Revolution—God, this was years ago, we were doing that kind of thing then. Well, as it turned out she didn't have much I could use, but she is beautiful, as you know, and this was even before her face was scarred. . . . The upshot is we fell in love and began living together, even though she was twelve years younger. I knew there would be problems, I expected them. I wanted so badly for her to be happy . . ."

He shut his eyes. "I even knew she . . . had other lovers from time to time. I overlooked it. She was a second chance for me. I blew it, I lost my first family and I wanted it to be right this time."

"But it wasn't this time either."

His eyes flashed at me. "I love her still. I'm worried about her. She's moved again; she's alone and she must be frightened. We agreed to separate for a year, to try it out, but this book of hers is generating more comment than I thought. She's gotten threats but we both know there are a million cranks for every genuine psycho so we . . . she has tried to remain cool. At least till that night you saw us at George's."

"I heard you split two, three months ago."

He gave me a steady look. His eyebrows had long dark curling hairs which lifted above their line toward the amber of his temples where a small pulse beat. "All right. Yes. We stopped living together in March. But we'd been seeing each other regularly until Thursday. Then you and she left the bar together, and when I tried to reach her last night she was gone."

I could hear myself sigh. "How did you know where to find me?"

"Heard you introduce yourself. You're well enough known this end of town."

I wondered—by who else besides the Feds. Had Angel herself turned him on to me? "All right. What can I do for you?"

"Whatever Angel wants, and one thing for me. I'll pay your salary."

"The kind of job she wants me to do pays one seventy-five per diem on the open market, did you know that?"

He flushed, then smiled again. "You haven't even asked what *I* want."

"And what's that?"

"I want you to find out about Rachel Stone. I might see my way clear to a thousand a month on a three month basis."

"Her mother?"

"Her grandmother."

It seemed crazy. "I'll think it over and give you a call." He told me his number and I wrote it on the back of the card my buttery friend had given me earlier.

It was one of those afternoons in May when you realize suddenly what's ahead: the humidity a noiseless jackhammer in your sinuses. Not that it was quiet. There was a picket line down the block. The trucks that get bigger and longer every year moved through streets which get smaller to warehouses more scarred pitted defaced where blackmen still unload and whitemen check bills of lading. There were overflowing garbage cans and rivulets of oily water. Once this was the city to me: the stench not only of commerce but of cultural exchange itself: the odor of one nation mingling with others, all held suspended in the choke and burn of the American machine . . . and it was to be mine, for I was a born American. So what else is new? And the collective energy, the pulsings in and out of the breath of millions together, working, killing each other, making money and love—I was a part of that, too; I was larger because of it, bigger than just Maria Katerina Guerrera . . . And now what? If I was lucky I might get a second-hand car out, a chance for two or three weeks on the road before I looked for the job which would take me to Spain as a tourist. Or this thing, terrifically peculiar, in which (according to Tarleton) I worked for Angel Stone as a secretary/companion or (according to Angel Stone) I worked with her as a bodyguard. In a curious way I felt I understood her better than he, but then I had to admit I'd spent only those four or five hours with her. He hinted she was breaking down which was certainly evident; question: how far down might she have to go? Had she bottomed somewhere in danger, or found friendly sanctuary? In general I was suspicious of any relationship in which one person explained the other to a third party, hinting secrets. It seemed like a good idea to find Lenore, ask a few questions, so I angled south toward Christopher Street.

There was a note at the door: *Leafletting Wash. Park Back at five.* My watch said a little after three. There was one other place I might go: the apartment to which I'd taken Angel Stone that night only a week before. Did I. G. Farb have a nine to five? There didn't seem to be any good reason to get inside except to ask how he'd heard about the vacancy. Or I could walk over to the park and try for a phone number from Lenore. I went back down the tiled stairs. One of the downstairs tenants was playing a Satie piano piece and its craziness pursued me south.

My feet always hurt when I walk in the Village; I think it's a psychological thing. It's always been a magic place to me. No, that's not the word: fantasy comes closer, and not always happy illusion. I started coming down with my girlfriends when I was at Performing Arts; it's what we all did on the weekends. You could get somebody to take you to a party or a bar and if you stayed together with your girlfriend you could both split when you didn't like it anymore. The guys understood, it was no hard feelings anywhere. We used to go down and find a party with drugs and load up and split and wander around until dawn and pick up somebody for breakfast and with the last of the high sail home around noon and sleep until Sunday dinner. I always said I spent the night at her house and she said the same. As long as I did okay in school my parents didn't care what else. How could we explain we spent the whole night looking into store windows at the beautiful and strange and ugly things people made and sold on Eighth? Or that we waited out front of a certain bar on Hudson where the folksingers drank, hoping to slip by the Irish bartender to the back room where maybe Dylan . . . Or describe how when the crowds began to thin between one and two we watched for prowl cars then slid up alleyways climbing fences taking possession of parks with the others like us all olive-skinned and young?

At the park, Lenore is leafletting with a woman named Cathy who teaches at a freeschool. Lenore is one of those who leads passers-by with a question: "Did you know the U.S. government has financed a hundred wars since 1945?" I smiled. "Yes." She looked up talking. "You can read about it . . . oh. Hello, Kat." I took the throwaway. "I want to talk to you, Lenore." She had half turned; now she stopped. "Sure. Here, take some leaflets." "No, I have to speak to you somewhere quiet." I caught Cathy's eye and she began to drift in amidst smiles and leaflets given to a man and a youth. "Hand your stack to Cathy, Lenore."

She obeyed, eyes flat, *the burned-out look.* Then why was she still doing it? I felt a deep pang at the front of my skull—something to understand. I took her arm and led her to a bench out of the stream of foot traffic. There was a murk of sun soaking the spot we sat in, and the trash can was too near and full for the heat. Flies rattled the air. It was hard to breathe. I had a monstrous uneasiness about Lenore; the thought of dissecting it terrified me, but any more of the past week's paranoia and I might wake to find I'd scared myself to death. I told her briefly about my recent visitors. She said only two things: "Slugslime. Did you tell them anything?" "No." "Well, if they come around again, get a lawyer." Then I said Tarleton had come by that morning. She began to question more closely; I recalled as well as I could. "Look," I said. "I'm getting pretty far into this thing without knowing much and disappearing acts creep me out. What's going on?" She shifted her head away, and I got a chance to watch seventeen pigeons fight over a hotdog roll. They left four feathers and half a dozen watery turds.

"I think you're right, Kat. I don't really want to know any more than I have to about it, so I guess I've been assuming you'd feel the same way. Ask me some questions. If I know the answers I'll tell you."

"Do you know where Angel is?"

"No. But I haven't really tried to get ahold of her. I've been leafletting—I get home so tired at night I just fall into bed. Know what I mean?"

I nodded. "Know why she left her apartment?"

She turned away again. There was a child to watch

now. He felt with his fingers on the underside of the bench across from us until they found something which he pried loose, inspected, and put into his mouth. He was chewing as he skipped away.

"It's complicated. There are two things operating. First of all there's the matter of the visitors—a lot of that going on lately. The word gets around; nobody ever wants to get that interesting—the idea is low-profile. I know it would freak Angel to hear you got pulled out of bed for a talk the morning after meeting her. The problem is you never know whether or not it's a coincidence. She had her first visit the night of the West Coast conference where the lesbians doing security allegedly beat up the man they found in the hall during the caucus. They got two of the women on felony assault; the trials are still pending and the women can't leave the state—it's real chickenshit. Then Tarleton calls her Friday morning and insinuates if she doesn't get in touch he's thinking of filing assault charges, and of course he knows about the other because it happened while they were still living together. Something has made him mad . . . or scared."

"So you figure she's just found a hidey-hole? But she has to come out sooner or later."

"Well, maybe not. She's been offered a job, you know. In California."

I added the number Lenore gave me to the others on the card, with a question mark. There was room for one more. That little card was getting informative; I slid it in my pants pocket, where I couldn't be searched except by a matron. Then I headed uptown on the Sixth Avenue bus. My feet were killing me, but there was something I kept remembering about Angel's apartment over the bialy factory, something I'd noticed but not remembered. I didn't make it past the freshly baked bialies with their intoxicating onion garnish until I'd eaten a couple, though, and just as well because a full stomach lifts the burden from the back and sends strength through the legs. What I'd forgotten was the new tenant's name, I. G. Farb. Was it possible? At the corner Garcia&Vega I searched the phonebook and found: Farb, I. G. 479 W. 88 496-7633. I decided to take the subway.

Angel herself answered the door. She didn't seem surprised. She had glasses on, her hair was twisted into a loose knot with a pencil poked through to hold it and her jeans were embroidered with spiny cactus blooming hot pink. Had she heard from Lenore? I thrust the bottle of champagne I'd bought at the corner into her hands.

"What's this?"

"To celebrate finding you."

She flushed and backed. I entered. I. G. Farb hadn't left much: a pretty but very worn Persian carpet, a couple of bowls of dried arrangements in the corners, some pillows to sit on. Angel had added a lot more: the cartons of manuscripts, all labeled by the same hand: FERTILITY G., RAPE & INCEST, MARY CULT. There was a gooseneck lamp from Woolworth's pooling light on an Olympia portable. She sank down on the cushion beside it, stuck a pile of clean sheets in under the carriage. "I'm sorry you had a hard time finding me." We shared the champagne.

It seemed to me she had decided to level. I was slappy with paranoia, my perceptions swinging so far at each new tidbit of information I had to struggle to watch the way her face worked around questions we put to each other. She said Val called on another matter and mentioned I'd left the group and it was her fault my cover was blown and she was sorry, which pulled me down: I realized it'd been hours since I'd even thought about what used to matter . . .

"Look," I said. "I may just be a candidate for the job you have."

"We are a fine pair of fugitives."

"Call it *strategic withdrawal.*"

She sipped and spoke. "Yes . . . of course. We are right . . . no doubt . . . and sooner or later. But? *Even a paranoiac can have real reason to be afraid.* The government is in paroxysm. I . . . have real reason to be afraid. I want to be around, there's work to do. I'm retreating . . . you too? I need help."

And that was how I wound up driving coast-to-coast twenty-nine boxes of manuscript, books and papers after taking Angel across the line to Newark Airport for a plane for British Columbia, where she intended to spend the summer making tapes of an eighty-seven-year-old Indian woman who told stories. The car was a new Buick station wagon, and I traveled with two other women who were going to attend the birth of one woman's sister's first child on a collective farm in Monterey. We shared gas and motel and stopped in New Mexico and watched Indians sell bracelets to white people. In Big Sur we all bought those tee-shirts which say I AM PATTY HEARST and that night after the farm dinner (it was the husband's night to cook) we slept together by way, I suppose, of celebrating our journey, the air warmly fresh in a half-finished cabin under bullpines. We made our love with fingers and mouths doing little slippery things to all the places that mattered, we tasted, we sang now and then to the moon watching us watch her. Angel's *Moonrape* had told the uses to which masculists put her, justifying their supremacy, and I thought of the sasquatch-tracks of the astronauts through the Sea of Tranquility, hitting a golf ball for Dick Nixon's entertainment.

"Hey," someone said. "How does this feel?"

It felt great, spreading urgent into all my hollows, tidal rictus, muscles firing wild convulsions, pinwheels in my brain. Much nicer than a punch in the nose.

# 2

Three months later—after trying to get in touch repeatedly with Angel and finally giving up—I received this letter:

Kat—
I imagine you prowling el valle grande, news of which had penetrated even to the outreaches of B.C. Glorious struggle, but I pity the farmworkers and the goons, that they should be killing each other instead of harvesting this fruitful mother of ours. During most of the time I've been here the bite has been on and some of the men were making five and six hundred Canadian dollars a day. Then a few weeks ago the fish moved south—or somewhere beyond the reach of these boats—and now the long winter begins, the drinking, the fights.

I have been very well hostessed and instructed this summer by Mrs. Willie Mack and Miss Darlene Noomnst. Their kindness has often reminded me of the night we met, when you were so good. Did you know that when the white man brought smallpox, and whole villages perished of it, that as soon as an Indian knew shehe had it shehe would go into the forest to die away from loved ones who would of course have otherwise been moved to ease the sufferer, with attendant risk of infection? They tried aconite, anchona, feverfew, *Valerian Vulgario,* they tried digitalis. Their own medicine was ineffectual, it was all they could do. I think I can understand what the dying ones felt; more and more since leaving the city I've had the feeling I was the bearer of some terrible disease of ideas which might have blown us to atoms. These months in the forest have cleaned me out, thank Goddess, and I think the visiting Lectureship is just the place to put my thoughts in order. What this means to you, friend and sister, is that you may consider yourself a free agent; the ghosts of the valley are different from the ghosts of the city and I am beginning to practice my own exorcisms. Michael tells me he has sent you checks each month, and if you will let me know what sum you are out of pocket for the sublet, I'll send it immediately.

Again, more thanks than I can say for your help; let me know if there is any way I can help you.

> In sisterhood,
> Angel

P.S. My grandmother Rachel Stone? Old Burma hand. Widowed young; went out with six-year-old son Andrew, my father to teach. Got into a scheme to transport agricultural products from the Hill States to the coast, some sort of missionary self-help project. Died rich. Sent me sandalwood fans, ivory elephants, lace hankies; and on my 21st birthday a gold wafer inscribed *per tu amica Angel*. Michael loves it, probably has it somewhere.

I wasn't prowling when I read this, I was basking in late afternoon sun under an oak tree outside the aforementioned San Joaquin Valley sublet, a modest affair: four bedrooms lanai sunken marble tub heated swimming pool designer landscape. It belonged to a professor spending his sabbatical in Saudi Arabia, translating tractor manuals into eleven Middle-Eastern dialects. Every Wednesday and Sunday someone came at the crack of dawn to water the landscaping; garbage collection was Monday and Thursday. The mail arrived a little before ten. Neighbor to the north, a doctor's wife, kept me posted on I. Magnin sales.

I reread the letter, getting mad and confused at the same time. Felt I'd been used as a moving-van driver, but that didn't really make sense; for three grand and expenses you could hire a Pinkerton escort and send it by Mayflower. On the other hand, I'd been instructed to drive the stuff here, settle into the sublet and keep myself available, and I'd done it; if they (it was clear now she and Tarleton were in this together) wanted to spend a grand a month for a live-in caretaker, I'd done my job and was, as Angel put it, "a free agent" again. I had twenty-three hundred in the bank, had had a vacation, and I was all set to tackle a winter's work somewhere *big* . . . or so it would seem. But it didn't. Something tugged my memory but no matter how many times I reread the letter the words just sat there, black and perfect and . . . cheerful. Was Angel Stone a *cheerful* person? The thought had never occurred. I tried to recall her face and could get only the redness at the roots of her colorless hair as she flushed, her lips with the white scar lacing their softness, ocean-colored eyes and the long white lashes curtaining them . . . Not a cheerful moment among all that extraordinary flesh. Yet she'd signed her name, and the postmark was Bella Coola, B.C.

What if I were to stay anyway? I got in the station wagon and went out to have dinner with Vincente Pesola Muzguiz, who according to my mother and his maiden aunt Veronica was connected to my family through my mother's father's sister's first marriage, and who worked as a janitor at the university and was studying nursing.

Four days later I was in the station wagon again, on my way under a magenta-streaked sunset past the science-fiction landing lights of the airport, to meet United Flight 189, on a tip from the clerk that Angel Stone's name appeared on the flight roster. I figured on a couple of things: she might not be on the flight; Tarleton might be on it; or both of the above. Vince offered to come. I said, "Stick to your beret, hermano." He told me the grapes of my grandmother were raisins. I said,"Your nose is growing toenails." Then later as I was standing watching the 505 taxi to the landing gate along with a U.S. marshal in his golfing jacket and three teenage girls in shirley temples, I thought that it was too bad we had so much to fight about, so many contradictions to resolve. I was not watching too closely as the passengers began limping from the craft like astronauts back from wherever it was they went. But I got a second look, and in that instant her face was lit with an expression so agonized, so distraught, it lept the distances between us and two thicknesses of plate glass Then she smoothed, bent her head. She had a tape recorder over one shoulder. She moved close to the man ahead of her, joined with a knot of walkers, vanished. The marshal faded, which pulled my eyes to his with as modest a glance as I could muster.

Next I noticed a woman in her early thirties, dark hair short, brushed into curls all over her head, pants and jacket faintly military in air. She replied to my eyes with a steady glance of her own, and the tiniest of smiles. She leaned gently against the corner where glass met wall, arms folded over full breasts. She was not a Chicana; she wore no rings. The shirley temples bounced on their toes as the deplanees moved through the gate. I had checked the other exits; they were kept locked except at boarding time. Relatives began to find one another; the line narrowed between the gateposts, belled and swirled; Angel appeared behind a man with a golf bag, and as she came through, as I opened my mouth to greet her, I watched her eyes slide into mine, hold, slide past to the black-haired woman's. Then she smiled. I heard her say, "It's been a long time." They shook hands and I caught Angel's eyes once but not again, and that once not long enough to tell a damn thing . . . so I stared them out of sight along with the U.S. marshal.

And I wound up giving Vincente a call. He said, "See, I told you. Come on over. Bring a bottle, rich lady." I drove down Belmont to an all-night and took the recommendation of the Nisei who ran the place and bought a small-vineyard Gewürztztramiener he claimed was better than imports. He grinned, "Behave yourself." "Oh yeah?" There was a sign on the wall: *Due to crime statistics in this area, the store does not carry change over ten dollars after five p.m. We accept checks with proper I.D.* There was a bonsai kumquat in the window, next to a Jim Beam steamboat.

Three men left the house as I was entering. I said, "Venceremos." One of them smiled. It was Vince's aunt's house; it had been condemned for a man-made lake and she had two months left to find a place. In the picture window of the living room she had orchids growing; a cattelya, and two cimbidium. She was in the kitchen washing up so I set the paper bag on the table, nodded to Vince, and went to say hello. She kissed me and asked if I had eaten. When I said yes she asked me how many weeks ago? I said noontime with Vince. She grunted and said now she would heat me a couple of tamales. I stood and watched her pluck the leaf-wrapped tamales from their porcelain dish in the refrigerator, her fingers like shiny roots. She was telling me about finding time during the afternoon to make them, and an especially good buy at the market, and the lady down the street giving her some fresh peppers. She was missing a tooth in her lower jaw, the molars on both sides above were gone and she wore a white banlon sweater. To support herself she worked at the Catholic hospital. Afterward, I watched the late news with Vince. He told me what was happening, what to think about the Governor, the President, the war, the latest scandal. I got mad at him three or four times but I didn't say anything.

He said, "When I empty the professors' waste baskets I think that you have got it made."

I said, "You think so? Those keys on your belt will take you into more places on that campus . . . that's real power." I wished he wasn't so defensive because there were moments I would have liked a reality check in this thing with Angel Stone and I couldn't take the risk. Later his aunt came in to tell us it was time to go to bed and he offered to drive me to the sublet and come with the car in the morning. I told him I could make it alone.

It was a little after midnight, the air warm as blood. I headed north to the old fig gardens, which were the new suburbs—stucco ranchhouses, brick colonials, redwood post-and-beams sprawling in this oasis of the San Joaquin. The car fled between corridors of spruce, eucalyptus, palm, and at the raquet club there were women in evening dresses. Then eastward, past shopping centers clumped like grapes on a vine, toward the newly-designated California State University, rude as an apple. Here men discovered how to make the desert bloom. Here also, stored in an office in a pre-fab building where I myself had put them in preparation for Angel's return, were the twenty-nine boxes of manuscript and books. In my pocket, the keys, signed out to Katerina Guerrera for Angel Stone. I parked the Buick in a lot about a block from the pre-fab which houses the Anthro department, locked up, and walked under dusty maples, my shadow moving ahead then leaping back at every light. This I remembered from earliest childhood, the shadow reaching, collapsing—like moving from one point of insight to another, understanding, pirouetting, dipping, swaying. Or as in the most primitive childhood anthropomorphism, where the shadow is self abstracted; thought-twin. I felt as if I were dancing with Angel Stone in the same way, our separate dances conjoined through no will of our own for a time . . . it was like this during my marriage—have I mentioned it?— and as nearly as I can see, it is the act of disengaging from dance, no matter how tortured, which causes most pain. The longer the dance, the greater the pain. You might try to remain dancing, hold the brightness, keep the bright ball bouncing. I unlocked the door, groped towards an inner office, unlocked, slid inside, and shut the door before turning on the light. The boxes were arranged on three walls.

They were closed with strapping tape, the kind with nylon fibers. A week ago it would never have entered my mind to look; now I felt like a vandal. I did not even know what I was looking for, or where there was anything to look for. Angel's strange behavior, her "cheeriness," her face in the plane door, her blank stare when I smiled—I realized again how little I knew about her. Then I understood how angry I had been since she cut me at the gate, and that I wasn't angry any longer, only tired. Perhaps she was nearsighted, perhaps she was absent-minded, perhaps simply a little un-together and dumb at times like the rest of us. Perhaps she was at the sublet waiting for me, right now.

She was not waiting for me; she was asleep in the room where I'd hung her clothes. Sleeping hard, almost feverishly, one arm upflung, now and then shallow fast gasps as if something were chasing her. Too many Indian ghost stories? So I listened longer and the strange sounds grew in intensity to low moans; her face was wet with the effort of nightmare; I had to touch her because the moans had turned to screams and I knew I was not listening to anyone scared of phantoms. Her arm was tense, her skin hot, and she only turned groaning and sank into quieter dreams. I poured myself the bottom of the wine and listened to the two o'clock news: we were killing each other in a dozen places that night, and I thanked whatever choreographer designed my fate I was in none of them even as I sensed it was all the same; that to know the death of another being was to suffer dying oneself.

And then when I awoke, she was waiting, her face bending full and soft, a cup of coffee in her leading hand. She smiled tentatively. "Like some coffee?"

She had found the Melita and the Colombian roast and the *moulinex,* I discovered, after struggling up in bed and taking the first sip. "I'm making breakfast," she said, and slipped through the door. The coffee contended with a little bit of a wine headache, lost. I felt suddenly awful, and once again angry. Then I noticed the sunlight stippling the ceiling, where sun danced on the water of the pool, reflecting upward: ah, hell with it. This country like that; lazily profound at center, as in

**31**

the Chicano saying: *I came out of the earth in the great Valley of the San Joaquin.* I could smell the food cooking. I threw back the covers and went outside naked and plunged into the water: eighty-five degrees, steaming faintly . . . then drew myself from two laps into air which raised a quick flush, thence to bathroom, to closet . . . and was in the kitchen as she lifted the toast from the machine.

We were on the second cup before we began to talk.

"I apologize for not recognizing you last night at the airport," she said. "I didn't think you'd still be here."

"You thought I'd pocket the three grand and split?"

"I didn't really think about it at all. I thought you would have plans for when the three months was up. I thought maybe you intended to go back to the city."

I shook my head. "No. I figured on working with you a little while. The way we talked about, remember? Friendly fugitives, companion, secretary, chauffeur, cook: what every working woman needs is a good wife, you said."

There came into her clear eyes a slight tensing, as from a vagrant memory which refused to halt, and it tipped me a premonition like that of her face in the plane door: that in her head images collided through which she was sometimes forced to stumble like a victim of casual violence. "I don't feel like much of a bargain."

She worked at her coffee cup for awhile and I got to think yet again about Tarleton paying me three for no work and how queer it was. "Look, Angel. If you don't want me around, say so. You don't even have to tell me why. But you've got to understand how strange everything is from where I'm sitting. First both you and

Tarleton beg me to work for you, then you split for three months, then I get a mysterious letter telling me to pack it up then you fail to recognize me when you meet your welcoming committee then you serve me coffee in bed. Tell me I've got my foot in the wrong shoe, but at least tell me so I'll know I'm not crazy. Feeling crazy makes me feel violent and I don't dig it."

She tried to smile and it was a determined effort: energetic, but not much energy. Then her eyes blazed and went wet and she fought that for a sec, then stood and went out of the room. I thought I had lost her for good. I was about to dump my grounds and pack my bags when she returned holding a piece of canary foolscap, closely typed. "Read this," she said, and vanished again. As I sat with my third cup, I heard her body *splunk* into the pool.

May 5th, 1976

Angel Stone:

I have received a message directed toward you from persons beyond who do not wish to reveal themselves directly. Suffice to say they are friendly, and very worried about your welfare. This message was originally revealed to me the evening of March 12th, when you were on the Dick Cavett show. At first I ignored it, but it has come three times now, so I am passing it on in hopes of getting some peace and quiet in spite of the fact that it will no doubt cause you suffering. I only suggest you can come through this difficult period through prayer and faith in the all-encompassing plan you and we are a part of.

The message is in three parts:

1. You have been marked for greatness, but The Way is difficult.
2. You will strike a man, you will kill a man, you will cause ten thousand deaths.

**33**

3. You have most to fear death while dancing; you must not forget *those whom the gods wish to destroy they first make mad.*

I urge you, Angel Stone, to heed this message and pray for guidance in this matter. It is not granted to many of us to receive instructions from the other side.

Yours in the Spirit,
Alpha Hoerung

Shaking my head, I went and found Angel stretched in a lounger. The sun was stoking hot. Her skin was very delicately golden everywhere that wasn't covered by terry-cloth sarong, and I thought for a moment of the summer she had spent camping next to who knew what icemelt stream tumbling out of who could picture what stark forested glaciated alp . . . then her brows collected and she sat, drawing her legs and arms up. I sat opposite, and folded the letter. "What do you think about this," I said.

"Well, I don't know. I float in and out of things. At first I thought it was some religious fanatic. I ignored it for weeks. Then that night we met—I mean, that is what I did, after all. I struck a man. I can hardly help waiting for the other shoe to fall."

"You know about gratifying expectations? How if you believe something will happen, you're likely to help it occur?"

"Yes, yes, of course. But that doesn't at all mean the letter isn't simply identifying inherent tendencies: have you never been angry enough to kill? And there's another thing, you see: I know who sent the message."

"You checked it out, you got ahold of this . . . Alpha Hoerung?"

"Well, no. But . . . "

"Okay, I'm listening. Don't tell me it was your father."

"My father is alive," she said. "That's a sexist remark. Everyone knows women do not need intermediaries . . . "

I practiced keeping my face neutral. *Everyone knows?* Maybe, I thought, she is simply a bourgeois believer in astrology and cults. Or maybe not. As Jung said of flying saucers: there are two possibilities and one is that they are real. "Okay. But did you get in touch with Alpha Hoerung?"

"No."

"Okay. That's something for me to do." I unfolded the letter and pushed it toward her. "Now lay out for me what you think this means."

I watched her face as she talked, she did pretty well with the eyes. A couple of times they slid around but mostly she was right on and I wondered why I was having such a rough time figuring her out.

"Okay, you say you have a feeling you know this person."

"Not really know . . . all I have is a kind of after-image of someone from long ago—I don't know where."

"A nurse? A servant?"

"Well . . . not really, but closer to that than anything."

"So you think this person out of your childhood saw you on tv and sent you this letter."

"That's just it. Whoever she was, she would have known . . . I simply feel it."

"Would have known?"

"About women."

The sun was very hot and she looked frightened. "How about Michael Tarleton?" I was sorry to have to say it.

She covered her eyes with one hand. The scar on her lip shone. "Why?"

"Maybe he's trying to tell you something."

Her eyes blazed full into mine. "You think that's his style?"

"Sometimes men get hurt and do things they regret."

"I suppose it makes more sense than thinking it was all accidental."

"You won't see him, then."

"You think that's all he wants?"

"You mean you don't know for sure."

"I don't want to see him. But the threat alone effectively censors me."

"That charge? Well, assault is assault."

I made a mental note to check on Alpha Hoerung and the supposed assault charge while the sunlight glittered off the pool and my tan got three shades darker. "All right. Now what have you got set up here?" I tried to keep from holding my breath at this tacit proposal that I stay.

"Well, he knows where I am, of course, if he's paid you. So I wrote Julia to find me another house. That was Julia who met me last night."

"Pleased to meet you, Julia."

Angel did not flush as I expected. Instead she slowly lifted both legs over off the chaise and stood. She reached a djamilla from the tile and pulled it on and faced me, hands on hips. "It's a holding action, I know that. I have just under eighty-four after taxes and a whole lot of work to do. Maybe they'll all get bored. Maybe somebody will kill the bastard."

After she swirled off I wetted again. Five get you ten Julia's find did not include a swimming pool. Mourning in advance even as I sidestroked half a dozen times

around the tepid water, now cool compared to the air, I thought about divorce, and how Angel seemed to have a bad case of the "disengagement paranoids" or—just in case Jung was right—a whole bunch of good reasons to look over her shoulder now and then. Or both.

That afternoon, while she was at the university, I did a little long-distance checking. Lenore said she didn't know whether there was a warrant but she would touch down with somebody who could find out and get back a. s. a. p.

"How're you doing, Lenore?"

A glittery laugh. "Done with leafletting, at last. Toward the end I was even passing them out in my sleep. But I'm glad I did it—good discipline. I'd forgotten some things. How're you getting along with Angel?"

"Up, down, in, out."

She chuckled. "Sounds passionate."

"Not so."

She chuckled again and rang off. I called information for Alpha Hoerung, Bronx, and learned there was an A. Hoerung listed at the address on the letter warning Angel. When I dialed direct, a woman answered: "Who is it?" I made her over sixty.

"My name is Katherine Brown. Is this Alpha Hoerung?"

"Wait a minute, just a minute." The receiver clunked on something hard the way a child might bang it down. I thought I heard voices, then there was only the static in the lines. I waited five minutes by my watch; hung up.

The danger was you could be so traumatized by a thing like divorce you lost your fine perceptions, got out

of touch with the viscera of experience, whose messages warned only of *real* danger. The organism might fall into paroxysms of sensation and psych itself insane. This was not the same as being burned out, but some place further in, way past burning—center hollow as one of those black holes astronomers tell us about, gravity intensely sucking everything to it. A little over an hour later Lenore called back: "Nothing. She's clean." And I stopped sweating a bit; maybe Tarleton was cooling. The phone was still off the hook at A. Hoerung's.

We moved anyway. The new name plate said R. Stiller but the image I got was I. G. Farb with his toe in the swimming pool. Predictably, I got a cold, or a flu, or whatever they were calling it that time. I have a theory. I think the left side of my body is my female side, and the right is my male side. For instance I can only get to sleep if I lie on my left, and of course night has always belonged to woman. This cold hit me on the right: eye, sinus, nose. I couldn't breathe on that side and even lying down on my left, female, side didn't balance it out. Pills wouldn't work. Whiskey helped a little, and so did smoke. For the better part of a week I stayed slightly drunk and slightly stoned. When Angel came home from teaching she made toddies for me and sat on the edge of my bed while she read her mail. Sometimes she read a part of something aloud: one piece was about beaten-up women and their children. She read in a flat tone, as if she were conjugating verbs:

An Irishwoman
tiny and skeletal
nods toward her
small sullen son

His sisters have
it worse though
Father has a Yale
lock on his bedroom

| marked | door |
| with the | he takes one |
| strap | daughter |
| on his | in with |
| back | him |
| and | every |
| legs. | night. |

All this was happening in the house "Julia" had found, which lay in the path of a proposed freeway. Eviction could come any first of the month, but it'd been six years already since the city condemned the World War II tract. Across the street the houses were empty, plants dying in unwatered yards, toilet-paper festoons over rust-fingered dismemberments of bicycles, wagons, washing machines, lamps washbasins recordplayers. At dusk the neighborhood children explored these ruins; as we settled for the evening news I could see them nimble debris, chuck stones through windows, run, jump, tag each other, shout; sometimes they ran the same thing on the tv; I'd forget the name of the place on the screen and imagine closed circuit, the half-mile-wide swath dividing city zones receiving First Battles. About a mile closer to the rotting center where government buildings and hundred-thousand-dollar statuary alike served as canvas for the street artist (FUCK YOU cheek and jowl with Viva La Causa!) was the house of Vincente's mother, only a few doors from that of his aunt. The houses of the mother and aunt were scheduled to be covered with water—an artificial lake with shorefront apartments. Sometimes I would try to visualize the lake, and saw a vast shallow enclosure with heaped banks, a highway cutting across like pontoon bridging a swamp. Construction by the U.S. Army Corps of Engineers.

What finally got me out of bed was the news clipping Angel showed me from Thursday's mail, in an envelope with no return address, Penn Station cancellation.

### Fire Victim Identified

Special to the New York Times, New York. The body of a man found yesterday in a burning midtown apartment has been tentatively identified. Coroner Rueben Henkel said the results of an autopsy indicate "real likelihood" the victim was Michael B. Tarleton, in whose name the apartment is rented.

"The body was so badly burned it made identification extremely difficult," Dr. Henkel said. He added that military records had been used to support the conclusions of his office.

Tarleton was a documentary filmmaker under contract to the Columbia Broadcasting System for the past four years.

The victim's mother, Mrs. William Tarleton, confirmed by phone from her home in San Francisco that she had been informed of the tentative identification, but declined further comment.

Homicide Investigator Arthur Wilson conceded that the autopsy revealed the man had been dead as long as a week when the fire precipitated discovery of his body, but refused to elaborate. He indicated that a thorough investigation is underway.

When contacted, CBS officials said it was not unusual for Tarleton to be gone on assignment for long periods of time, and that no one knew his exact whereabouts in the past two weeks.

1) Tarleton killed himself (why?), and a week later by a curious coincidence a fire started, conveniently burning the body "beyond recognition." 2) Tarleton killed somebody else like him and returned a week later to burn the body. 3) Somebody killed Tarleton, etc.

4) Somebody killed somebody in Tarleton's apartment to make it look like 1), 2) or 3). Who, why?

I took a long look at Angel's face, what there was to see under the hand spread tightly over her eyes and forehead. Lips gray, mouth slack. She was breathing in little audible gasps, hyperventilating probably. "I feel sick," she said.

"Do you have to vomit?"

"No."

Then there was the matter of the date. A week before the news item put it at September 14th, the day Angel arrived to be met by the statuesque Julia. Which of course meant she could have been the somebody of 3) or 4) above. Some sack of snakes Angel had dumped.

"It was utterly bizarre. He came into the office about three . . ."

"He?"

"Dr. Kaltfeuss, and he said, 'I'm terribly sorry about . . .' Then he just stood there looking at me through his whizkid eyeglasses and I knew something just awful had happened from what was going on in his face as he realized I didn't know what he was talking about. And then he said, 'You don't know?' So I said, 'No, what is it?' And his mouth was horrible, like some gruesome slug was trying to force past his lips and he said, 'The secretary told me. You better call her and find out.' I felt utterly naked: he knew; I didn't, and something awful had happened. So I called the secretary and she wouldn't tell me what it was, just gave me a number to call—my lawyer's number."

"In New York?"

"Yes."

"Did you reach him?"

"Her. Yes. She said she's been visited by New York

**41**

Homicide and had a call from the District Attorney's office."

"Just like in the movies."

Angel looked hard at me: I could see her pupils leap large. "Yes. Only it's real."

"That's what we all say."

"We?"

"Everybody who gets involved in . . . accidents. I'm not even going to ask if you know what's going on, so please don't volunteer. Did she tell you to get back?"

"No."

"Did she want to know where you are?"

"Well, she asked, but I got the impression she didn't really want to know. She has my university address, of course."

"So you didn't tell her."

"No." Now Angel rested the bridge of her nose in the hollow of her palm, running fingers up into her hair. Her eyes closed. She stood, left the room, returned with what looked to be a weak Scotch/water. "I think I'm coming down with what you've got."

"With what I *had*," I said. "I've got too much to do to be sick anymore—but don't let that stop you . . . and enjoy yourself. I'll lay in some chicken soup."

Looking back, what I said seems cold. But I hadn't been figuring on murder.

It seemed like a good time for some on-the-spot. I drove over to the U. and made a call to Aida on Potrero Hill from the English Department lease-line in the faculty mailroom. The secretaries were Chicanas and left me alone. A thinly-bearded youth, forehead iridescent, smiled a weak smile and hitched a bony hip onto the counter to read his textbook offers. I didn't know how I felt about him so when I got Aida at Pan Am I asked her about her mother and she said *Mother is fine, can you come visit* and I said *yes on the way back from the East, when is a good time?* Then I copied down the numbers she gave me. The bearded one left; replaced by one with electric hair, bruised eyes and thriftstore tweeds. Aida said, "I can probably get you on the milk run if you're here at six-fifteen. First class okay?"

I could feel myself grin. "Champagne breakfast?"

She laughed. "Whatever you're woman enough for."

We're both transfixed by our paranoia. I wonder who's listening on Aida's end. And now coming through the door the chairman of the department, who gives me a hard stare then seems to shrug away his question as another more pressing image tempts his mind. I think I know why I'm paranoid; it's because I'm about to move further out than I have ever been. Imagine me getting involved with the longlegged whiteman's children—Angel, Aida—jiving them like the movies . . . yes everyone Aida talked with was some kind of *customer*, and the language was of commerce: was I woman enough? Again the stretch as I see myself about to hurl three thousand miles to ask as many questions as I could think up—of as many people as I could get to listen. The old thing we had is long gone, we're all scattered to individuals again and winter's gonna be cold so even though there's no one out there any more to solve my problems, there's gonna be somebody with the right *information,* if I can just if I can *just* find the right buttons to push.

I drive home slowly; it's getting cool and the flesh of my arms flushes. I'm prepared to think this is a sickness feeling, warning me back to bed but at the same time the message *you are moving deathward* penetrates, pulling my brain into its sparking kind of flush, near-sexual: *no.* Who wanted Michael T. dead? Why? Was it a trickle of accidents, like me not tending to the one favor he'd asked, that I look into Rachel Stone? Maybe up and down some invisible hierarchy everybody owed one to Tarleton. Maybe that was why he was dead.

Or maybe not. Maybe he was dead because of something *he* did. Like finding out about someone named Alpha Hoerung? It seemed too thin for murder. Suppose it was accidental, then it could be dangerous to act like there had been foul play. In the books the private eye always got to look at the body, it was a big help. It was too hot—a hundred and three on the Equity Savings Bank—and the food chain at the shopping center had a boycott picket around it, pinioned at corners by sheriff's blue flashers.

At the house Angel was asleep. I wondered whether to wake her and explain I would be gone a couple three days but she was peaceful this time, no upflung arm, no moans, no scream. I lit a cigarette, maybe hoping she'd rouse in the flash of phosphorus, seeing instead as long as I could hold the match how softly beautiful she was, fresh as a child . . . except where the mugging scar ridged white through coral lips moist with dreams. The match burned my fingers; I realized my heart was pounding.

I tried to reach Vince, but his mother said he was out of town till Monday, she didn't know where. I finally wound up writing a short note and propping it on the coffeepot:

Angel—I am going to the city to ask some questions. I'll call in case you want me to run any errands. Take care of yourself—

                                                             Kat.

44

# 3

On the flight east I talked with the stewardesses. They were talking strike: reservations clerks, flightcrews, pilots had struck. The stews said things like, "The airlines can't function without us" and/or "If we went out they'd hire another batch from the airlines schools." I tried to explain why that wasn't so, that their support increased the power of all employees, themselves included, but it was a hard go. From the seat in front of me: *He* knows *you're contrite . . . has to give a show of authority . . . to dump the noshows.* One of the stewardesses said she was always sick after a tour, had to sleep a day and a half before it wore off and she could think again. And that led to talk of jetlag. My senses filled with the swabbing cotton of flight. In front . . . *got to you when they rattled the chains, eh?* Silence. Or rather the sub-mechanical percussion of the upper air and all those filaments stretching either side, making sound solid as a swallow of milk. Below, the Rockies erupt pearly babies' teeth from the pinkgold Great American Desert. The kind of clouds only the Japanese have ever been able to paint grow in midair like birds' nests. Over Kansas they turn Watteau to heap gold tinged, iridescent as the last rinsing of blood from porcelain. *Thing is, I feel I did what I had to. I would do the same thing again. . . . Watch who you say that to, luv,* says the man in front. The first-class compartment is upholstered ruling class gray. I thought it would be interesting to look at their faces. The men in front appeared to be bureaucrats of one level or another, lawyers probably. Then I had a moment of claustrophobia, a sense of utter subjectivity to accident. The cabin was dark, porthole eyes shading black to light like heavy-lidded Walt Disney hounddogs. But cleaner, the darkness touched with glints of aluminum. I'd heard stewardess phone pilot the passenger weight as the engines revved at Oakland: "Seven six zero zero." At onehundredfifty pounds each it came to a hundred and fourteen bodies. There were hardly twelve people in First; did that do something to the balance of the plane? I'd tried to sense it during the takeoff. The stewardesses turned waitress and were serving lunch to Economy. In front of me the men began to talk about sentences, and I shrugged back into my raincoat. I listened to the engines for awhile and felt paranoid. I stood and let myself waddle to the magazine rack, felt the eyes of the men on my back, then nothing. When I returned they didn't even look up. I had never seen them before. So then I decided I was *too close,* beginning to fantasize;—*the strain toward omnipotence*—I was sucking off the madness of Angel's trip which song and story said was the way life was. Maybe she had something with her Alpha Hoerung, one had met everyone in childhood, we weren't just atoms in ether. Over Illinois we started to get into heavy lowlevel smog.

In the city, the tourists had all gone back to work. Everybody was saying that next to spring, fall was the loveliest season. People were buying imported sweaters and brown leather shoes, looking a little like it was war-time. Lenore insisted she was out of the leafletting trip and then asked if I would help carry some downtown to a teacher's trial *"just* to deliver them." So we went down and I talked for a minute or two under the yellowing trees near the courthouse with Cathy and a woman named Janet. Janet asked how I was doing with Angel Stone, so I ran it down.

"Well, that's interesting," she said. "I worked with Angel on and off for a year in a very peripheral way; took a class from her when she was just Ms. Tarleton whose husband was from a racially-mixed marriage like my background, and I wanted to see—and then I began to hit on she was very naive, really convinced right would prevail and she had nothing to worry about. Which I guess is what happens with *her* background. But it knocked me out at the time: seemed like she lacked one of the basic instincts. For instance from the beginning when she went to speak I would go with her because she would always miss the freeway exit and wind up lost twenty miles down the road and have to cancel. So you'd have a bunch of people gettin mad. But her driving slid me round the corner: tailgating at ninety, like that. I wound up doing the driving, is what it amounted to."

I asked if she'd heard anything about the fire in Tarleton's apartment. The picketers were into the second hour, a slow Ourubour; Lenore talking with arm-banded monitors along the line. Janet wrinkled her forehead as if I was interjecting something that had happened a long time before. "Oh, this 'n that. You know about rumors."

"Like what?"

"Well, the newspapers said it was a short circuit in the air conditioner. It'd been running steady for a week, they figured. They said he died of liver failure due to infectious hepatitis.''

"He? They were sure?''

She gave me a queer look. "Tarleton. They identified him from Army records. Didn't you hear any of this out in California?''

"We got the initial story yesterday.''

"But you knew he was working on a piece about drug addiction at Quantico?''

"Nobody told *me.* "

The woman named Janet drifted to join Lenore.

"You see, this is just what I mean: this is the way Angel's manifesting to you; with me it was not having my kind of survival instinct.''

"But we've got to keep trying with these people; we can't just let them drift away, they're too powerful.''

"I don't need any more heroes, honey, I need organizers. And I need heroines like I need another hole in my head.''

I would have walked away and I probably should have but I said, "Maybe I'm trying to organize Angel Stone.'' She started toward the picket line.

"Anything you say.''

I nabbed Lenore, reminded her of what she'd said about being out of the leafletting trip, and we got back on the subway. Rattling toward Christopher, I asked her the same question I'd asked Janet, and she, too, seemed to soft-focus backward further than the actual fact of a week. "Usual rumors.''

"So I hear. Like what?''

"Well, the most interesting one is that the body isn't Tarleton's at all.''

"Oh?''

"You see identification has been from records.''

"And who did *they* get to volunteer to be the body this time?"

"Come on, they can get any kind of body in any kind of shape any time they want on a phone call. You know how many people die in this city every week?"

"Because he was making a documentary which would blow the Marines?"

"No." She looked at me with a smile on half of her face. "You really want to find out how paranoid we all are?"

"Try me."

She was silent. She shook her head.

I stayed on the subway to A. Hoerung's address just over the line into the Bronx. It was a twenties oasis-style Hollywood apartment with a *Piano Lessons Given Here* sticker on a downstairs mailbox. I looked up A. Hoerung and went up to 4C. A spidery-frail old white woman answered on the third ring, peering through the chainlock, taking my press pass and giving it a close look under the fifteen-watt entrance light.

"I've come about Alpha Hoerung. I called yesterday. Are you Ms. Hoerung?"

"Why no, I'm not." She faded from the door and I was afraid I'd lost her, but in a second the door opened *sans* chain. "What did you want to know?"

"Could I come in?"

"Well, I'm just fixing Adelbert his tea . . . "

"I can talk while you work."

She led me down an equally dim hallway spotted here and there with sepia prints hardly a shade darker than the beige-painted walls and woodwork. Adelbert was in the parlor reading the newspaper. He looked up but did not get up as we passed, as if I fit some category of visitor the ancient spider woman entertained. We went into the kitchen. My eyes were getting used to the dimness. I sat in a painted kitchen chair and watched her arrange bread on a plate. The table top was beige enamel with green around the edges; the kind with leaves that slide out and pop up. The chairs were green. "Now. What was it you wanted to ask?"

"I wanted to talk to Alpha Hoerung if I could. I'm a reporter. People are interested in hearing about psychic phenomena these days, and I was told she sometimes makes predictions."

Her eyes snapped to mine, liverdark in candlewax face. She wet her lips. "Well, my goodness. You didn't hear about the accident?"

I closed my eyes. "The accident."

"It was just after Mrs. Finegold—our oldest neighbor—called about the man who had been standing outside the door so long . . . but then the police, they said they'd checked that through and he was only a Bible salesman . . . a blonde man . . . anyway they—the police—never got the driver. There was no one there to take the license number."

"It wasn't like the movies."

"No, though I always said it was wrong of Daddy to keep her from marrying him; she loved Dickie Mullighan, you know. Just because he was a divorced man . . . but that was forty years ago. I'm sorry I guess I'm sounding awfully . . ."

"I see. And she was killed?"

"Yes. She's taken to wandering these past few years, you know. I couldn't keep my eyes on her all the time, I have Adelbert to watch, too."

The kettle began to boil and she poured a bit of water into the bottom of the pot, rinsed it, added tea leaves and more water. The quilted tea cosy was beige, printed with green ivy. "I think I'll let Adelbert open the paté tin this afternoon all by himself. Would you care to join us for tea?"

"No, thank you. Just one more question, please. When did your sister pass on?"

"Well, I think they broke her heart when they wouldn't let her marry Mr. Mullighan. That was when she went out to Burma. Actually, Adelbert doesn't like paté, but I have to get his iron into him. He likes little sweetsour gherkins wrapped with summer sausage. But if you mean dear Alpha's body, her soul left last April eleventh. The daffodils were still in the stores."

Angel answered her phone on the third ring. "Hello?" A sleepy voice.

"This is Kat. Look, I need some explanations fast."

"I'm dying with this flu."

"You sound sick. Have you had some soup? Plenty of juices?"

"Yes, but I'm . . . "

"Good. Now take a minute or two to explain what the hell is going on."

"Do you think it's wise—over the telephone?"

"Shit, lady, if they were that efficient we'd all be dead or in exile. But if you think someone is listening, I'm capable of understanding metaphor . . . "

"I didn't mean . . . "

I could feel a flush crawl into the roots of my hair. "Baby, I think you're a little bit of a racist. Why did you lie to me about Alpha Hoerung?"

There was a long indrawn silence, but I was tired of hiding my anger. Then her voice came. "All right. She worked for Grandmother. I just figured she was crazy, but then when Michael . . . I panicked, didn't I?" Another pause, then her voice gathered. "Portia told me I should view the pound of flesh, that . . . Shylock was going solely on three fingers. You follow?"

"Yes, yes."

"But . . . well, if they have three fingers, that says it, right?"

"Maybe. It's a problem in topography. If the average fingerprint map has forty peaks and valleys, then $40^2$ is one of our values. Then assign characteristics: whorls, triangles, and run the whole thing out as an equation: there are 6.4 billion sets of maps around, and an awful lot that look similar. That's why you want to know the name of the country, the color, the age, weight, sex, etc. Then it becomes *positive* identification. And I'm not even exercising the paranoids: things like switches, vanishing records. Do *you* follow?"

"Yes."

"Okay. Look, I'll call Portia to arrange the details. How can I get in touch with her?"

"I didn't mean it to be this way. I feel so . . . normal. I feel as if I've been sucked into other people's compulsive fantasies."

"It's a crazy life. I didn't say *we* were crazy."

"Then what is it, why can't we escape?"

"I thought you knew, Angel. As Emma Goldman said, 'It is organized violence on top which creates individual violence at the bottom.' "

She came back on that. "Oh." She seemed to want to say more but all that came was, "Well, I'm going back to sleep. Ask Lenore about Edgar Allan Poe."

"I'll check it. And by the way . . . "

"Yes?"

"You don't have to worry about hearing from Alpha Hoerung again—at least not this side."

There was a pause, and she hung up without saying goodbye.

When I went to see Lenore to find what on earth Edgar Allen Poe had to do with Angel's lawyer, she raised her black eyebrows and said, "Ain't you got no cultcha?" then went to the bookshelf and handed me a thin volume titled "The Raven" as she wrote on a slip of paper. The flyleaf said E.A. Poe and was covered with names and addresses. She popped gum, told me she hadn't had a smoke in eleven days, and handed me the folded piece of paper.

"Who were those people who did the apartment switch with Angel last May, Lenore?"

"Old school tie sort of thing. Good for overnights, has a short half-life for serious use, unless whoever's looking for you is months behind."

"Where did you go to school?"

"Hunter. Bacteriology. Easy to get jobs and clean work; if you don't want to deal with live cultures you just say so."

"And Cathy?"

"Barnard. English Literature, Women's Studies."

"Angel?"

"Berkeley, Boston. She studied with Mead, you know."

"And do you know a woman named Julia: about thirty, dark, full figure, five-five or six? She's out in California right now."

"Yes, I know Julia. She teaches in the psychology department."

"What does she teach? Do you know?"

"She's into some aspect of behavior modification. Look, Kat, I bailed out. Angel tried to tell me one time that the story about opening Pandora's box was an object-identified male fantasy about lesbianism and I said *enough! already* . . . do I need Pandora? I need to get into med school, that's what I need. She said, 'You're right. Just get me somebody else I can trust.' So I got her you. I tried to make it clear . . ."

"You did. You don't hear me complaining, Lenore, I'm just asking for information. What is this big project she's working on with twenty-nine boxes of manuscript?"

"She referred to it as the Codex. Or if she was frustrated by it all, the Kotex. Basically Code X—the female chromosome."

"How long has she been working on it?"

"Not very long, really. A lot of manuscript isn't her own, you know; it was given to her shortly after *Moonrape* appeared."

"Do you know who gave it to her?"

"All I remember is it came by United Parcel Service, just before winter solstice. For a couple of days I remember thinking it was a whole bunch of Christmas presents. Her people do that kind of thing."

I went to the phone and dialed what she'd written on the scrap of paper. I got the secretary, who said Counselor had left the night before for Washington, where she had to testify. I got her address in that town, thanked, hung up. Lenore was in the kitchen end of the room, opening doors, getting out food. "I'm starved," she announced. "I got to talking with this butcher, you know, and he said he sold all his lamb's liver to restaurants, they sold it as calf's liver. So I asked him to save me one. Have you ever had lamb's liver?"

"I don't think so."

"Stick around, I'll make us a little something. There's some sherry in the bookshelves."

I poured two fingers in each glass and checked out the new offerings on the bookshelf: There was less Marx than there used to be, and more Mao, and my favorite

Hanoi 1967 pamphlet, *North Vietnam against U.S. Air Force*—the one with the tiny woman in the black pajamas bringing in the huge rumpled American flyer. But mainly there were a lot of books about violence. Rape; war; causes, results, examples of, theories about. She even had a copy of the quarterly Angel read to me from, and I found the passages about the whipped boy and his less fortunate sisters. I punched the tapedeck and Brahms' Sonata #1 for Violin and Piano wound from the reel. I fingered the *oro fino* and went to watch Lenore cut leeks.

"Nice sound."

"It's the third in two years. I don't buy them new anymore; I wait a couple of days and go down Amsterdam Avenue and check the second-hand stores. If they haven't got mine they've got somebody else's. It gets old fast. But the street's fairly well lighted and this building is still respectable and I get to watch the never-ending spectacle of human passion coming from the 'residence hotel' near the corner."

The knife flashed for a long while and the delicate dialogue of violin and piano nimbled its diminishments as her leeks grew finer and finer.

"What kind of relationship did they have, Lenore—Angel and Tarleton?"

She smiled with one side of her face. "From prostitution to marriage, eh? Your mind works like mine."

"Have you ever been married?"

"Same as. I lived with a man six years. Broke up three years ago this month, matter of fact."

"Why did you break up?"

She whisked eggs and cream. "Well, he started managing my time. It was after I graduated: I didn't get a job right away, I was in shock, I guess. Anyway for a couple of months I did just lay about, and he began to tell me what I should do each day. He had excellent arguments, too: I was getting fat, I was going crazy. So for a while I did what he said I should do, and then one afternoon, while he was at work, I found myself wandering around a Woolworth's. I had twenty-eight cents. And everything I could buy was something I had no need of. And the things I needed cost more. At least that's what I was thinking at the time. I mean I regarded myself as quite enlightened, and all of a sudden here I wake out of a walking dream and I'm talking to the assistant manager, asking him if he had any black dolls. I can't even get him to understand until I say Nee-grow. Because my anger had focused on the toy counter, the war toys, the cheap plastic shit, the pink faces of the baby dolls. That's when I knew I had to change my life.''

"And you went down to live with Wendy.''

"I'd met Wendy by then so I moved in with her. There were five women in the apartment, much too crowded. I learned a lot about kids, though. I'll never look at a woman with small kids the same way again—I had been far into the tv shuck on that score.''

"Were you there when Wendy had the fire?''

"Yes. That was when Laurie and Cybele moved out. Their room burned. What a mess! Laurie had just gotten a six-hundred-dollar stereo, and that burned too.'' She poured, filling a baked pastryshell, popped it into the oven. Then she laughed. "I had an appointment the morning after about disability. I'd tried everything at that point—welfare, training programs, foodstamps. What with the fire, all I could find to wear was one of Ronnie's muumuus. And you know how big she is. So I wandered into the worker's cubicle and started in about the fire—trying to explain why I looked the way I did, you know. Well, she decided I was crazy. I mean really.

She certified me for sixty percent." She laughed again. "I probably was at the time. None of this was funny then."

"What do you think about fires, Lenore?"

We sipped the *oro fino* for a few moments.

"They happen when people extend themselves too far. Every time, seems whoever suffers has let too many details slide. I think it's that way with all the disasters all up and down the line."

"Do you think that was the way with Tarleton?"

"Well, Michael . . . was a very driven guy—always pushing to see how much things give. That's why he got as far as he did. He was obsessed with his family background the way people are when it's mysterious— unknown white father, unknown because his mother was at the time a prostitute. She was resourceful and intelligent. She was able to stay away from drugs— anyway she later got married—a World War II veteran, Eighty-second Airborne—and sure enough he was called up for Korea."

"You're well informed."

"There is a film, you know. Michael called it 'the only serious film I ever made'—his family history. He worked on it off and on: he probably decided to do the Quantico thing because he had some lead he was following for the film. He's like that. Once when he was drunk he told me he knew who his father was and if times got hard he would put the arm on him."

"Do you think he was telling the truth?"

"At that time I was into transactional analysis, you know. It really colored my perceptions." She thought, then giggled. "And there's always white-skin privilege. I thought he was writing a life script in which he could be a hero because he was of divine parentage. You know, the illegitimate son of the king. The Kunta Kinte

syndrome? I didn't see how it could hurt, except I guess it's pretty hard to relate to somebody who's looking up his family coat of arms. I think Angel tried—she certainly has the background. Her father keeps her in new cars, you know."

She was doing intricate things with the liver, pressing in herbs and dusting flour while butter foamed in an iron skillet.

"What about the difference in age? Twelve years, wasn't it?"

"Actually fifteen—Michael shaved three years. And he looked younger. If you mean he was a father figure I'd have to say, more Pygmalion and Galatea—me Adam, you Eve. It didn't seem to bother Angel too much until the book came out. That was the beginning of the end."

"Yet the last time I saw him, Tarleton claimed he loved Angel very much."

Lenore nudged the sauteing liver. "Set the table, would you? We have two minutes to go."

# 4

A party: in an offbase row house near Quantico, Virginia, they are getting out the news: VICTORY FOR VETS. Geronimo and Biglip are turning the handle of an old Gestetner in air pungent with duplicator fluid and sweet opium, which Moose uses to keep a smile on his lips and a song in his heart as he wheels his chair in place and watches the Evening Report. Above the tv:

> Freed, the prisoner can build the country
> Misfortunes are tests of a man's loyalty
> To worry about the common good is a great
>                                   merit no doubt
> Let the prison door open and the real dragon
>                                   will fly out.

Uncle Ho's face stares from the skyblue poster next to his quatrain, alive in black ink. Rainbow explains carefully to me that I should not pay attention to Charlie Jack when he shouts *eat the rich* because he took one in the head so he doesn't know what he's saying. Rainbow has very clear earnest eyes and he seems concerned that I might not understand, so each time he makes his message simpler. Finally I laugh: "Eat the rich? They are unfit for consumption," which either offends or persuades. Anyhow he moves away. In the corner sit the two women I came with, handing off a bottle of Mateus. Rona received an Undesirable Discharge for "personality problems due to character disorder" after two years as an M.P. but Melly is still in, clerking for the Marines at Quantico. They both have the distracted gaze of the permanently depressed, and on the way over to this decaying Georgian hidey-hole, Melly let it down: "When I'm at work I count the hours. The minutes. I can't keep my eyes off the window. Most of the men I work with are assholes and there isn't a single one I'd want to so much as have a beer with." The men in this room, our brothers of the left—are they any different?

I smile; a tall blond man approaches and offers me a can of Colt .45. "You knew Tarleton?"

"He was making a documentary about drugs at Quantico."

"That was a cold day I heard about him being dead. We need more like him. On base, half the troops are on the nod all of the time. I mean, these are Marines, m'am, this is peacetime."

"Drugs on base?"

"Fort Benning Georgia may be the military suicide capitol but Quantico *vee a* has got to be Smack City. And Headquarters keeps going on about how this is supposed to be run out of smuggled film canisters of drugs."

"So you're writing about this in your paper?"

He shakes his head. "Please don't tease, m'am. Right now we are working on a balance formula: the good news and the bad."

"Victory for vets?"

"Disabled vets are going to get more clothing pay. That's fifty-two thousand vets, and their annual allowance will be up from $175 to $190. They get the allowance because when you wear prosthetic or orthopedic appliances there's extra wear and tear on your clothes. Like this." He hiked his right foot forward and there was a click as it lifted. I could see the wear line on the trouser leg where the artificial foot laced on. "Also it'll mean I get an allowance toward the purchase of a specially equipped vehicle, I get a break on VA mortgage insurance and when I die of complications they're gonna reimburse for the cost of moving my remains to the nearest national cemetery."

"That's the good news."

"Yeah. Now for the other stuff: Fort McClellan Judge Advocate General dropped charges against the forty-six-year-old colonel who was accused of raping the twenty-two-year-old recruit. While on the other hand at the Sierra Army Depot the C.I.D. is investigating a female M.P. S/4 on sodomy charges brought by a female officer at Fort Gordon."

"Sodomy by a woman? It sounds physically difficult if not impossible."

"That's what I thought too. And at the same time the military is protecting officers from sexual attack from enlisteds, twenty-nine percent of military families are eligible for food stamps 'cause they're so poor but instead of raising pay the Pentagon is phasing in the neutron bomb. And that's all the news . . ."

"That's fit to print?"

Geronimo filled the door. "Weep no more, troopies. We need collaters and staplers." Rona and Melly rose from their conversation, pushing up their sleeves. Geronimo and Biglip appeared, took custody of the wine. The abandoned mates were passing smoke so I moved to share. The tall blond man stared round the room: "Twenty-five cents to buy into some sloe gin." I got out my quarter. The reefer was torn from what looked like a Marlboro filter and on the floor between us a red and white pack said: PARK LANE. Geronimo winked. "A good brand, awful hard to find nowadays." He showed me the lion seal of the Royal Cambodian government like a blue excise stamp on the pack. Someone put on an Allman Brothers album, the blond man returned with the bottle. When the newspaper was ready, two of the men stood buttoning bundles of newspapers into their shirts, first the backs, the fronts untucked, then the fronts palmed under the belt and the backs: like bulletproof vests, like the vests during People's Park, the battle for the liberation of Berkeley. They took long swigs and went into the night to deliver. Geronimo said, "This has been a winter war from the start—it's hard to remember what we started with. We've been infiltrated three times by my count." A brief silence. "And you folks, what are you interested in lately?"

"What do you know about Burma?"

"Oh, they're beginning to talk about Burma, are they?" A hard chuckle and a prisoner's pull to efface it, his hand moving across his lips pulling his face straight. "Well, that's where the dope's at, all right. Crossroads of the Golden Triangle." He rooted around among ten feet of paperbacks to pull forth a small square label in cheap faded ink DOUBLE U* O GLOBE BRAND NO. 4. "That's the Hill Tribes, m'am, and they been running opium and fighting wars for a thousand years. We're just a blink of the eye to them. Backed now by all the Kuomingtang cadre who were caught in the north in forty-nine when they took Chiang's pants off the foot of the bed. We're talkin' Asia now, m'am, they got ten times the people we have and the flag of the People's Republic is the rising sun, y'know."

Charlie Jack stumbled over with eyes which seemed maybe unfocused, maybe a little crossed, grinning his stubble away from a crescent of stained teeth. "Wanna arm wrassle?" I said, "I don't arm wrassle with anybody who eats people," and his eyes went empty as the blond man took him aside. "Whad' she say?" "Take it easy, man, you're blowin it."

Geronimo said, "Don't want to arm wrestle?"

I said, "I'll arm wrestle you, if you'll give me a book to put my elbow on." I started to roll my sleeve.

He looked straight in my eyes and smiled. I smiled back. He handed me a dictionary. I figured he'd been feeding paper to the Gestetner about as long as I had. We got down and settled on our bellies. The book gave me almost half an inch and he let me have it. I knew then I would take him. His face got a little red and he held for a while but then he let me have it, bouncing back and to his feet the moment his wrist touched. He laughed short and hard. "Watch her, she's strong." I would have left off but Moose roused from his wheelchair. "Let her try Sandy—if she takes him, I'll give her a go. There's plenty of us here, must be one man enough . . ." Charlie Jack held out a banana to Rona & Melly and asked, "What do you think of that, girls?" To which Rona replied, "Well, it's got a nice curve on it, but it doesn't look like it would hold up very long" and Melly sang *soto voce*

> Hey meester can I bite your banana
> It's so nice and firm
> Hey meester can I bite your banana
> And watch you moan and squirm . . .

While the blond man—Sandy—got down and our palms were even and he took me. Like rolling off a log. Moose let out a long peal of laughter but nobody else laughed. Rona was nudging Charlie Jack in the ribs with his banana and he had his mouth open. Sandy

leaned toward me. "What did you say your name is?"
"Kat." "Kat, you're strong, for a woman."

So I had a hangover when I met Portia for lunch. I was surprised to find her a motherly person, and was grateful to her for coming down to the train station to eat with me. "Try to talk Angel into making the identification," she said. "Legally Tarleton is in limbo, and you can never tell when someone might decide to subpoena her just to tie up the loose ends."

"Nobody knows where she is."

"They will soon as they run down my long-distance log." She smiled, her elbows spread, hands entwined before a cottage cheese plate.

"Do you know about Rachel Stone? Last time I saw Tarleton he told me to look her up. Angel says she was her grandmother, lived in Burma, died rich."

"How very interesting. I'll have Ann run that down when I return." Counselor did not smile. She ate a prune. She removed the pit and set it on the edge of the plate.

"What about Angel's folks?" I asked.

"Her mother is dead. Her father's name is Andrew— he's quite prominent in certain circles."

"Money?"

"He has it, of course. He's in the sort of . . . business which does very well: public relations, offices here in D.C., San Francisco, Mexico D.F., Vancouver. Half a dozen offices in the Far East, let me see—Rangoon, Singapore, has Vientiene fallen yet? Bangkok, Hong Kong, Taipei. The Andrew Stone Company, perhaps you've heard of it."

"No."

"It is what's known in the . . . intelligence community as a *cover*."

"I see."

"I can see that you do. We all have to come to grips," she continued. "It's been going on for years; there's no privacy anymore. One learns to cultivate a sense of righteousness, an awareness of public scrutiny. There's no reason we shouldn't be able to show all our actions in honesty and assert our freedom of choice." She smiled and added, "Do you always look this bad in the morning?"

"I spent the night with some vets over by Quantico. They said it was a party but actually it was a working drunk."

"Well, I suppose everyone has to spend a night or two in a barracks now and then, otherwise you stop understanding war movies. Tell me, what are their amusements these days?"

While I told her she ate her cottage cheese and canned peaches and watched my face.

# 5

I arrived back in the San Joaquin Valley at four p.m. Friday, called the house; no answer. So I spent six-fifty on a cab to find this note propped by the coffeepot:

Kat—

Want you to know I'm concerned that you seem to feel we aren't communicating fully. Maybe it will help you to understand if you look into the box numbered 12.

I have to be out of town for a little while—I'll keep it short as I can, and would appreciate if you would take over the classes referred to in the folders on the kitchen table.

I looked to see three file folders.

If I have not returned by the 24th, please inform the chairman I have been detained out of town and you will be taking my classes until I return. I spoke with him about this already; it's just for his information. Use your judgment based on the guidelines within; nobody knows less about what I'm trying to do than I.

In sisterhood,
Angel.

I don't know what I expected: with Angel you couldn't expect to come back after six thousand miles to slippers and a fire. What I got was a medium thickish oaktag folder with booklists, class rosters, notes, sources, and the rest of the paraphernalia of the teaching professional. And a plan, a simple and easily understandable and remarkable plan for the teaching of anthropology.

By asking her students to create a culture and bury it, she asked all the important things: their problem was the answer. I understood suddenly why she had been able to scoot cross-country into academic retreat, and a little bit more about how she would always be able to do it—would have more and better offers the longer she was around.

I thought again about the blond vet Sandy saying of Tarleton, *That was a cold day I heard about him being dead.* Sitting in the heat of the valley I felt cold, and wondered where she was, what doing.

Through the kitchen window I cold see a tarantula crawling under the pomegranate tree. The big gold Buick wagon rested in the car port under a cape of tokay, muscat, and emperor vines fruiting fat clusters dangling from a trellis. I opened the coffee pot, but it was clean. The stove was cold, the house somewhat stuffy but not stale. I figured her for a six hour start on me; we might have passed in the air terminal. In the bathroom there was a fern, inked price $12.95 + tx. There were half a dozen furry rugs on the wood floors, which were dusty in the corners. Giant cushions in their original plastic bags—about a hundred and fifty dollars worth. On a square table a nice old bronze lamp with curved Tiffany glass sides. No price tag. A chrome Bentwood rocker also without price tag. In my room my foam mattress pad was covered with a gold and salmon Peruvian blanket and there was a mirror-blouse in hot pink atop. That made me smile; she got the right size. So I went down the hall and looked into her room. She had half a dozen ferns and cyclamen spotted on more of the square teak tables, a handmade quilt for a bedspread, the corners tucked neatly around the foam pad. At the foot of the pad sat her sleeping bag. I tried to imagine the kind of bed she and Tarleton had slept in: certainly nothing this austere, more a temporary encampment than a room of one's own.

The phone rang: Vince. He said certain activities were being investigated by the Justice Department and some of the people were beginning to worry Grand Jury and some were having visits. They were talking a letter-writing campaign, to get the issue into the newspaper, so would I help a few of the people with their English? He asked me how my trip was. I said I would come by the next night. Vince said he would get a hold of some people, I should bring a bottle if I wanted to drink; his mother was going to cook some chicken. *Okay, Vincente.* I went out to the car and got the keys from under the mat. The tank was full; Angel was thinking of everything. I wondered where she was. The evening was cool and bright, the moon waning. I thought for a moment of *Moonrape*, and its close chronicling of the moon in human experience, the almost-indictment of the ending, where blame began to be meted out like lottery tickets. The car started easily and I backed, eating a bunch of muscats, the grapes so sweet I could only manage them one by one, a honey-edge in my teeth. The campus was deserted when I parked in front of Angel's office building and went up.

Number 12 was labeled HERSTORY. It was still sealed. A couple of boxes had been opened, however: number 29 BELLA-COOLA-TLINGLIT and number 27 unlabeled, which contained film canisters. The labels on the film canisters were "Michael T.," nos. 1-14, and "Angel

Dancing" nos. 1-7. That was a lot of film. I wondered where I could get a projector—the film was super-eight. I wondered whether it was wise to take the boxes from the office. Wise or not, I couldn't camp in the office to go through hours of film and hundreds of pages of manuscript. Still, it was enough decision to concentrate my thoughts on the actual moving of the boxes until details began bouncing in my head. I felt, how to say? in the shallow waters of that same neuroticism, straining toward omniscience: why need to know? I was a spy in Angel's life and she for some reason desired to be spied upon . . . could you call spying something covertly invited? . . . The manuscripts in no 12 were lighter than the film canisters but I had a sudden terror I was carrying boxes of rocks, and muscles of my middle back began hooking. I locked the boxes in the back seat, returned to check the office and call Vince. "Hey Vince, I do this every time with you . . . " He told me to meet him at the media co-op in a half hour.

First I watched "Michael T.," the projector beamed on my bedroom wall. I brought in a couple of pillows from the living room, made a smoke, drank half a six-pack and fell asleep about midway through. Which was probably good because when I woke up I realized I really wanted to see the last reel, an answer print. It began in wobbly black-and-white footage of a gaunt pretty black woman in an apron. She was laughing and giggling, pushing out at the eye of the film, covering her mouth. No sound. Then a series of documents: birth certificate, report cards, diplomas, news clippings. Then photographs, four minutes of wedding in color, tightly shot loosening into two minutes of reception, faces hands mouths clothes teeth in soft grainy yellows—the yellows, I thought, of his skin—in which

Angel's was the only true whiteness, moth in candle-light. Then a series of pastorals, a southern landscape, soft green valleys coming out on miles of orchard; then Atlanta row house sagscreened, the color values high, a younger Michael . . . maybe a cousin in a Marine uniform . . . then with Michael, the film wobbly in some helper's hands, Michael and Michael's cousin grinning ear to ear, the cousin darkskinned. Then, most puzzling, a long study of an anglo in his early sixties looking younger, walking a golf course, addressing the camera freely. Smiling, gesturing. Some of his words could be lip read or at least you felt you could . . . mainly there were the clues in the face: a certain eagerness after a question, swift opacity, and turnings aside. Then a series of swings, tightly cut, the golf club a vicious weapon under firm control. Last, a scan of a tombstone, "In Memoriam, Rachel McKinley Stone, 1889-1969."

The reel ended. I took it off and went to make myself something to eat. Brown rice, tamari, a jarful of sesame balls, and I brought in a bunch of emperors. There was a bottle of white wine but I felt beer-bloated and my head was ringing from what I'd seen. It was almost two but I couldn't think of sleeping, and realized I hadn't been feeling this way in a long time—this inexhaustible energy with the body subordinate. I listened to the news—the Candidate in a swing through the Southern Tier—ate my rice, and returned to thread the first reel of "Angel Dancing."

It began with a tripod shot of Tarleton unloading picnic gear and an old Zenith shortwave radio high in what looked like an upstate New York meadow, early spring. Then cut to Angel undressing, camera handheld, moving around her as she removed sweater, skirt, stockings, shoes. Her skin was like snow and her hair somehow even lighter, tinged graygold at pubis. She posed arms-out like a ballerina and started what looked like an improvised minuet. Not a particularly graceful dance, rather it was stately and there was a mildly prim smile on her lips. Then she ran toward the camera: Look, goosebumps. A cut of Tarleton, grinning and waving his arms: Faster, dance faster. He was in black—turtleneck to trouser cuffs—but wore track shoes and bounced on his toes as he demonstrated. Angel again: à go-go—then moving wider, camera letting her rove for she always returned, her face opening more on each arc till the flush began to light her breasts and throat. She was still cold, you could see it, and something one level deeper whispered from her eyes as she approached the lens which stoically continued to record her movements even when she broke from dancing into writhings and running excursions, body pumping open and shut, moving blood to crimson and warming her skin. Then the reel stopped.

I put on the second. Opening: the same, except now we were in the desert, cactus brilliant in lemon sunlight. Angel disrobed except for a pair of mocassins. The dance began. Her body seemed a little less supple or she was less willing; as the camera ranged it picked glints of blue snow in ledges under cliffs. Angel was running. Tarleton was letting her move far, far out so she became only a speck. And then returned growing slowly to a flushed smile. But she wanted to stop. Cut to Tarleton, burlesquing a slap on the buttocks. She dances again, arms over head, a belly dance. The camera records her gyrations, the tension of breasts and hips. She tires and sits. She defies the camera, which circles. She puts her head down. A yellow hand enters the frame with a nubbin of cactus which spikes silver whiskers on the smooth white buttocks and now she is up and furious, swiping her cheeks with her hand, running at the lens so like the gaunt woman of the film "Michael T." it becomes a satire on itself; she has to keep coming to threaten so her rage drains to a grim smile. Then an amber hand reaches into the frame to caress her breast.

The third reel is set in the mountains, towering snow-capped mountains, icemelt stream, cedar and hemlock in heavy stands. Angel bathes in the stream, which is gray and green, so clear you can see every rock of the bed; she plunges in and comes out gasping eight, ten, twelve times, like the silver-haired anglo of the earlier film and another vibration to sort . . .

There was one last reel I would have run just out of curiosity because I was too tired even to care any more but in the corner of the box under it was a plastic sack with something knotted into it and I probably wouldn't have thought anything except that's a way to carry powdery things like drugs, for instance. Right away I woke up. There was about a hundred grams, light brown and faintly gummy. I felt a little sick going into the kitchen, finding a candle, and bending one of the stainless steel spoons to hold enough water to tap in a hit to see what heat would do. The water turned tea-color but at bottom there was residue: tiny tarry nodes and a lump of what was probably milk sugar. It took a long time over the flame for the dark heroin to dissolve and almost boil before the sugar melted, swirling into promises of dark dreams. Something for everybody—for the hillside farmer and his family a cash crop, guns for the guards and payoffs for the warlords bringing the raw opium to be refined, and then the endless doublings of price as each middleman took one hundred percent off the top. The annual crop the farmer got five hundred dollars for, cost the addict her/his part of a quarter of a million dollars. Something different for everybody: money, power, dreams, and for Michael Tarleton—death.

It'd gone light outside. I went into the kitchen and put some bacon on, whirred some coffee beans to a medium-fine grind. The earth under the pomegranate tree was washed with early sun; a boy of eight or nine squatted there making designs with a stick, looking up at the kitchen window now and then. I went to the back door.

"¿Que tal, hermano?"

He brushed straight black hair away from American eyes. "Bueń, graĉ. Speak English?"

"Yes." I was smiling. "What can I do for you?"

He stood. "The other lady?"

"Angel"

"Yes. She said I could watch the cartoons if our set is busted. Okay?"

"Okay." He slipped past to the living room. In a moment he had returned. "Hey, did you know your set isn't color?"

I told him to keep the sound low and to turn it off when he was done watching and went to finish breakfast. The bacon was slightly burned but the eggs were good . . . *Strictly Fresh* the carton said, telling the truth for once. The carton labeled HERSTORY was sitting by my bed. It was the box she had invited me to look at and instead I had spied, stealing the images of her life. She'd never know how much I knew about her. Or I could suppose she knew me better and left the opened boxes as invitation. An invitation to the dance.

# 6

I called Vincente to tell him something had come up which unfortunately prevented me from carrying through the remedial letter-to-the-editor workshop and listened to him crawl through the receiver with curiosity. Not that he asked me what could be more important than *la causa*; no, he said *bueno, andale, otra vez.* Which must have pissed me off a little, because next thing I knew I was asking him how he would go about finding out if somebody had a medical record of hepatitis. His suggestions in descending order: 1) ask the person, 2) ask a close relative, 3) ask the family doctor, 4) ask the government . . . so I thanked him and said *mañana . . .*

Then I sat for a long time and thought about the plasterboard wall and the plastic teapot clock and how many millions of dinettes there were with plasterboard and teapot clocks. What was forming in my head I couldn't at first make out: mainly I think I was very angry at Angel for pulling me in but there was absolutely nothing new about that. What was new was realizing I'd lost hold of it all being an exercise or an action or a trip or a job. I was so mad I decided if I couldn't find Angel to shake I would get ahold of Julia and rattle her teeth.

She lived in the back court of a complex of garden

apartments, vines and semi-tropical shrubs crowding cobbled walks between pools and statuary. It was a great place for a rape but at noon under that killer California sun I couldn't imagine anyone getting up enough blood. I mention this to give you an idea of my frame of mind, because it changed real fast when Julia answered the door with a big smile and a "Come in, I've been expecting you." Also that was my first good look at her: a medium-sized dark-haired huge-eyed woman in her thirties; ripe, it seemed to me, very ripe. She had on a caftan and a gold ring in one ear, inconspicuous enough so you weren't really aware of it until you looked for the other—and barefeet with lacquered nails. I felt suddenly very gritty and realized she could outflank me with a wink of one of her long-lashed dark brown eyes. While I was thinking all this and also how she was probably twice as smart and certainly a lot better educated than I, she got me over to about eight feet of silver velour sofa and sat me down to wait while pouring a couple of glasses of iced tea. Which she set on the coffee table with the silver-veined plate glass top next to the silver cigarette box as she took the sofa a few feet away.

"Did you have some questions about Angel's instructions?"

That made me mad again. "Oh, no. Perfectly clear."

She smiled. We sat and sipped iced tea through glass straws. I didn't know about her, but a million thoughts were running my mind and I couldn't hang onto any long enough to make a sensible question. Finally I settled for the obvious. "Do you know where Angel is?"

"Yes."

Simple enough. "Where is she?"

"I promised I wouldn't tell."

The line I had invented for this situation was *you peo-*

*ple are a bunch of verbal motherfuckers and I mean literally* but she spared me having to get myself up out of all that velour for some kind of final farewell scene:

"Let me tell you some things about Angel Stone?"

And she did. Beginning with the usual sordid run of luck: when Angel was seven, her mother's breakdown and suicide orchestrating failure within the context of monogamy: pressure for male heirs, marriage scripting. I'll spare the details, except to say she was not told her mother had suicided until she was twenty-one. As a young adult, then, she turned her newly-educated head toward the contradictions of her mother's life, operating on the premise that error came in pulses, forming a pattern of which she was a part. I'm not going to tell you I didn't feel sympathy for her, from deep inside the languorous freedom of my own family, in which so much of the time Ideals were maintained even though the shape of the Structure was somehow always taken for granted. Working people can't afford not to be Marxians, and if there was ever a family man . . . But the Stones, as persons of property, had so to speak invested their marital relationships as carefully as blue-chip stocks and after Angel's mother was unable to rectify—through a second, male child—the error of Angel being female (secondary sterility was the medical name for it) one recalled that she was not an heiress but simply beautiful whereupon the beauty began to fade. Well, I don't mind fairy-tales even sad ones so I listened to Julia's rap but at the same time, nicking the edges which are supposed to be hard on this kind of old-fashioned American dream, was another reality which was a high class wolf ticket, a rationale for something, I couldn't figure out what. The more you paid to see the wolf, the more mangy the dog you were shown, the fancier the story the ticket seller had to front. Like *this is the* oldest *wolf,* this *wolf has survived three earthquakes and a tidal wave.* "What's the connection with Tarleton?"

A solemn brilliance flashed briefly under concealing lashes. "The whole thing was tragic, and now it must be put behind."

"We're satisfied with the identification?"

"We'll never know what really happened. That's the way it is with these things, and they can ruin a life."

I was believing probably ten percent of this line, and beginning to get irritated again. "Forget Tarleton. What's your connection with Angel?"

"We've been friends since college."

"Any business dealings?"

"Just a scholarly exchange of ideas. Oh, and now and then we try to put together a grant application."

"Such as?"

"Well, learning problems related to sexism, role stereotyping, patterning of various kinds. Angel was doing background work this summer in British Columbia. The one we're working on now is cooperation cadres in which we attempt to get the maximum number of persons to establish primary bonds within a socially viable context. The group Angel studied had a developed variety of sexual practices each individual was expected to pass through which insured primary bonds in approximately eighty-five percent of the group. We want to see if we can create such an environment."

"Why?"

I was hooked but didn't know it until well into the ten or so minute rap Julia laid out along the general lines of "destroy oppression by moving beyond dyadic relationships." Physical sexuality was okay in general; she envisioned early and educated sexuality, movement toward group sex, etc., etc. I didn't realize how charming

Julia's abstractions were until there was a thump of flung-back door and a voice it took me only a moment to recognize, which seemed to call out with freshly unfolding wonder each time I listened: "Julia? Why are you saying these things?" and now she was at the door, blond head flung chin high holding out an empty wine glass. "I couldn't bear to listen any longer. I want a drink." And she walked toward the kitchen.

I think I'd just gotten too tired to be mad. Julia said, "Why are you sighing?" in a slightly suspicious tone, I thought, which made me understand how she must feel. What a bunch. If you could ever get them to hold still long enough . . . In a minute Angel returned. She had on some kind of almost completely destroyed antique garment which looked like it had been designed in the forties to take out the garbage in. Her color wasn't bad, but it wasn't good either: a sort of medium I-am-hanging-in beige with weenie mauve streaks building under the eyes. Which, incidentally, she wouldn't let me catch, slumping instead into a chair across from the sofa and propping her forehead on her extended fingers. "I went to the funeral—it was ghastly. There were a whole lot of people I didn't know; the only ones I recognized were his mother and his brother. I know they saw me but they didn't make any sign. I was afraid to go over to them. I was just about the only white person. They all ignored me. There must have been close to three hundred people there, all acting as if I didn't exist. And I can't blame them. They must hold me partly responsible, I can see that. If it hadn't been for me . . . But it's hard to handle these things well. Michael and I just couldn't carry the load; we had so little time together, and so much tension. We messed it up because we weren't communicating. When I remember, it seems as if we were animals grunting and groaning with each other, knowing we were in pain but not knowing how to talk with each other about it. Nightmarish. But that's really what happened, and why I'm here. I feel as if it's some kind of freakish accident and I wonder if I'll ever get back on the track."

While Julia clucked reassuringly I thought it over. Any way, it was marshy going, a continuation of half-realizing what's happening lengthening into soft margins and slicing currents. With the shades drawn against midday sun, the planes of her cheeks muted young and her body in the clinging housedress seemed almost brittle.

Did she know what Tarleton had stashed in the carton of film? Had she killed Tarleton? Generally I am of the theory that you have to be pretty well organized to kill somebody, no matter how shitty and bad they are; and if they're bigger or older or male there are additional problems. Not that Angel wasn't organized on a personal level. But there was something about her that was to-the-core lovable, and nobody wants to feel capable of loving a killer. Do they? Ah, it was mad. I let myself sink further into the velour as Angel sat shying a glance at me now and then, and Julia moved her hand on the silver cushion like a cautious calligrapher.

When the idea came, I was startled by its simplicity. "You were the last person except for the murderer to see Tarleton alive, weren't you."

I couldn't even buy five percent of the startled look and "how did you know?" that she gave me.

"You tell me." I heard my voice being tough.

While she sipped and thought it over and told me her story, her eyes met, caught, caught and held mine. It seemed she was telling the truth. I only mention it because there are a couple of problems connected with telling the truth; one is you have to know what it is and the other is you have to realize that any invention is going to work out even more grotesquely than the most bizarre reality. Basically, she described a spur-of-the-moment decision at the Vancouver airport to fly not south but east, to confront Tarleton and resolve her fear he might attempt to bind her legally. Portia had begun divorce proceedings for Angel, and there was talk of a restraining order. The summer's field work—research into women's masturbation clans in a remote reserve of Coast Indians—had gone so well she felt up to facing him, and without calling any friends or her lawyer she got into a cab at Kennedy and had herself taken straight to his apartment. She remembered this because as the meter ticked she began to worry whether she had enough cash and was chagrined to find she only had a dollar over for the tip. Tarleton was continuing to live in the apartment they had shared because of the cutting room he'd put in and she remembered the strange feeling searching for the key and hoping he hadn't changed the lock. And then inside, her things (which she'd never thought of that way before, rather as things she'd brought to them both) replaced by new (his) things or else still ghostly present as voids.

But everything was clean and neat, as if he'd made bachelor's peace with himself; it wasn't that, rather a dry, pared-down almost stark quality to the rooms where her things had, it turned out, been the soft, warm, colorful things. She said she sat and thought about this and lost track of the time a bit before realizing she should try while the opportunity was there to find a couple of rather harsh notes she had written after the red-haired woman—the one with Tarleton the night she slugged him—told her about *them.* As she looked through the bedroom she was amazed how tidy he'd become; the usual stacks of newspapers and the bundles of ancient letters nowhere in sight. Finally she wound up in the cutting room, searching drawers. At this point she realized she was no longer looking for the notes, which had probably been destroyed long ago, but simply for a clue to how their break had affected him and she rather liked what she saw. She remembered staring at the splicing table and finding tears in her eyes recalling his shoulders bent over the gossamer film, glasses almost off his nose at the tip while he concentrated celluloid into focus. This image, so in contrast to the ones marking for her the last brutal months of their relationship, made her feel guilty that she had hated him enough to violate his privacy, and she had just flicked off the light over the cutting table when she heard the bolt of the police lock slide and the front door open, bringing with it the voices of two men.

One she immediately recognized as Tarleton's but the other was unknown to her, and she gasped air to calm her heart at the same time listening desperately for words. Impossible, however, to catch what was being said except that by the tone she suspected the other was black; Tarleton's voice was higher and thinner when talking to whites. Up to this point she had half toyed with making her presence known, confessing and apologizing, but it had been a lesson of their relationship that around blacks with whom he was working—interviewing—professionally, he did her no favors at all. She mentioned an occasion of this rather early in their relationship, when a weapons courier from Detroit told Tarleton to get the pussy out of the room so he could finish his story: "She looks like she's got a big mouth to me." And he told her to leave, which she did, incensed that the Detroit "brother" was willing to boast of his actions only to other males. In fact, though her perspective changed, theirs might be the same, still. By the time she realized these things, it was too late to move, even if she had wished, and she had to remain silent and hope they did not come into the cutting room. Her thighs began to shake, so to have something to do (she was afraid to sit down) she inched her way to the wall behind the door. Her heart pounded again, and as she softly pawed the air for obstacles she felt utter helpless dread, such as went deeper and beyond the fact of two (possibly) hostile men who might surprise her.

"I was so terrified I was afraid I would burst if I didn't get out of that room and I must have jogged the door. But anyway it opened and I heard Michael say, 'Well, all right, go get the stuff . . . ' And then the other man left the apartment."

"Did you get a look at him?"

"No. I couldn't keep my thighs from shaking. I was afraid he'd notice the door had fallen open."

"Could you tell what was making you so frightened?"

"Well, the Quantico thing. I mean, perhaps he was making a contact."

"In New York?"

"I don't know."

"Then what happened?"

"Well, at first I was afraid he would come into the cutting room to do some odds and ends while he waited for the man, but then I realized even if he did it was all right, because I am just as strong, and then I realized I could leave at any time. I'd try to be quiet, but if he heard me, well, I was close to the front door and I would simply run and let him figure it out. So I stepped into the hall."

"And?"

"Well, there's a place where you can see the foot of the couch and since I was almost out the door anyway I just glanced over out of curiosity. And I could see his feet. They looked strange."

"What do you mean?"

"Oh, he had his shoes and socks on, but one sock was wrinkled down on his ankle and the shoe was partway off. It just didn't look right. And so I went closer until I could see the rest of the couch and he was lying kind of passed out. But as I was standing there trying to figure out what to do I realized his eyes weren't entirely closed and were moving slightly as if he were trying to focus or something. I must have stared at him for half a minute, waiting for him to speak. But he didn't. So I left."

"I don't understand. What are you saying?"

"Well, it seemed to me he was nodding out."

"You mean he was addicted?"

"No! He never did more than snort a few times when he and I were together. It's just . . . you can't talk reason to someone who's on the nod. I mean you can talk to them but it just brings them down, you may as well save your breath. At this point all I could think was how dumb I'd been to take my summer high and waste it in the city. I couldn't get out of there fast enough. I found an independent cabby who took traveler's checks and sat in the airport until I got a seat on a 727 for San Francisco. That's how rattled I was, because I hate those big aluminum foil jets; all I can think of while I'm in one is the quarter inch of wall between me and twenty-five thousand feet of altitude. And how if anything interrupted that skin we'd all whoosh out like a busted carton of eggs." She swallowed wine. "What do you think?"

"Look." I no longer had to pretend, I was angry. "You're paranoid. You got some ideas why you're paranoid . . . and . . . " She bent her head so far down I could not see her eyes, only the chalk-white lashes and the scar ridging white through the tan. I would have let her think it over even longer but she looked like she'd just been slapped. "I know why I'm paranoid."

When I pulled the knot of brown drug from my pocket and sent it skidding across the silver-veined plate, her brows lifted: she knew what it was.

"In the boxes?" She barely whispered, the room stilled; then somewhere else a human voice appeared to reach out in a strangled, muffled way to . . . whom? Julia picked up the heroin in two fingers, inspecting it like the instructions on a gas mask.

"You knew it was there."

"No." Angel's voice high and thin for the flick of an eyelash. "I was afraid . . . and I didn't want to look."

"That's fine, good thinking."

"The . . . message . . . from Alpha Hoerung, it made me terribly afraid."

"You went to the boxes."

"It was because I had a dim recollection of this woman who worked for my grandmother—no name, just a kind of afterimage of an old . . . "

"Spiderwoman," I finished for her.

"Yes. You see my grandmother was . . . robust—at least that is the way I remember her—but there was, now and then, this other . . . wraithlike person . . . who was always just . . . around . . . when grandmother visited."

"You think it was Alpha Hoerung."

"Well, because the first ten boxes I received were filled with records of my grandmother's business, plus old letters and Society of Friends literature. Fascinating, actually: the record of a working woman's struggle to wealth. Quite Horatia Alger."

"But your grandmother's been dead for years."

"Yes. It took the longest time to figure out how they had gotten to me, and I finally decided it was the companion-person, only I couldn't remember her name."

It sounded okay. "Keep telling me the truth, Angel." I gave her name the Spanish pronunciation. She flushed. She bent her head. "Si?"

"There's a lot . . . I can't remember."

I could hear my pulse tick. "Keep trying."

Julia shifted. "You *are* a little bit of a bully, Kat."

"This *is* a little bit more serious than a punch in the nose."

Angel put her hand back over her eyes. "There's . . . something I can't figure out. I keep trying to put myself in Michael's place . . . "

The name fisted between us. "Michael?"

"He was not an addict. He was working on a documentary."

" 'Drugs at Quantico.' "

"More . . . "

Julia set the knot of brown back on the table. "Is this Mexican?"

She was smiling. I smiled back. "Possibly. It's unrefined, in any event. Not your number four white smack."

"You can smoke it?"

"Smoke it, shoot it, snuff it, stick it up your rectum, I've heard all kinds of stories. The reason you don't see much of it around is it's so much bulkier, harder to smuggle. When it shows up somebody's taking more risks than usual. Something strange is going on: if a lab blows or is busted it may slow things down for a while but you don't all of a sudden get a lot of unrefined junk from your corner dealer. That's talking something much more profound."

"Like a change in government?"

"That would do it, I guess."

"The U.S. military in Guam confiscated almost two tons of heroin when the Thieu government was airlifted through to the refugee camps." Angel spoke in a buffeted voice.

"It's better than cash, pound for pound much more valuable than gold, less flashy than gems."

That was when Angel's glass broke somehow, wine spilling like blood over the veined glass.

I wish I'd had a dip in the freeform pool beyond the bronze fawns and a whole lot of shrubbery, because it was all of a hundred and two and maybe if I hadn't been cruising with half my head just then I wouldn't have been pulled over for a registration check. The patrolman's face looked like somebody had managed to get a bowlful of mashed potatoes to stick together and as he moved his large body I saw he'd been pushed too fast into sports as a child and it had injured his bones. He called me *miss* and took my papers to the radio for a call-in which made me nervous enough to be glad I was clean in California. So it came as a real shock when the dispatcher's voice crackled back that there were three parking warrants totalling eighty-seven dollars on GRE 981, Buick Suburban Gold 1975. Well, of course he had to haul me in, after another twenty minutes while he figured out how to do it. He took his shades off to read, and in his eyes was a show-me-how-and-I'm-your-man doggedness. I could picture the coach taking him aside at the high school awards banquet and whispering into his ear with whiskey breath, *Billeh, ah don't b'lieve you got the phys'cal stamina fuh pro spowt . . . Wah don't y'trah Lawnforcement?* It was fine with me; gave time for the towaway to show up and meanwhile I got a chance to work once more at—yes—figuring it out. Too tired to be mad. I knew I hadn't put the shiners on the car, which left Angel and/or some other unidentified (friend?) person.

The bent jock plied his black and white between palm trees planted long enough to give a solid respectable look to neighborhoods moving not so slowly toward re-development. Houses and lots small, one-level frame dwellings; the kind of area with a garage sale sign every other block in front of used dinette sets, baby furniture, slightly broken dimestore lamps and racks of cleaned and pressed discount store clothing. I felt pretty comfortable in the back of the car, remembering other times when it had been more than parking warrants and I'd been handcuffed. At the same time it's twice as weird to be busted for something you didn't do because if you didn't do it by definition you don't know what it was you didn't do. And if you don't know what it was you didn't do then how can you know you didn't do it? So I thought again about parking warrants, and when and where I might have gotten three. What it amounted to was hypothesizing a real big wind able to pluck tickets from under the spring-loaded wipers three times in the three months since arriving in the sunny south. No. Eliminating Angel temporarily, why would she loan the car to a person likely to run bad karma on it?

While this was stomping through my head we pulled into the garage at Police Headquarters and when I saw the matron waiting I realized there was more going on than parking tickets. She led me to an interrogation room and left me there. It was a small room with a low ceiling, painted tan. There was a simulated wood table and three chairs so I stacked the chairs on the table and lay down in the space made vacant. Not enough room really to stretch out, but I wiggled around till it felt okay and began breathing in my abdomen in-out, 1-2-3-123456. In a moment my heart slowed and I started from the balls of the feet relaxing my way upward into thighs and buttocks and carefully up the spine to the shoulder blades. Then fingers inward to shoulder blades, feeling bis and tris separately, finally up the neck into the jaws and cheeks and pulsing off scalp. Then I manipulated my spine, did a cobra for a while, did neck rotation and spine stretching and when I'd cracked every joint that wanted to I lowered into a modified lotus for a few minutes quiet reflection.

Maybe this sounds too easy. But what the hell it's do something or have the crappy jail environment crowd in on you. It's a creephole and it's meant to be; there's the whole thing about deterrents and, while you could argue that one all day, there's no doubt in my mind one whiff is enough to keep most folks from bending any more laws than they have to for survival. This was my third arrest, and that meant I hadn't been deterred, obviously. Maybe that also meant I was on some kind of bizarre death trip associating with ghouls like him who entered just then followed by a short smiling partner and the matron. Actually I only heard them, my eyes looking inward at the moment; heard them and then silence, presumably as they took in the scene. The silence lasted for about ten seconds and then the screech of chairlegs as they were set down and the short one in the middle said, "Very Kung Fu. Would you get up now?"

So I sighed and opened my eyes and very carefully so as to avoid vertigo stood to face them.

The matron sat but the rest of us continued to stand until the middle one hiked a hip on the table edge. Then his partner sat and rearranged his jacket over the gut gun in his belt holster. It was so clear to me they meant me to stand without ever saying it to my face that I deliberately walked to the remaining chair and pulled it away from the table to sit in. But then when I sat down I didn't get a very good view of the matron's face so I moved the chair until it was between her and Shorty. Now I couldn't see the ghoul, which was fine with me. He shifted to get a better view of me but the room was just too small. Too bad. He wound up propping his cheeks in thumb and forefinger, as if he was afraid his mouth would betray him.

Shorty spoke again. "Are you comfortable now?" I think it was a try at sarcasm.

"No. I want my phone call."

"You people know all the rules, don't you." I think this was supposed to be an insult.

"Do I get my phone call?"

"The line's busy. There was a bombing, you know. A man died. He left two young sons."

"I didn't know that."

"Funny you didn't know, because all those warrants are for parking within a four block radius of that bombing. Very funny."

To tell the truth that lifted my scalp. Either it was outright bullshit to shake me down for something bigger in such a way I'd be grateful as hell to accept a charge of smuggling nonaddictive drugs or some other such shuck and they'd get to lock me up for awhile (*why?*), or true. The fact is once they get you charged with the right felony they've got you for at least three years and fifty grand and what the hell if you prove you weren't even around at the time, you've been broken. All that energy put into fighting a machine so vast it can only roughly estimate how much it costs to run itself, services by bureaucrats as interchangeable as flashlight batteries . . . even if you won you lost because there's never any way to make up time. Example: a university computer center is fire-bombed and completely destroyed. The fire engines come, the police, a crowd gathers and is held back. Half an hour later a black man is seen running from another building near by. He is arrested. Turns out he is the janitor in the Center, claims he was in the building when it went but he didn't see who did it. He is tried and convicted and sentenced to three-to-five on the basis of not very conclusive evidence and since he's in a state with indeterminate sentencing procedures, it's possible he'll never come out. The "crime" is marked solved, the janitor becomes a convict—who knows? maybe he really did it—ripples up and down, time passes, another man done gone.

"Are you going to give me my phone call?"

"Where were you the twentieth, twenty-first, and twenty-second of this month?"

"Don't you even read the Miranda flashcard any more?"

"Why bother? You already know what it says. Anyway the Supreme Court changed the ruling."

"Well, I'm not going to answer your questions. I've given you my I.D. and I want to make a phone call."

So the matron accompanied me and I called Vincente's mother. He wasn't in but she expected him back any minute. Could she take a message? I gave her the address. On the way back to the interrogation room it occurred to me they were birddogging Angel pretty close, because otherwise how could they pull those warrants within a week of the actual citation? I was trying to construct a witty rejoinder to what was beginning to seem an inevitable question, "Will you tell us what you know about Angel Stone?" but the matron led me to the desk sergeant and I was charged with failure to give a left turn signal which is a moving violation carrying twenty-five dollars bail. In view of the fact I hadn't done it I was a little pissed but not very. I mean, it was better than any of the other possibilities.

I wound up calling Vince's mother back again and this time he had just gotten in. "Hey, Niña—are you okay? I'm just about to come down."

"Yes, it's all taken care of. Just too much to explain over the phone. Don't come down to this slimy place, I'll take a cab and see you later." I hoped it didn't sound like a brush-off especially since he was the only person in town who could be counted on. As for Angel, I desired her, wanted to be near her, but we weren't tuned into the same station.

"Hey, you should let me pick you up."

I was about to ask him to cool it when I changed my mind.

"Okay. But not here. I'll be at the first coffee shop I find headed north."

"See you in twenty."

The coffee shop was one of those city-center places with a blind newsboy and two overweight cabbies at the counter, and a burger cost two bucks. I ordered one with fries. When it came it looked like what the kids call a "Hearstburger"—you open it up and there's no Patty inside—but I finally found it slid off to one edge of the Thousand Island dressing coated balloon bun. I wondered who was getting the rest of my ration that day. It took me maybe half a cup of coffee to bring it right back home. It takes a little explaining: I'm not much of a reader except for the basic stuff and so it took me a long time to realize that there were some things I read that made me angry, and some things that made me peaceful. When I read that women are considered better candidates for lobotomy, since afterwards they are tractable, cheerful, and more adapted to tedious work like housekeeping, I got mad. When I read "1,936 'Bombing Incidents' Reported by FBI Last Year" it made me feel good right to the bone. The stuff that made me mad I called my Atrocity File and the other stuff I called Cosmic Giggles. And then I watched them balance out. One time I heard an aging member of the Israeli Irgun say, *Excess of atrocities is counter-productive.* So now I thought about the price of meat and out of my Atrocity File popped the statistic I'd been unable to forget during September of 1974: that Rockefeller's weekly interest check ran into six figures—in effect every Monday morning he had a tenth part of a million dollars to spend. I was picking gristle from between my upper left third and fourth molars and reflecting on how many bozos that would buy when I realized it had been three quarters of an hour and no Vincente. So I thought again quickly—yes, we'd agreed first coffee shop north. That made me nervous, it was getting to be a habit—so I took a couple of deep breaths before I stood and went to pay my check. The skin between my shoulder blades felt funny, a little warning pressure. Just one of those days when everybody's after you. Still any warning will do to move my feet; I hung around too long once and it put me in the hospital under charges of "inciting to riot." And then another time I hung around and wound up being subpoenaed by a Grand Jury. That time, three years ago, I figured I knew too much and split and glad I did, even if it meant I couldn't hang out in Illinois till Thanksgiving. So this time I hoped Vincente was all right and got myself to a phone booth for a few long distance words with the lovely Aida-who-works-for-an-airlines, to set a date for my visit. But first I called Julia and told her to do something about getting all the bad paper off the car or else sell it.

I felt like a refugee knocking on the eggplant-purple lacquered door of Max's big house on Potrero, and I wouldn't let Aida give me the big hug she had waiting until I got a shower. "What's up?" she smiled. I could see Mickey through the doorway to the living room with its sweep of plate glass overlooking the city. Judy was on the stereo, her last concert album; Mickey was smiling. We waved. "I'm in the middle again, babycakes. I don't know how I do it."

She grinned and led me down a deeply carpeted hall to her bathroom. As I watched myself undress in all the mirrors my eyes stung from the silverfoil walls and naked bulbs and then adjusted. It had been a while since I gave a close look. I'd gained a little weight during the summer and now I could see it was coming off. The tan was okay, it didn't do to be too dark in southern California unless you were trying to be invisible. The swimming had kept me pretty well muscled. I did some flexing and turned to find Aida smiling, holding out Pernod on the rocks. "Still lookin' good." That made me blush. She always could make me blush.

Later we spent two stoned laughing hours ransacking the house wardrobes for something for me—*Your clothes,* Mickey said, *will of course have to be burned*—and we all thought I looked demure in white bells and canvas midshipman's summer dress jacket. Aida tucked a lace-trimmed hanky in my left top front

pocket—*Have to be careful which pocket you put it in,*
she added—and I tied a red silk headband around my
brow. *C'mon,* Mickey said, *Max told us to be there at
eight-thirty on the button.*

At the restaurant the maitre d' was expecting us and
led to a banquette at the back of the large room with red
leather and white linens. "Anything you like, and enjoy
yourself." So we giggled and ordered prawns and crab
and Caesar's Salad and Weibel Cellars Haut Champagne. Max was part owner, a good restaurant cook
who didn't cut corners and did his own purchasing.
Everything was fresh and if he couldn't get it he didn't
use substitutes. It was wonderful to eat so well without
having to look at the other side of the card where the
prices were and I got to feeling so good I almost forgave
Rockefeller. But I couldn't quite, because it wasn't
Rockefeller who'd cooked it, it was Max.

After Max joined us and we sipped through a pousse-
cafe the guys offered to take us bar hopping, which
seemed like a good idea. So we left Aida's MGB in the
parking garage and took Max's ancient Mercedes.
"This car is getting so creaky and loose I'm afraid I'll
come back and find it's all oozed together in a great big
burgundy-colored puddle just like one of those illusions
you see advertised in comic books. Poor baby." He
fussed with the ignition until it glowed but when he
kicked the starter the engine purred like a silk thread
run through the fingers. I let myself sink into the leather
seat which through the years had hollowed like the
pocket of a catcher's mitt and Max caught my eye in the
rearview mirror. "Who are these folks you're running
with now, Kat? I hate to see you waste your talent."

I thought that over as he pulled up in front of the
Powder Horn and the attendant—eighteen and black—
took the car off to park it. I was still thinking when we

got inside. And then I even forgot I could think. The decor is frontier 'n' leather, and after the new fashion the bar is vertical, four floors ranging from sawdust and bullshit to rivergambler and antebellum queens. You already know the service is slow and the drinks are outrageous. But on the Western Saloon level the act is great, a willowy guy with a rubber face who is a marvelous Billie the Kid. And when a soft-eyed lumberjack with blond hair/blue eyes came over to say how nice it was to see ladies in the bar I could barely bring myself to say, *Goddess made women: Rockefeller made ladies.* Then Billie went off to his dressing room and an impersonator came out to do a lip synch and Mickey yawned and we gathered ourselves after the first song. It seemed even possible he hadn't liked the way Max barked laughter at Billie's act. Whatever, he had Max take us to the Onyx, near U.S. Army Post Presidio, an uneasy blend of biker and uniform trips. I'd heard about the place but you would never think of going there unless with someone who'd gone before. It was said a newly-appointed commandant of the post frequented the place the last weeks before his stabbing death in his on-base bedroom. The bar owners had been offered a choice: sell or we close you down. So they sold. Now the sign said *Club Presidio* and there was so much leather inside you could smell it. Leather, and about ninety-nine earrings and now and then a smiling brawny fellow with a leather thong around his neck where something heavy hung inside his leather jerkin. Some of the chaps had eyes empty as a place between the clouds and some hid their eyes and some only had one eye left, but all together they added up to a cold hard wind on the back of my neck. And even so a great beautiful vacant smiling lout in black tailored capeskin came to tell us how nice it was to see girls in here, and to buy us a drink. So what with explaining about girls and boys we stayed rather longer than we had planned and Mickey explained how before there had been a glassed room at the end where the bikers parked their machines in view of the bar and there was always a muffled thunder of perfectly tuned engines.

I thought about the uses the military made of gay people, trading on fear of court-martial and the guilt of being thought "deviant" to coerce the gay soldier to demonstrate super patriotism and willingness to do hardship work as proof of "normality." While at the same time the perverseness of militarism and the contradictions of the culture—which called us to fight for peace by waging war in a dozen places each day—met in bars like these. With gentle passions, off-duty troops waited for someone to explain why they had been trained to kill, and who the enemy was.

"Who do you think cut the Commandant, Max?"

He turned to me. "I talked to an older biker who claimed it was a woman, but they hushed it up. I only heard it because I listen to the news on the way to work, and at five a.m. sometimes you find out things about generals you don't find out at five p.m."

Mickey blinked slowly. "Seems to me . . . didn't they get a guy for it, a noncom with a gripe?"

And now I remembered dimly, too. "He was a Chicano. About a year and a half ago."

"It's funny the way these things get forgotten, isn't it?"

"Yes," I agreed. "It's very funny." I thought for a second about Tarleton, about his amber skin and hooded eyes, his brown smile . . . *what do you think about families, Kat?*

On the way home Max played Moody Blues and we all looked at the sky, which tried real hard to be starry and almost succeeded. We'd left the lights on low and so when Mickey uncorked the sandalwood massage oil it seemed friendly and familiar to undress and rub each others' bodies. We'd done so before, we knew about contracts and telling the truth. About one-thirty Max began to yawn and a little while later he went to bed. Mickey said he knew a way for the three of us remaining to get off at the same time—involving four silk scarves with Aida and me facing each other joined at wrists and ankles. "Oh, Mickey, how decadent!" she cried, eyes glistening. He grinned. But I? I don't know . . . I did it. Oh yes I rolled on the floor against Aida's long gold body while Mickey talked and touched, delicious threats wise hands. "Isn't it interesting how you *girls* went along with everything I suggested and now I could do whatever occurs to me? Ever think about that, Kat?" His pointed face, his large amused eyes, his large and calloused hands, his B ticket longshoreman's wiry body pushed between Aida and me and he laughed. I felt her fingers against my own but everywhere else was him, even his long chestnut hair in my face when I wanted her blondness to remind me of Angel. He laughed some more and grabbed us round our waists and brought his knees between our thighs into all the madly firing nerves and slippery heat of our sex. First he didn't have an erection then he did and Aida and I dangled laced by wrist and ankle under his grin. "You are," he said softly, "completely in my power." Well, of course we had to show him we were not, kissing long and keen till fluids danced and pounded and the frontier was once again crossed to that mindless place orgasm dwells, blind and tidal. I loved it. I got off, I did, it was real good. They were so cool and I wasn't, I was ridiculously grateful and they shut me up, laughing and carrying on. I wished I could be more like them and less obsessed with Angel, because they really were good people, better than her in being able to give, expecting and wishing to give. Then it seemed to me I was being unjust, for Angel Stone knew what she knew.

In the morning the house was rosy with sun. Max was long gone to purchase and Aida had left at six for a flight to Boston. Mickey and I sat over coffee and he told me things he would pick up the gun for:

a. If the "consenting adults" laws were modified oppressively, as for example if local governments got back into the sex law business. "This is something we have to fight every generation."
b. If the country went more at war, he would go to the barricades. "Another continuing struggle."
c. If it became difficult to live the good life he and Max and Aida were living. "If I couldn't work in my studio, if I had to do what somebody else thought was *better* for me . . . I'll be damned if I'll suffer so the Pig can fart on silk."

I told him about Hearstburgers and then discovered I'd worked backwards and told him about the "interview" and before I knew it I'd gotten clear to the story Angel told, and the funeral and Julia and then all of a sudden I was talking about the films of the night before. He was a great listener. He smiled a lot and when I finished he said, "Do I have your number?"

I told him I didn't have a number. I told him I wasn't at war; that I tried and it was unhealthy for living things. He told me there were no spectators, everyone participated whether they knew or not. I said yeah. I said I thought it was weird how people seemed to want power and he laughed the way he did the night before between us only in the daylight his mouth looked thinner and less soft. "What are you—accusing me of being macho?"

"Maybe. Are you?"

"Maybe. What'd you have in mind?" His eyes flicked over me and there was no trace left of the night before.

I thought about how fast it leaked away, union of bodies—worse than words, the flesh utterly unsatisfiable. "It's too easy for you—you're white, you're a man; anytime it gets tough you can jump back into the ruling class, become an invisible drone."

His eyes glittered. "Don't put me in that whiteman bag, honey, don't you dare. Why do you think I'm queer? Dig it, really dig it, because I'm a worker, too, that means I have to work with all these other people some of whom think queers should be exterminated. You can hear that—you're pretty butch yourself."

On the way to the house in North Beach where Tarleton's mother lived I thought about loving women and sometimes men, something about respect and trust, something very important about it that it could build and burst like a dam and flood everywhere through people; and I could have *believed,* except in the Mission District people were still dying in doorways at nine a.m. and on Geary at nine-twenty-nine I watched a hooker solicit her last? first? john, a fattish fellow in his forties, with a hairpiece and sunburned skin.

# 7

At ten a.m. I was walking up a forty-five degree North Beach street looking for three-seven-three-two, which turned out to be a trim gold and brown stucco circa 1920, lace window curtains, potted plants. It was the house Tarleton bought on his G.I. bill, where he and his first wife were living when Angel came into the picture. He was a second cameraman then, taking a course on film from U.C. Berkeley extension. She was commuting from her parent's house in Hillsborough; one night when the car came to pick her up she gave him a lift; a matter of a few miles, but long enough. In the back of the brougham chemistry occurred, that catalytic excitement where one and one make three. Not to say they fell into each other's arms immediately; they were both too carefully raised to omit obligatory social acknowledgements. Imagine the shock and surprise in Hillsborough, the alarm and dim forewarnings in North Beach. Now, according to Angel, Tarleton's mother lived in the house, but when I rang the door was answered by a very tall black woman about my age, her hair turbaned with the same African print as her dress, cheeks and forehead highlighted with umber cream, her large unfriendly eyes kohl-rimmed. *"Yes?"* Not to say she was hostile, though her tone hovered close. I was getting a crick in my neck from looking upward from my five feet four inches to her six and some so I pulled the press pass I'd given myself when I still belonged to the paper and she said, "Wait a minute please" and I guess went to talk to somebody. She did not forget to close the door, so I looked up and down the street. It was a real nice neighborhood, a lot different from Harlem or Watts or Hunter's Point, but it had that fragile quality any deep-city block has. One more piece of trash in the gutter, or a couple of yelling kids chasing each other and the whole place would suddenly seem a touch squalid. Three or four more buildings with peeling paint and an unkempt old person sitting in a basement doorway, too many cats and dogs, not to mention a neighborhood addict and a garbage strike and the place would be gone . . . but right now the turbaned woman reappeared smiling slightly as if I'd passed at least the first test and ushered me into the front parlor where Mrs. Tarleton sat draped heavily in black, her dark hand resting on an open book. Her companion sat next to her on the cut-velvet sofa so I took a chair at the side.

"My name is Katerina Guerrera," I began.

Mrs. Tarleton answered my gaze. "I know who you are. Michael hired you to look out for Angel before he died. Are you still with her?"

I thought she might kick me out, but I had to be honest. "Yes."

She nodded as if she had known anyway. I was beginning to remember her younger face from the film and now and then some of the earlier delicacy of jaw and nose shadowed through, but she had put on flesh since and under the present circumstances it wasn't surprising she looked pretty grim. "What do you want?"

"I'm sorry to come to you so soon after . . . the funeral . . . but I am trying to consider how to protect

Angel from any possible harm. If I just knew more about what happened . . . "

The companion gave me a hard glance for that, but she didn't say anything. Mrs. Tarleton looked down at her hands, then back to my face. "Such as?"

"For instance the hepatitis—was your son ever infected?"

She stared evenly at me for a long time before she answered. "You have some illusion you are going to solve this crime, don't you. You actually don't realize we have our best people working right now . . . "

She might have said more but there had been an almost invisible pressure, a mere shifting of weight against her thigh perhaps. And then the kohl-rimmed eyes of the younger woman sweeping up to hold mine as she smiled her way through the line: "I think what Mrs. Tarleton is wanting to have understood is that we are in no sense deluded about the seriousness of Michael Tarleton's work and life, and we understand their implications. We are investigating the matter very thoroughly." She recomposed her face smoothly.

"I of course expected you to say this and never for a moment did the thought cross my mind you would not do a complete investigation—I would like to help in any way I can, but right now I also have to be concerned for the safety of Ms. Stone. Do you see *my* motivation?"

She gave me a cool smile for that and it suddenly seemed like we might get along someday. Mrs. Tarleton broke in. "Michael had the best care when he was a child. His health was perfect. He didn't even have a filling in his head. My husband and I made sure he had everything he needed. He took a degree and he fulfilled his military commitment. The police, the coroner, the press would have you think that because his skin was not white enough to pass that he was automatically some kind of junglebunny addict. Well, I'm sorry for them because he was a good son and always respectful to me and treated me right. The image they see of him is what they want to see."

I stayed long enough for a cup of tea and to hear three sophistications on the line: that Tarleton had uncovered more than the military could stand to have revealed about the involvements of high officers in international trafficking and that he had been murdered because he would not stop working on the project; that the hepatitis cover story indicated the collusion of the N.Y. coroner's office in a crude attempt to portray Tarleton as a needle freak; that the apartment had been set afire later when the assassin realized Tarleton might have films of the Quantico project. Please understand this analysis developed from the facts known to them which they conveyed to me; they were, it turned out, intending to publish their findings and, if a substantial case appeared, to press charges. I wished them luck with their judge.

North Beach was trying to have one of those sunny afternoons which used to be so common—or was it just that I was younger?—and it seemed right to walk out Columbus past the Italian delis to the little park where everybody used to come then to eat pastry from the shop across the street. And to Signor Repetto with the celluloid prosthesis and the hundred-pound sacks of coffeebeans which he roasted each day in an enormous brass cauldron. I bought a canneloni and watched women. But today I could only muse on Tarleton's mother sitting other days long ago in a park like this, if she was lucky enough, with the infant Michael, she knowing in important ways the idea of family was not working and would not for her with the father of her child. I looked

**103**

at young mothers in flowered prints pushing strollers or carriages each with a moonfaced grub translucent with newness and wondered how many of them would be able to hold together, the Mommy/Daddy/Baby of the American twentieth century. It was the unit of commerce, a consuming unit whose products were infants and emotions, a cultural coatrack to hang notions of human nature, an unconscious mechanism to maximize feelings of individuality to the point of vertical alienation from anyone but Mommy/Daddy/Baby. In which of the multistoried shafts of the financial district only a mile away did Daddy work? Did Mommy dream of a house in the country? Did Baby hear the tidesuck of *us we my* in the blinking dark? I've said I was monogamous once and by now you've probably guessed with a woman, so I can say the relationship permeates all kinds of couplings; if you don't want kids it's pets. My mate—I'll call her Nord, for we had nicknames, the whole bit—was an overweight Jewish woman whose people had money from the auto salvage business and lived in a candybox house out Pelham Parkway whence we repaired pretty often for huge meals, clothes, and to borrow a car for the weekends. We were both in school and she covered a lot of my expenses; I thought her generous in a way Christians simply weren't—with possessions and money a real socialist. She told me how smart I was, how beautiful, until I believed her even as I resented being placed in a position of proving/disproving basic assumptions about myself. Her parents called each other "Papa" and "Mama." As for our sex life we hardly knew what a clitoris was and so wound up having about as much fun as a newly married hetero couple, which is to say not all that much to judge from the jokebooks. So while we satisfied the quotas on romantic love and got along well into the bargain we had this enormous contradiction which was we were living out relationships we weren't even aware of; essentially monogamous and completely consumption-directed. What happened was she met an older woman—twenty-seven at the time—named Topper, who was the daughter of a clerk of the fifth U.S. Circuit Court of Appeals, moved in with the woman within a week and it was in fact I who had to bite the bullet. Like any divorce it hurt like hell, and it took me years to even begin to figure out what happened. Like Angel and Tarleton? You could get terribly sucked into the individuality dyadic relationships promised, each for each—you could delude yourself you were free inside your own doors when really what you were was simply unconscious of how what you did in the privacy of your rooms was a reflection of the need society had of you.

To listen to Mrs. Tarleton and her companion at least a terrible crime and possibly an unwitnessed martyrdom had occurred. I could readily see why the mother would respond to unwitnessed martyrdom as an outgrowth of her own Mommy/Daddy/Baby experiences, her sensitivity to the uses to which society had put her energies. For the companion also it was part of a pattern around which some considerable skill of handling had accrued by nature of incessant practice, generation after generation of dead children. Did anyone any more want to raise humans to it? In 1973, in California, two-hundred thousand women killed living tissue and the state paid for it lest both showed up on welfare rolls while lesbians continued to say love women not men we're better lovers and you won't get pregnant (it was Gertrude Stein's centennial) and the Church deathrattled *Abortion is murder! Murder! Murder in the first degree!* So I

thought about Murder and Martyrdom and Men and
Michael Tarleton and Angel Stone and Monogamy and
Hillsborough and Women and Drugs.

All I knew about Hillsborough was straight out of the
papers during the Hearst thing, all those montages of
rainy lawns and wind-whipped awnings and drenched
network reporters. There was some moderately sophist-
icated stuff on the makeup and origins of the SLA in the
underground press, but nobody managed to crack the
Hearsts at home, though Steven Weed appeared to
make a White Rabbit try. So the first thing I realized
was that there are different parts of Hillsborough, and
that some of them have what my people would refer to
as a "small mansion," that is to say less than sixteen
rooms. But even the small ones have their sweeping
lawns and curved drives. The one marked *Stone* in
chrome on polished basalt looked as if it had been there
for about as long as it took the first member of my
family to get to college; it was a very tailored Bauhaus
model which had apparently defied rusticizing.

I pulled the rented car into the only vacant spot and
let her get a taste of parking between an 320 SL so antique it had clearly been in the family from first purchase and a two-year-old Volvo 1800 ES, air-con-
ditioning and sunroof. I didn't know what she'd do, but
if I were in her spot I'd climb up their license plates.
Then I went past a whole lot of shrubs which could only
have been cared for by an Asian gardener who had had
them at his mercy for about a hundred years. Against
the highly finished white cement walls and stainless steel
and glass they seemed stricken souls trapped in a vegeta-
tive eternity. By the time I rang the bell I felt like Icha-
bod Crane pursued.

An aproned black woman appeared, looked suspicious, handed back my press pass and said she'd been instructed to say there was no comment on the reports Mr. Stone was intending to resign. I filed that under "I" for interesting. She accepted the note I held out and departed silently in white nurse's shoes. She did not neglect to close the door.

The simply dressed woman in her forties who appeared next invited me into a hallway mirrored floor to ceiling with frosted insets of strong geometric shapes outlined in a dark walnutty wood. The woman smiled. I'd call her handsome and for a moment I thought she might be some other stratum of employee, but I've seen too many servants to mistake the longlegged stance of someone who plays tennis and so I asked, "Mrs. Stone?"

She continued to smile in a distracted way. "Yes?" I watched her eyes shift almost imperceptibly to the platinum filigree watch on her very lightly tanned wrist as if to hint meetings and committees and then her eyes found mine. They lit in a curious way—I hate to give the wrong idea, but it was like watching a pinball machine register a score, or a radar display sweep hidden objects. "You're from Angel, aren't you."

She shortened the *a* and stressed the last syllable— Ann*gel*—and I thought about that as she led me into a living room which looked like a set for "Guess Who's Coming to Dinner". There were about seventy yellow chrysanthemums in a Chinese vase decorated with a goldfish in four strokes sitting next to piano music on a contemporary Knabe which seemed hewn from a single block of cherry; but that was just the background for long cream silk sofas with huge down-filled cushions and low round cherry coffeetables with claw feet and a lot of wool rugs striped cream and yellow with silver threads shooting intermittently toning the room less formal. We sat on two sides of a cherry round and I watched her light the first of the four cigarettes she smoked in the course of our conversation, taking each from a cup of dimpled crystal and lighting from a little black disposable lighter. The ashtray was bronze.

"You care for her, don't you. No I know she can't let us know where she is. This terrible thing! Her father is so worried about her . . ."

"She's fine. I saw her yesterday."

"Oh, I'm so glad to hear that. They came to talk to Mr. Stone and made some accusations. He was very angry afterwards."

"From the Federal Bureau of Investigation?"

"I gathered they had to do with . . . sexual practices. And of course it's true about the rapes."

"The rapes?"

"The white women kidnapped from the streets, taken off and raped repeatedly by groups of black men. I know of a case in which the girl was held for twelve hours and raped by more men than she could remember in a house where there were white women pregnant, who came and watched. But to suggest Angel is involved in this sort of thing!"

She looked a lot less like Katherine Hepburn now, and her finger trembled as she lifted the cigarette and set it carefully between her lips. "We were living in a dangerous illusion when we accepted Michael into the family. I see now it was terribly innocent of us to think we could take the most brilliant member and assimilate him without also getting the people who pushed from below. And some of those people are simply . . . criminals, or verging on it. I think Angel is still innocent about this. At least she is being cautious for the first time, I'm grateful for that. It worries her father so. I've never been able to impress on her . . . "

"When you say 'criminals,' what crimes are you referring to?"

She ground the cigarette against one of the neo-Grecian nudes in the frieze border of the bronze ash tray. Two of the inch-high perfectly formed naked women disappeared under ashes. "Why, there are three kinds, in my understanding: crimes of personal injury, crimes against property, and crimes against human dignity. To say that something is not a crime because it's done in the name of politics!"

She seemed on the edge of something very interesting but as I counted the naked ladies and tried to think of what would push her over, her hand reached for another cigarette and she steadied, frowning it lit. The room was so quiet I could hear the base of the lighter click dully against the polished wood. So that's what the reporters meant when they said "the quiet suburb of Hillsborough." Where one could be a woman in mid-forties who knew what terrible things happened, in fact even knew a person to whom they had happened, but had never had them happen to oneself—although one's step-daughter, by some fault of upbringing, some error of heredity, was closer and must be watched or she would go over the edge down into where all the pushing began.

"Tarleton was involved in politics?"

"It didn't seem so at first. It's *quite* confusing. We had a delightful time with them the first six months they were married. Then he was offered his own film unit and for some reason that meant he had to base in New York. So each time we flew east on the way to the

Aegean we'd have a week in Manhattan with them . . .
Isn't it tragic about Cyprus? There were the most
charming villages there and they have been decimated.
Men are great fools.''

She puffed away on that thought for a moment and I
looked at a small museum-mounted tapestry depicting a
peasant bending to harvest wheat as the Grim Reaper
hovered over him with a scythe. For good measure the
word *Mort.* had been woven over the scythe and Death
had a hideous grin. The peasant was also smiling . . .

''You visited them in New York?''

Tapping the ash from her cigarette she shifted and
looked at me. Her eyes were vividly dark brown and I
thought of Angel's clear blue ones. But then this was a
step-mother; they weren't related by blood. I wondered
for a moment about Angel's mother's eyes. ''We'd do
some holiday shopping. They invited us to their apartment, quite a nice apartment in a building of studios.
The entire front was glass and they had some very pretty
plants. Angel was very much quieter than she had ever
been, less argumentative. I put it down to the fact that
she was finally able to write full time. When I heard
they had moved because Michael needed more room I
was sorry.''

''So she wasn't really changed, simply quieter.''

''Well, our last visit was when I realized how far
things had gone. She was quite changed.''

''In what way?''

She gave me a shrewd look but continued: ''I suppose
one might say that the visible manifestation was her
drinking. A certain spiritlessness. It's hard to define.
Michael on the other hand was blooming. There was
just something terribly perverse about it. She seemed
under a strain, even though when we did get a chance to
have a few words alone she was just as . . . unequivocal

as ever. Her father didn't notice anything so I put it out of my mind. I tried to warn her!"

"Warn her about what?"

"Well . . . " She snuffed the cigarette. "The nature of the interests she had aligned herself with . . . "

"Which were?"

She looked at me as if I were mad, or a fool, or insulting her. I smiled and leaned forward. "Please understand, Mrs. Stone. I work for Angel, Tarleton hired me. For three months I babysit a jillion boxes of manuscript while she's off being a scientist in British Columbia and then she comes back and things look like they're working out. For two days that way, and then all of a sudden it starts raining troubles and Angel is in hiding and apparently frightened about something. Originally . . . "

"Well, you see, there's your problem right there. You were hired by Tarleton."

"But Tarleton's dead."

She reached a third cigarette and flicked it burning. "All right. I'll tell you what I think," the second or was it the third Mrs. Stone said. "I think men don't plan carefully enough. Then they're astonished by what happens. It's sad, really." She kept the lighter in her fist, tossing it now and then. I always notice when people arm themselves, however symbolically, and decided *no* on the end of my speech she'd interrupted: the part where I was going to come right out and lay on her she hadn't said one *real* thing so she better have some facts before she started pushing a scenario as perverse as Tarleton involved in some kind of politically rationalized rape squad. Her implication this sickness had pursued/driven Angel west was even more bizarre. But there was a further, totally personal and private reason I couldn't say any of that, and her name was *Barbara*.

I knew Barbara when we had the *dozo* in Madison and again two years later when she and a brother named Pi were active in the L.A. area. The people in Barbara's house were heavies to my eyes at least partly because of the almost cultic obsession with sexuality they exuded in their clothing—leathery, nudistic, significantly accented—the women big-eyed waifs in harem silks. And to witness Barbara, who only twenty-odd months before had been a sophomore student taking self-defense karate now manifest this gutter ripeness, had been mind-bending for me. When I asked *what* and *how* she smiled from the other side and invited me for a night. So I asked *was that how it had been with her* and Barbara ran it down for me. I hadn't thought about her in almost a year, but now I could see her—like Angel's step-mother a wiry brunette who smoked nervously—as with egoless eyes she had told me what happened.

Barbara began, I recall, announcing I was going to hear the story of her life. But she started with her arrival in L.A. where she went—you guessed it—to try for a job in the movies. She wanted to dance. Well she got one job and an almost promise she'd get a bit part before running out of money so to support herself she decided to go topless. And that led way out Santa Monica Boulevard where she met *a different type of person,* into just generally a faster harder trip. It hadn't bothered Barbara; she'd figured all the trips were getting faster and harder, even the slowest softest ones, because the energy some people were beginning to define as collective began torquing under pressure of Greed Culture, she called it, and the *gimme* scenario bleated from all sides. She had an offer of two hundred a day to do a skinflick and rejected it as too clearly moving deeper into the belly of the beast . . . But pressure persisted, the suck into a somewhere and one evening in the company of the straightest guy she knew she was taken to a house much like the one Mrs. Stone and I now sat in—in other words big and old and comfortable—and over the course of a very long evening she found herself naked then making contact with other naked people and finally simply forgetting everything and letting things be done to her. One of the men was black. There were more and more of these times. With different people. She found she had to know some people better than others before she could be comfortable with them but everybody was real nice, everybody seemed to understand. She gradually put it together that there were really six people living in the house: four men and two women. One of the men was Pi. She was the newcomer at the house, interested in fitting in, going along with what the others did. Now and then two or three of the men would take off and be gone for a few days. She realized what they were doing. It didn't bother her, she wanted to help; she figured she could drive. When she said so, the men gave her a lot of shit and laughed at her and one of them called her a cunt which made her so mad she walked up to him and kicked him in the shin, decking him. Everybody thought that was pretty funny and one of the men started singing softly *Have you got what it takes?* which was a signal for a come-on in the house so to get out of a tense situation she accompanied him to one of the upstairs rooms.

She told me she would never forget the ceiling which was black, here and there shiny in patches, or the bedspread, which was pink and red and purple chenille in wave patterns. He told her they were going to *work her down,* they'd done it with the other women, it was something they did and they would be able to find out what they needed to know so to trust her with the group's safety. It was not like other times, when they'd informally focused on one person or another in a kind of intuitive round robin but spinning out evenings over a week or two; *she* was the focus and the time was *now*. She was naked but they didn't take all of their clothes off; she was told to take certain positions . . . she said it was all a dream-like extension of the way it had always been in the house, the precedents of each extreme act established one time or another so after the first couple of hours she would look up with a rejoinder on her lips into the face of someone with whom she had done something so like what was happening now, only a little different, that the words died unspoken. But eventually she began to tire and wanted it all to stop. She had been with Pi and Long John and Kip and she was more than a little sore and when the one who called her a cunt, the one she kicked in the shin, came and stood against the wall and watched she got scared, realizing she had understood the violent core of his trip, that she had been instinctively avoiding him. And yet she was afraid to cry out that she was sorry because then she would lose it, *it* being belonging to this place which was the most exciting yet. So when Kip left the room and there were only Long John and him and her and he came over to say, "She doesn't want to do it with me," she was so relieved she began to shudder. She scarcely had the sense to begin to struggle when the two men grabbed and trussed her like an unwilling concubine and then there was nothing to do for hours and hours while the afternoon died and she wept trying to find pleasure but it had been eternally altered so she cried instead hysterically for them to stop. Finally when she was forever past asking anyone to do anything ever again and they had done everything they could think of wanting to do to all parts of her body they went away and sometime later one of the women came in and undid the bootlacings (she was already stiff) and she spent the next couple of days in bed. When Pi went out next time she drove for him.

Somewhere in the Stone mansion a clock began to stroke the hours. The black woman in the white nurse shoes was at the door asking when Mr. and Mrs. would eat. So I thanked the Mrs. for her time and drove my rented car back toward town.

# 8

All of this left me without much appetite, but my stomach was screaming *conspiracy to obstruct nutrition* so after getting completely lost in Hillsborough (all mansions look alike to me) I was willing to pull in to the first steak house. No difference: you can tell where the suburbs begin in any American city by checking business routes for meatnpotatoes joints. This one had waitresses in red velveteen micro-minis, yards of ruffles and tight black lacings over their breasts. Mine was a blond wig chirping, "Hi! Welcome to the Red Lantern Inn. What may I serve you?" But when the New York cut broiled rare with fries and tossed green came, same as every bland number—frozen, processed, precooked, canned—a little something done to every part so even what was fresh tasted hybridized to be shipped half way round the globe, I remembered Vince telling me how the produce was developed. Machines could process, you could tell just by the flavor of a vegetable whether it was grown by agribusiness, sprayed, harvested, trimmed and shipped, each step an incremental profit for some few at the top of the pyramid while those below got eye-appealing tasteless vitaminless insecticided pulp. His eyes had flashed. "Anyone who works in the fields knows the managers spray right up to picking—have to, because each year the bugs get more resistant. They say so what if it causes cancer—when one worker drops out of the line another will fill his place." I looked around and tried to think positively.

There were about a dozen tables occupied by families with subteens and in the corner a couple with baby. I'd forgotten there were still men around who cut their hair so the scalp shone through, a moment of boyhood promise memorialized, themselves forever a kid on a skateboard. As if somehow the body was just a blown-up sad replica of some more innocent time. The wives lacked muscles: simple as that. Some were tanned and slender, some pale and puffy in the middle under dacron/nylon/banlon permanent press polyester and plastic. The kids were clean, dressed like miniature parents. Everything matched. Everyone worked, too: you could see in their eyes this kind of display took a lot of effort. Maybe it *was* Mom's night off but she'd worked half the day to swing it. Yes, they all worked at jobs, were hard-core nuclear families, each a house, car, vacation vehicle, each a color tv, washer/dryer, basement freezer. It made me think of what Alan Watts said a few weeks before he died: *If all there is to life is being born, growing up and getting married so you can have children and watch them grow up and get married so you can be a grandparent—then it is not worth living.* And what was the other coin side? Angel and Tarleton and Julia and all the rest of us socio-politico-sexual-intellectual deviants? Once a dyke said to me, "Know what I want written on my headstone, kid? *She was queer for ideas.* Har har haw haw haw . . ." Yet the ability to abstract is maybe the most dangerous quality of the human mind pulling real bodies into real physical conflict with here-and-now. It was some strange paradise in which no one talked to anyone else except for

"Bye now! Hope you enjoyed your Red Lantern dinner—visit us again soon!" Okay, I thought as I paid my bill—so it isn't anyone's fault, everybody's just doing what they think is right. So what was wrong with everybody (white) looking the same, wearing the same clothes, running the same line of patter? Was it any different anywhere else? Fact was, the barest idea of people having relationships outside of Mommy/Daddy/Baby was so recent the problem was only beginning to be firmed under the word *alienation,* referring to conditions under which an impenetrable barrier to expression of feelings had been acculturated. I stepped into the ladies' room which was pink . . .

My face confronted me in plate-glass wall mirror with anger lines seaming, brows pulled tight with all the drivel of dinnertime thoughts. Over the hill, lines gathering silently in the folds of mouth, nostrils, and eyes, reminding me how my brain shaped my universe. Who the hell are you to say, my mouth asked. How do you know they don't have an answer you've never even suspected? A cat on the prowl—what kind of life is that? The lines announce, their verdict not subject to appeal. Why the tight marks at the nose—what's the smell you don't like? One woman's odor is another man's profit, who the fuck are you but a crazy dyke/dumb cunt just like they say in the thrillers? I tried to find a single redeeming feature. The teeth? pretty nice, cost many dollars, straight, white against my dark skin. Hair? yes, black feathers against ears, tendrils almost to collar. But the *lines.* I tried grinning into the mirror. That's right you morbid bitch—*smile.* Get a little fun in your life. Be fruitful and multiply. A song in your heart, a smile on your lips . . . Who knows how long that resolve would have lasted, how my life would have been changed, if it hadn't been for the man who was waiting for me when I got to my car?

My own fault. There'd been a little light in the sky when I went inside so I'd parked away from the bunched middle-American cars near a clump of half-grown coast pine marking the back edge of restaurant lot and announcing the beginning of another shopping center glinting dully beyond a deserted five-year-old gas station, its plastic beginning to shred in an onshore wind fingering from the ocean beyond smog. And I noticed another car parked next to mine since I went in. I just didn't put two and two together to get the meaty bozo in a poplin golfjacket—who, as I slid the key into the doorlock of what I was coming to think of as Connie Car (I mean I really was trying to be friendly), stepped fast to my right wrist, hooking it somehow backward in a way I couldn't scope till I heard a *click*. By then I knew and if I didn't there was his voice telling me "this is a gun" behind the heavy thing jabbing my liver. I hadn't had time to want to scream but anyway he set me straight, his calm voice announcing as the other cuff clicked my wrists together, "Move it into the trees." Which I did. Hadn't even gotten a good look at him, that was how bad a spot I was in, but I judged him six feet at least, and his footsteps were heavy on the tarmac. So I got real scared for a moment until I breathed my way out. There was a professional finish I couldn't place—but yet not official in any way, the cuffs plastic numbers I could tell now as they rubbed tighter. So on the off chance he was simply a common garden rapist I asked as we came into the under tree darkness, "Why me?" I guess I should have screamed instead. What he did was trip me onto the packed clay and meager grass of what I could now see was a large and concealing clump, the kind kids would use to smoke in while their Mom shopped in the Safeway, kind a dog would make part of his rounds and drunks would use. But there wasn't much time to think. I'd let go with a cry when I hit face first and then found myself sucking desperate air from an explosion of pain where his foot connected with my ribs. Just lying gasping back into the world was suddenly enough, while he leaned over, a crop-headed blur, hissing, "Any more and you'll get that in the face."

Not that I could do a fucking thing: he was a pro all right. As the smell of the ground made me nearly puking sick he unzipped and skinned my trousers to my knees and then knelt on them. I couldn't move a muscle, trying to work out some way to deal with what was happening. I tried breaths in my abdomen until I could open my eyes just a little. My right cheek stung where it rested on the ground, and it was so dark all I could see was the phantom of his jacket as the wind rustled the trees. He knew just what he wanted, and just how he wanted it: the message was crystal clear and the price was my face. He used a rubber, but I don't think it was to protect me from pregnancy. There was an odd tentativeness to his manipulations, as if his hands were not fully under the command of his brain. Yet he was acting to plan: no pauses for station identification. Even as I broke down from the breathing I'd used to avoid pain from the tearing of tissue—he barely skipped rhythm. He said something once, and he came in a series of mounting gasps like a mute, twisting my body into the clay. He made only one mistake which was to use the gun in a way I cannot forget, which necessitated rolling me onto my back; so I got a look at his face, which was of a well-tanned white man in his forties, thick-skinned and a little heavy in the jaw. He told me to shut my eyes and I did. He straddled my neck. He told me to lick it real nice and I did. I waited until he began again his terrible gasp, the crotch of his trousers against my mouth as I opened my eyes. He arched into the grim night, a stark profile—man with gun, death ecstasy—and I strained to remember all: the leftward tilt of pointed nose, the scar under jawbone, the tiny tattoo on the meat of his left palm like a tally *one two three four* hatch *six seven eight* . . . if I'd been able to say anything I would have told him to kill me unless he wanted me to do it to him, but the time he took to shove up and off and zip his fly wasn't enough to give me the breath I needed even if he'd turned loose of the gun, which he hadn't. I think he said, "One more chance. Tell that to your friends" before he left me to figure out who they were.

With adrenaline clarity in the hard white light of pain I ran down my list of friends: try a chorus of "Killing Me Softly" mooging into Phoebe Snow—"have mercy on those men with no feelings." Some of the faces were of the smiling dead and some were of friends at addresses marked *emergency for memory only* but Angel was there too and even Julia's face blossomed. For a while I drifted: something about marines and men in berets and others in windbreakers and business suits, and all looking for . . . Suppose they were looking for Tarleton, but somebody else got there first so now they were down to looking for his associates, trying to find out how much everybody knew? Suppose the burning of his apartment a week later was no accident but rather an attempt to shut down Tarleton's entire operation, to short-circuit something he'd built which was strong enough to survive his death? The brown powder—there was money in that. It had blood on it. You would have to have a pretty long lead to protect it from its point of origin in whatever delta city in whatever pro-west country with access to the poppy fields. You would have to have a secure way of shipping by the carton, and it was almost as heavy as books or papers . . .

Then the voice echoed in the sudden dark inside my skull: *tell that to your friends* and I remembered his gun and how the hammer snapped on the empty chamber when he held it to my head and then I seemed to come up out of a long heavy dream back to life, and it was cold and dirty.

I've been hurt worse and it wasn't even my first rape if your operating definition for rape is "forced sexual intercourse." But these things are *como se dice* memorable. Most of the women I've talked with were raped in their teens, by a date or a friend's brother or a male teacher with a wife and four kids. That hardly fits the stereotype of drooling crazed beast so most of the time you even wonder whether to call it like it feels. Suppose you do object when the father of the tots you babysit silently grabs you like a drowning man gasping for air and comes, his trousers open slightly, semen spilling onto your lap while his mouth leaves other liquids on your averted cheek? What if he says you led him on? Not that there would be any doubt in the eye of the beholder if I yelled for help and one of the fatnbrave folk standing confidently under the lights of the steakhouse actually responded. The best I could do in the first few minutes was to turn ever so carefully onto my good side, shoulder and knees, which left me bareassed in the breeze. The rapist knew that, of course; he was as I mentioned a pro, one of the minority into creepo fantasies: not too hard to imagine him ripping apart live chickens in his brain's deep as the ejaculate voided. And using my body for this perversion. I felt simply filthy, soiled beyond salvation, near-helpless on my knees, crawling as best I could in search of a broken bottle to attack the cuffs. I can't remember when I heard the last car leave; I know I was crying and at one point I lost the New York cut and frozen fries all over the parking lot, cursing and damning the suburbs until I located broken glass and could work back onto my side feeling the glass slice here and there as I took it up. As my hand and wrist got slippery and behind closed eyelids popped small brilliant fireworks the whatever-it-was parted and I found myself holding in sticky fingers a set of dimestore toy cuffs cutely reinforced with plastic tape. Like boys pulling wings off flies . . .

Connie Car looked great to me and it was too bad about the blood on the upholstery. I drove around I don't know how long until the shaking stopped: something about every place I saw to pull into to wash up having too many male faces in the windows. Finally I stumbled across a sign pointing Hospital and figured why not? To the admitting clerk I said I'd fallen down a flight of stairs onto glass trying to save a cat. She didn't believe me of course . . . and I went to sit from 12:40 to 2:05 while the on-duty staff sewed up an abdominal knife wound fortunately shallow and pumped a woman for iodine while her pimp and his buddy tried to get past the nurse to talk to her. It was fine with me: I got to use the bathroom and that good greensoap and I felt a lot cleaner after washing out my mouth and everything else I could think of. I had a lot of cuts, but nothing deep, and most had stopped oozing by the time the intern came into my cubicle. He was short, balding, running to fat at thirty. He looked first at my chart then at me. He smiled. In an accent so bad I could barely make him out, he asked: "¿Habla Ingles?"

So I smiled and in my best Spanish told him the testicles of his grandfather never descended. Seeing we had reached an understanding he began his examination and after only three attempts I was able to make him aware of the fact that my ribs were cracked. He kept asking "¿Tengo dolor?" but I couldn't help him out. When the nurse came in he told her to give me fifty mg. of demerol, which took care of my problem. I didn't feel a thing during the x-ray, and aside from using tape instead of an elastic bandage there wasn't much to complain about. It came to forty-seven bucks so I added that to the list I was compiling on the man with the funny tatoo on the palm of his hand and turned Connie homeward just in time to see the sun rise over the Tehachapi.

# 9

The demerol wore off around Modesto and by the time I pulled in under the grape vines my ribs were gigging at every breath. There was no one around to hear in the car so I let myself make a few noises now and then not that it helped much. But I wasn't prepared for the sounds that came out of my head in the silence after the car engine cut. It took me a long time to get to the door and dig out keys—my hand with all its queer little red mouths kept doing spaghetti until I managed to hang onto the knob in one of the passes made by the hand with the oozing wrist—longer to get inside to the cabinet where the whiskey was. It tasted awful but it kept me on my feet into the bedroom. That was what really frightened me: to fall and have all my crushed splintery things mangle. Each injury carries its own paranoia: when I had my knife wound (a dumb accident—Youthful Folly) it was the spurt of blood and the vivid pain of ripped muscle which terrified me into mortality. I lowered myself carefully as an injured animal onto the pad. I was an injured animal; I had been reduced to that. I tried to feel angry but it was too late or too early. I even tried to be glad I was still alive but it hurt too bad. Finally I just tried to fall away into the blackness all around me and that worked.

I woke to Julia's touch and it was dark outside. I had dreamed of slicing hotdogs with a very sharp knife, *snik snik snik*. Julia was wearing a burgundy velour turtleneck, brown suede trousers and boots, and her eyes were merry. I felt if possible worse: she looked so gorgeous that under normal conditions I would have felt honorbound to make her aware of all the possibilities but now I could only groan slightly and grunt my way onto an elbow. Her eyes clouded, her brow puckered. "You have cramps?"

*Among other things.* I nodded. It was impossible to breathe. My side was one long ache and it brought out the sweat on my face. I wished Julia had stayed home for a change.

"I think I have some codeine," she was murmuring, searching her handbag. "Here . . ." holding out a brown plastic pill bottle. "I'll get you a glass of water."

It didn't make any difference to me; I couldn't keep my head up any more and I took the opportunity of her absence to grit my teeth and ease back. I was feeling rude enough to do some dumb thing to offend her—there's no escape from certain impulses.

She brought the water and I swallowed three of the half-grain tabs, hardly noticing that she put her arm under my shoulders to help me until it was time to lie down and one of those unfortunate noises crept out again. When I was back she sat on her very beautiful buttocks and gave me a long look. "What happened to you?"

That made the sweat start again, while my head ran half a dozen replays of unforgettable moments and I felt each part of my body all over. "I was trying to rescue a cat."

She gave me another long look. At least I think it was a long one because that's all I remember, except that when I woke screaming in the middle of the night she was still there. A regular Florence Nightingale.

In the morning she was gone, but there was a napkin covered tray with orange juice cornflakes and milk. The juice was okay but the cornflakes didn't make it. There was a note under the milk pitcher:

> Dear Kat: You have an appointment with Dr. Genevieve Perigot at three-thirty. I will come by and take you there.
> —J.

Maybe I shouldn't have been so flattered she'd take the trouble, and maybe I didn't need to feel paranoid she was setting me up, keeping me in line. Maybe I should have told her all the wandering freaked-out fantasies of blood and violent premature death which had hunted me the long ride back, and told her I had but one life to give and I was going to shop around a little more before I decided on my favorite charity. Probably I should have said my body was sending warnings collect, making me an offer I couldn't refuse namely *you quit or I split*. I put it down to the memory of her face in the glow of the nightlight as she bent and stroked my terror away, easing me back to where my body could mend. It wasn't the kind of thing you pass off with "thanks, babe, I needed that" and still hang onto the human thing it's supposed to be about in the first place. She was trying and it wasn't her fault I couldn't straighten out in my own head what the smiles invited.

We went to the doctor's and she waited outside. Dr. Perigot was a small dark French woman who wore spotless whites and questioned me in a soft accent about what happened. I told her what I thought she needed to know but her eyes kept after me for more. She wanted to know what he looked like and I told her that too. She asked me how I felt and I said I thought I was okay, a little confused, maybe. She wrote me a couple of prescriptions—"you must promise me now to take these"—and said to stay in bed until I stopped hurting, and to come back in two weeks for another x-ray. I thought she was through, then, and turned to get my clothes, but she stopped me with her hand and I sat back again on the examining table. "Where did you get this scar?" she asked, pointing to the knife wound now healed to a thin white smile in my upper thigh. "An accident." "And this?" pointing to my shoulder. "Another accident?" "Yes." "And this?" "Yes."

She drew back. "You are very young to have so much accidents."

I took a second look at her then, and realized her hair was carefully colored dark auburn and her skin was finely webbed with minute lines, her shoulders bent. It had been the brightness of her eyes which fooled me into thinking she was younger. On an impulse I asked, "Do you know what's going on?"

The curve of her mouth changed slightly but that was all. Her gaze which had been over my shoulder moved slowly to meet my eyes. The curve of her mouth changed again. "I beg your pardon. You are speaking of?"

"Julia. Angel Stone."

She had taken out a sheet of paper on which was the outline of a human torso, back and front, no sex. She began to draw a smile scar on the upper thigh of the torso's right leg. "I was in Indochina in '54," she said. "We could tell the cadres because of their scars. At first I simply noted that some of the civilians had more scars, and that they were admitted to a separate ward and when they were out of danger the Paras took them away. Later on of course I found out what happened to them. Then I wondered why they would come back again and again knowing that there would be a time when the examining attendant noticed how many scars there were and ticketed them for the security ward. And then I thought that it was something you could never know. When the line was crossed it was too late, but before how could you know? It required a different perspective to see the pattern. *Vous comprenez?*

"Yes."

She finished the drawing and labeled it neatly at the top: Guerrera, Katerina. "How old are you?"

"I'll be thirty in a couple of months."

"And this is the first time you have received an injury into your torso?"

"Yes." I hadn't thought of it that way.

"You are lucky. Let me tell you this: more often now law enforcement officers are using the shotgun and in revolvers, the dum-dum bullet—you know it? And if you are shot in the torso it is very often fatal." In her soft accent this information brought the hair up on my neck.

"Are you telling me . . ?"

"I am not telling you anything except perhaps it is wise if you are ever unfortunately in a position when there is a police officer or especially a sheriff's officer who is about to fire at you to make it as plain as you can that you are a woman, shout, show your silhouette, anything you can think of. It may save your life."

"Or?"

Her lips rearranged. "Or perhaps it will not. I lost a twenty-two-year-old Chicana last week: she was inside the police line for an hour before the ambulance arrived. I was only in time to sign the death certificate. Her hair was cut short, like a boy. I keep trying to see the patterns . . ."

Julia stopped at a drugstore then drove straight to her place, where she piled me into a chaise longue with pillows and pills and a stiff drink. It hurt me to have to turn down the refreshments, but some of the pills were antibiotics and the others were barbiturates so I asked her what the hell kind of doctor she was to make the patient keep track of the medicine and she got a little mad and that turned me on. Then she grinned and went to fix dinner.

I watched the news: it was the week the world fell apart again. Otherwise business as usual: the stock market up slightly, prime rate down slightly, unemployment up, housing starts down . . . It put me to sleep.

I did a lot of sleeping the next few days, and in between grunted around Julia's quiet apartment looking for something to read to keep away the aches and ugliness of healing. Also to hold off thinking about a lot of things, all of them pretty terrible. The problem was I either permitted the flow of conjecture while I was awake or suffered nightmares so intense and logical that each unwilling sleep turned into restless struggles. Part of it was no doubt because my ribs were so fuckin painful I couldn't drag smoke into my lungs and after fifteen years of increasingly steady Kools habit I was tampering with forces I permitted long before to get beyond my control. Julia brought me economy packs of cinnamon gum which was okay—something about the bite of the spice—but which finally turned my mouth into a definitive sweet poisoned pit. I felt like a rotting Shirley Temple. Mainly I think the evil proceeded from that other encounter, the one with Angel's step-mother, steeped in my battered body and nourished by my own knowledge. It seemed bizarre to lie between satin sheets in Julia's spare bedroom—the same Angel had used as recently as Saturday—and think such a scenario as this, but it added up.

Suppose Tarleton, by everyone's estimation a basically good guy gone wrong, found out something nobody wanted him to know at Quantico and when they told him to lay off, he decided/was forced to take up the gun/defend himself? Suppose the people he turned to for help said sorry wrong number because he was married to Angel, i.e., a white woman. It was an ugly picture, but it had room in it for all the weirdness—the work Tarleton was doing at the time of his death was "motive" enough for anyone's pervo phallacies: shit is money, the fix is always in. This man they'd loaded up and thrown in for free the cremation, not quite the French connection.

At least that's the way it seemed during the day; at night I also had this dream . . . There are several women involved, among them Lenore and Angel . . . dressed in the shambles-clothes of the secondhand store they climb mouldering stairs past verdigrised walls crossed with the slogans of anomie: *I suck cock* F*U*C*K Y*O*U Chulo Eats it. In a big room they are beating a man whose face I cannot see; there is a tape recorder in the corner, eating his screams. Lenore tends the tape; in her eyes I see the reflection of cat's eyes so I know I'm there. Flames begin framing a platform, raked like a stage, where now one of the wraith-women lifts in her hands a scrap of something bloody; laughter like a drumroll rippling upward again screams which die to an image from long ago: Korea, corpses of G.I.'s with their genitals stuffed in their mouths by their killers, the sisters of the women they raped northward above the

**131**

parallel. In the corner Lenore clicks off the tape recorder, closes the cover, and slings the carrystrap over her bony shoulder.

Most of this was the second day; the third I felt a lot better for about four hours so I got up and dressed and out to a place I know where I purchased a .38 Police Special revolver for about twenty bucks more than it was worth, but he threw in enough ammo so I could have gone right back and killed the fucker if that's what I'd bought it for and that's service, I guess. On the way home my legs began to shake so I knew I'd done it and got right into bed. I was asleep when Julia came in as I had been the night before but this time she woke me with a tray.

I ate my way through a quarter of a pound of ground sirloin and half a baked potato before she said anything, sitting owl-eyed and with her wrists crossed over the bone of her kneecap. Then she perked a grin.

"I'm pregnant."

Fortunately I had nothing in my mouth at the time. "You?"

"Angel's idea, actually. I want a daughter."

"Well, that's . . . far out, I guess." I could feel the flush begin. "I mean . . ." Suddenly there was an enormous space between us, a Grand Canyon of emptiness, and the childhood inarticulateness built like fog as she became educated lady and so I took a couple of careful abdominal breaths just to the point of ache and the scene settled back to focus. "If you are happy, then I share your happiness."

She inclined her head I thought a little shyly, which was pleasant, and then looked up, face changed back. "You went out?"

I ransacked for recollections of the morning; had I left my purchase out in the other room? No—under my clothing. "You're not into James Bond, are you."

She laughed. "I prefer Agatha Christie and Dorothy Sayers. Call it a shrewd question based on circumstantial evidence: your bottle of phenobarb is missing from the nightstand for the first time. As if you took it somewhere with you . . . ''

"Guilty, yer honor. And dumb. I felt like shit when I got back."

Then she did something which really gave me the fidgets: she came and sat on the foot of the bed, and propped on one arm by my knees. And while I couldn't say she was actually touching me, my pulse leaped and she smiled at me and blew my mind out to where the Venusians threaten with their sensual rites luring dumb cats to mysteries and masses.

She smiled, her lashes swept. "You don't trust me, do you."

If she had touched me then I would have been off the mattress like an astronaut, probably Valentina Tereshkova. "Let's do something—backgammon? Chess?"

"I don't understand."

I shook my head. "Woman, you turn me on. I see you and I want to . . . fuck you. Does that shock? Not like a man does. I want to wipe all that out of our heads. So you say you're pregnant and it knocks me back, I didn't catch that drift. Do you see what you're doing to my brain?"

She bowed her head. "It's reality."

"Yep." I stretched my legs and got over on one side to try a Kool.

"You shouldn't smoke."

"Right." I lit and drew and I think I faked okay. She

waited until I was good and sorry I had lit up and continued.

"I find it very frustrating to deal with you."

"Maybe you should stop trying . . . to deal."

Her crossed foot swung to a small but steady beat. "What do you propose?"

"Well, first of all I've got a pretty good idea of what happened, and . . ."

"And what was that?"

So I filled her in not on the dream but on the daytime speculations and she asked a couple of questions and nodded here and there. In return she said Angel had left for place or places unknown to rough out the book she was beginning, and that my first class was a nine a.m. She told me she'd take me and introduce me to the students, and about what had to be done in a way I could understand and how to do it 1-2-3 which reassured me and how to explain to the chairman which armed me and on the way out the room kissed me on the forehead which disarmed me. The only thing she didn't do was warn me—a most important thing, maybe the most important thing of all. And I can see that she felt she had no choice, because if I had known Michael Tarleton put Angel Stone's name on his checklist of the new corridor, Burma to State-side—figuring, no doubt, he'd be there to sort the mail—I would have hit the road like a scalded cat. And of course I can't blame her for putting Angel's life over mine—I felt pretty strongly about Ms. Stone myself.

# 10

It was one of those brittle, bright fall mornings and if you squinted the palm trees on the boulevard looked like advancing soldiers of some as yet unidentified force. The road was thick with work-a-days and then further out near the university with students carrying books under stadium-coated arms: plaid was big, something about accentuating breadth of shoulders. Every third male looked only recently returned from lumberjacking. Most of the women were in modifications of the no-clothes look: poured into synthetics revealing sweet little feminine curves all over the place. The color scheme was early bo-peep. All this was happening under a sky not quite purple or green or orange but very close to all at once, you might call it bruise blue. There were enough of those days when the bozo on the tube advised us to try not to breathe today except within ten feet of the Pacific Ocean and then only with an onshore breeze that my diaphragm contracted a little just checking out the odors, which were diesely, greasy, sulphurous. In Hindu religious painting hell is represented in shades of red and green; animal demons and men with the heads of animals are joined in ghastly orgies, greedy-eyed and lecherous. Where the school began was a notice *You are entering the campus of a California State University property of California State Board of Regents* and maple trees flamed autumn carotenes while the grass was cut to within an inch of its life.

Julia parked and we walked. This campus like every other had its marks of Cambodia, Vietnam, Chile, Lebanon, Soweto. The campus police wore loaded pistols, there was a lot of cyclone fence and the newest building looked like part of the Pentagon. We got a bunch of sullen, tied-down looks walking the corridors of Science, but the Anthropology Department seemed merely dusty and small, its secretary nose deep in a paperback titled *Mistress of Emory* whose jacket displayed a lot of a hard-faced starlet in red velvet. Over the desk the clock said 8:50 and all of a sudden I got sweat nervous. Inside Angel's office the cartons lurked. And it looked like she had gotten a couple more, one marked "Tactical Separatism" and the other "Hex." I wondered what they had in them. A poster with a line drawing of three women announced:

> See
> That no matter what you have done
> I am still here.
> And it has made me dangerous and wise.
> ****
> You cannot whore, perfume, and suppress me
> anymore.
> I have my own business in this skin
> And on this planet.

. . . and on the wall in front of the desk where it seemed from the marks on the blotter a typewriter had sat pretty recently a yellow and black sign WOMEN AT WORK. Well, that made me feel better for a minute but when Julia glanced at her watch and began to pick up her things my knees started to knock. It reminded me of Angel the night I met her at George's Downstairs and I thought maybe she hadn't been as drunk as I figured; maybe she was just terrified.

"Nervous?" Julia was smiling, striding pace for pace.

"What makes you ask?"

"You're biting your lips."

So I stopped that and just as well because they were beginning to smart and before she left she told me the one about God creating Adam and then looking him over very carefully and shaking Her head and saying "I can do better than that."

So I went to the class and listened to their plans for a culture to bury (their god was an astronaut) and then I went back to Angel's office and lit a Kool and stared at the boxes marked "Tactical Separatism" and "Hex."

I stared at them for a long time and when there was no longer any thing else to think about, I wondered whether they contained more of the brown powder.

Then I locked the door and took a couple of tissues from the desk and looked on all sides of both boxes.

Both were still sealed, but whatever outer wrapping they'd had had been removed. They were heavy cardboard file boxes, the kind which would hold manuscript. The heavy strapping tape which sealed them passed all around each way. It would be impossible to open and reseal them without arousing suspicion. I sat with knife in hand for a bunch of long minutes and tried to think who would mind me opening them (Tarleton? Angel?) and then I went over to the one marked "Tactical Separatism" and cut the tape.

I found nothing. Or maybe it's closer to say I found a lot of paper with words on it.

Then I went off to the rendezvous with the eight caucasian, one negro, female(s) and found them dismissing as socially trivial their first idea to create artifacts of an amazon culture; they intended to sit in for a women's center with childcare facilities.

And then I returned to the office and stared at the box marked "Hex," for a long time because I was sure I was wrong by now. But it wasn't any use. I opened it, too. I thought, *I'm maybe two weeks behind them. And they have found me already.*

The air conditioner was set too low and I shivered. As the strapping tape parted I wondered who besides me, Angel, and Julia had access to the office—Vincente the janitor? the campus patrol?

Inside, layered like sand bags around a mortar emplacement or brown sugar on a supermarket shelf, were neatly-sacked pillows of brown powder, gram weights noted in dark scratches on slips of flimsy paper taped to each. The only thing that wasn't a sack of brown was twisted into more of the flimsy paper like a piece of taffy. I untwisted it open to find a smallish coin, heavy only because gold is nineteen times the weight of water, and read on its face: *Per tu amica Angel.*

I put the coin in my pocket and tallied the weights on the pillows. Near as I could tell there was almost twelve kilos of drug and I wondered how long it would take, now that the corridor from poppy field to addict was open, for the ethnic Chinese chemists of Rangoon to set up their refineries so they could tranship the less bulky refined white drug.

I repacked the brown powder and taped the lid shut with the see-through stuff from the dispenser, then I restacked the boxes so "Hex" was behind and on the bottom. Then I went out to the main office and roused the secretary from *Mistress of Emory* long enough to discover one of the delivery services had brought the new boxes, she didn't know which, that there had been an invoice which she put into Ms. Stone's box, and that she had given the delivery person the brown envelope as instructed in the letter from Ms. Stone's husband, which she had unfortunately thrown away, not thinking she would need to prove anything. This was shortly before school started, wasn't it a shame about Ms. Stone's husband dying?

Back in Angel's office I put through a call to Portia's (*Counselor is not in just now, will you talk with someone else? Ann? Yes. Ms. Margolin is in.*) to listen to a fast rundown and an amused voice: "Rachel Stone left a foundation, established 1949 some twenty years before her death. A nonprofit corporation, its purpose 'to further, by the transfer of qualified persons from the United States to the Republic of Burma, the relations between these two nations.' Basically fellowships, travel and living allotments, for 'technical assistance in agriculture in the Republic of Burma.' Alpha Hoerung, secretary, Adelbert Hoerung, treasurer. That's it."

"Ms. Margolin, that's beautiful."

"Really think so? Sounds shady to me."

"Oh?"

"Well, it says in the registry all the stock is invested in something called Trans-Burma which isn't even listed and yet last year the Rachel Stone Foundation found fifteen point three million dollars somewhere to give away."

"Mmm. That is a lot of peppercorns."

"Wait—more to come. An item in the *Post* yesterday—The Senate Select Intelligence Sub-Committee refused to confirm a report it was investigating seventeen family foundations and trusts to determine whether they were used as conduits for funding of Central Intelligence Agency activities in foreign countries. Among those mentioned . . ."

"Very spicy."

"No denials yet, but there are bound to be. This is the stuff that decides who gets support and who doesn't."

"Support?"

"Endorsements, funding. It's impossible to find anyone in that town with clean hands, but some are able to maintain the illusion better than others . . ."

I went to the campus snack bar and got a sandwich that tasted like somebody's left foot with the sock still on and watched the students. There were the usual blear-eyed Middle-Eastern students (tuitions paid by some slightly *louche* consular patty-fingers with vested interests) who might possibly be arrested as they stepped from the plane bearing them with their M.A.'s homeward. And the Asian students busy working who *knew* they would be arrested when they stepped from the plane . . . and the Africans, who knew better than to get on the plane in the first place. Here and there also covens of women in levis and workshirts embroidered flowery yet always somewhere the fist the Venus mirror. And my mind flashed to the notation (Progressives) Angel'd made behind the listing of Group C. Then the invisible ones became visible: the vets, humped here and there like mushroom spawn in some fertile dungheap, their khaki jackets so like the earth it was as if they fisted nameless from some place beneath the annealed concrete of this crackerjack bauble. Talking, often, with some older professorial person wearing shirt and tie or at least sweater and slacks, also bags under eyes gaunt cheeks and a way of glancing half over the shoulder. These older white men: what did they fancy had happened to them? They knew they were being played the villain while the dictatorship unfolded, they the radicals, commies, addicts, spies, traitors who must be caught before the country came clean again. They knew their only power was the pen. And they let themselves be sucked into a word-trip with the boys in D.C. but the Feds got to hold the dictionary. Maybe it was just that they'd always thought they had a piece of it. Then I watched the students again, how they had a guarded look—had they seen too many people pulled in? *Had they themselves been pulled in?* Did they now seek inchoately for the next pressure point, and was it the demarcation between the sexes? The boys in clogs, the girls in levis, had they lost the fine sense of what was right and fitting for each sex so necessary to maintain the old lines monogamy (which had been breached already)/coupledom/heterosexuality/marriage? I turned at the sound of a small clear voice.

"Hi. Are you Kat?"

The voice was I hope permanently attached to a perfect woman even smaller than I with a madonna's face altered very slightly strange by her eyes, which were black and faintly unfocused or perhaps merely set one higher than the other in her skull so it seemed she might have been incautiously squeezed in infancy by some giant hand. She plunked a bookbag into the seat beside me.

"Julia described you perfectly. I knew it was you the minute I walked into this hole. I'm trying to get ahold of a tape recorder, I have to rerecord some tapes. Julia's trying to get one for me. I've been working on this torture thing, you know—by the way my name is Belle, glad to meet you—and I did some interviews in Canada but there are certain parts I want to edit out so nobody will get in trouble, for instance there was this one guy who was talking about bombs and blowing stuff up and I think that could be misinterpreted. And then once when I yell at my daughter—Mercy—I don't mind if people know I yell at my daughter, but I don't think it fits into the interview, if you know what I mean. Goddess I feel paranoid today. You're laughing. Everybody always laughs at me."

"Well, I'm sorry, I didn't mean . . . "

"That's okay. See what I want to do is get this material on the air—I think I can do it through the student station, and at least the people in the area will hear it. AID-funded, CIA technical assistance—and so many of the victims are women and children. Electrode-shock, rape, beatings . . . "

"I follow you. Can I get you a cup of coffee?"

Something happened to those strange eyes then; they moved and returned to my face while the delicate nose pinched at some hint of an odor and the lips decided how to moderate ideas tumbling into birth. It was a complicated expression and I had respect for it. I'd risen but I sat again.

"Thank you. I don't want to be alone right now."

So we sat quietly and thought about that for a minute or two until she ventured a brittle laugh so tiny it sprang and died between only the two of us, although one of the narks—older males enrolled for criminology credits—lowered his paper and looked our way.

"I just got out of jail an hour ago. Did you know that?"

Her eyes did the thing again and then they glistened

only as long as it took her to sniffle seriously into a wadded kleenex. "Yes. They took me in. They know my car, they've been hassling me for months. So when they told me to walk the white line for the videotape I thought 'I'll show'm.' So I walked nice as could be away from the camera and when I got to the end of the line I turned around and I dropped a curtsey and I said, 'My name's Belle, and you want to know why I've been arrested? It's because I'm for life, liberty, and the pursuit of happiness.' Well, when the judge saw that he laughed and dismissed the case." An easier sound bubbled up from inside her and as she grinned her face lost its strangeness.

"That's a victory."

"Yeah, 'cept I'm scared to drive now, they did that. When they gave me back my car my legs were shakin so bad I could hardly find the brake pedal. Pigs."

"That was only an hour ago?"

"Yeah. See, I'm still shakin. You are Kat?"

"Yes."

We sat and thought about being terrified or at least I did, and I wondered if the ones who pulled her had the rapist's grin of the man in the poplin golfing jacket, the man with the tattoo—and then I realized I had thought of him and was not sweating, although I suddenly felt my ribs twinge. "In a few days you will be better."

"I don't like the way they smiled when they took my address. I live alone with my little girl."

"You believe that of the police?"

We thought again, seeing the flash of teeth and the sidewise proud smirk of the tormentor. And if the policeman who'd taken her address came after-hours to date her and she refused and he threw her down on her own bed would he perceive it as rape or think simply that she was asking for it, to be alone without a male protector? *Tell that to your friends* . . . So I looked into Belle's queer eyes and saw that she was a friend and told her about it.

In the midafternoon Group C stumbled into class like they were auditioning for a sequel to the "Night of the Living Dead." I'd been supposing behind closed blinds with the lights off, running it past inside my head: it all led back, somehow, to the celluloid images: Michael T's mother, the documents, the brother/cousin, the wedding, the white golfer, the tombstone. At a point in the film—say the wedding—there was a reality-shift, and what had been one kind of family experience bulged strange and hard. And then the clean tight images of Angel's dancing, maybe a little arty and forced in terms of idea—okay, he couldn't write a story line—but somehow . . . reverberent. Messages about the way consciousness is constructed, if you will, with the camera the medium. And then the whole flip side: the video documentary interviews the vet claimed he'd made at Quantico, the brown powder, the Rachel Stone Foundation, all of these tapes gone now, most likely.

Suppose he'd married Angel rather innocently, if that were possible, because she was beautiful, intelligent and lovable. And then he'd lifted the corner of the family carpet and underneath was a CIA front bringing, first, arms to the Kuomintang as Chiang scuttled south; then, opium from the hills to the city refineries. It seemed too enormous to imagine, yet pieces of the puzzle were beginning to fit. It was standard practice of the CIA to establish Americans who'd lived abroad preferably since early childhood in "proprietaries"—and a transport system with an agricultural tie-in was part of the pattern favored for developing nations. But Vientiene

**144**

and Bangkok and Rangoon were on the other side of a lot of water, and that made a big gap: Andrew Stone in his San Francisco office was no simple stooge of any Asian warlord, merely the medium of some kinds of commerce not much talked-about in the press.

The evidence so far was painfully circumstantial. The names of two doddering colonials, some heroin of poor quality, one dead man and a rapist with a tattoo—it didn't add up to much. Pretty standard, in fact: Andrew Stone as Daddy Warbucks was no big surprise. There must be more—something that angered Tarleton deeply and sent him to track down the family wealth with the eye of a real muckraker. Was it simple greed for power? When and why? Did it start after the marriage? From the DAR and the Great Mother to drugs at Quantico was not a single step: when did the journey begin, and where?

By five o'clock I'd had the course, had sweated through my clothes and dried off and sweated through again and I smelled so bad to myself that when Julia picked me up I sat way to the side of the little silver Peugeot and just watched all the other commuters watch each other drive home. There was a purple haze over the Valley, and the sun was sinking into it like a rotten pumpkin. Every third business establishment along the strip of traffic was a liquor store; every fifth sold furniture; all seemed uniformly half-prosperous, as if the original owners had died. I wondered again what happened to Vince that day he failed to show at the coffee shop. There were no brown faces in the cars around us, few Asians; we were headed toward the best suburb. I watched the road and then I watched Julia watch the road: she had a very softly rounded nose and

I wondered whether it was her own. Mine was what they called aquiline—narrow at the brow, high in the bridge. You couldn't call it a true *American* nose; no starlet would be permitted to keep it. Julia's nose she would be allowed to keep. Then Angel's face burst through my brain so I shivered and felt a little sick—*damn romantic attachments*—and to bring my thoughts back I asked myself what about Angel's nose? Does it pass, is she truly one of the American Girls or is her origin hiding out in the middle of her face? I wondered again what her mother looked like . . . a beauty, they said, but without money of her own . . .

"Bad day, Kat?" Julia turned into the landscaping and a drive miraculously appeared; she parked in a spot six inches larger all around than the car and we disentangled ourselves toward her apartment. The sun shimmered little wiggly lines like paramoecia under a microscope; sunset was all the colors of burning oil: cameo palm trees implausibly framing primordial ooze. As we walked the scent of oleander clogged the nostrils and the management put the lights on, those cute items hidden in clay temple bells and under toadstools. "Yeah," I said. "I guess you could say I had a hard day."

"What happened?" She bent over her keys and I thought she must be a little nearsighted, the way she held them close to her face before bringing the proper one to the doorlock and clicking the very solid sounding tumblers through their metallic dance.

"I've forgotten."

She waited until we were inside for that. She turned on the soffit lighting and threw her cape over the back of a chair. She set her briefcase beside the small foil table which held the phone and in a moment I heard the chime of glass on glass, and the soft thud of the refrigerator door. She came out carrying two: something medium brown on the rocks. "Here. Do you want to tell me before or after you bathe?"

"After."

So I took a shower of sorts around the tape my Spanish-speaking friend had installed and it made me feel a little better not to smell so bad. The gravel cuts on my cheeks were crusted black and beginning to lift at the margins and my wrists and hands itched under their new scar tissue, but it was only the ribs which really bothered and even they had gone to dull ache. In another week it would begin to be hard to remember how much actual pain there had been and in fact when I looked at the scabs and shiny scars my stomach no longer lifted and turned; pretty soon I would be all mended, and Julia would take me back to the little house of R. Stiller where the tv set wasn't color where—by now—probably all the expensive plants with the price tags still on them had died from lack of water.

"You look clean." Julia had changed into something silk and long. "I sent out for dinner—even the thought of handling raw food makes me faintly nauseated."

"You really are pregnant."

She smiled. Her teeth were small and blue white, the kind that are pretty and soft. Then set her drink aside as if it smelled bad and began to drum very softly with the fingers of her right hand as her eyes drooped and I thought she was fading into a nap but when the doorbell rang she was on her feet in a single movement, and at the door with her purse. The delivery boy was a cheerful fool who seemed to be listening to an inner rock & roll turning his sentences into gasps between unshared melodies. "Y'hear about . . ." he said, but the rest moved inward while he fumbled with bills, eyes flicking up as he tried again: "I heard . . . " Julia was smiling a pretty-lady smile it would have taken a crowbar to demolish. "What did you hear?"

But I never found out because just then the phone rang and if Julia's face hadn't begun to fall apart looking at me, the phone, then me again I probably would have let her get it. As it was I don't say I made a leap, but I got there pretty fast anyhow and picked up the receiver. A voice asked, "Angel?"

I said, "Yes?"

It was a man's voice. "Julia?"

I said, "Yes?"

Silence, then a click and Julia was beside me, the delivery boy gone. "Who was it?"

I was wondering about that myself, trying to fix the quality of voice, not really an accent as much as lengthened glottal stops and a loss of certain fricatives. "Somebody for Angel. When I said yes, he hung up."

I watched her fingers unfold the grayish paper wrappings around what turned out to be a "Mexican" dinner consisting of tamales and tacos and chiles rellenos. I didn't even want to think why Julia had ordered Mexican food for me, I was afraid I wouldn't like her. Where the hot plates sat on the plate glass table they fogged the glass. There were two bottles of Carta Blanca beer. I had had no idea I was so hungry.

But then every scrap was gone at least from my plate and Julia, her lips an almost smile again, was offering me the taco she said she could not possibly eat. And when I shook my head she piled all the debris back into the paper bag and just like that the dishes were done.

"Pretty soon I'm going back to the house, Julia. Maybe tomorrow." I wanted a cigarette very badly. I poked my right hand, the hand that needed to hold it, between my crossed knees.

"You said you were going to tell what happened today." She was smiling again, her brows lifting into fine dark crescents. Her silk thing had opened slightly in front and in the soft light her skin was quite creamy. "You're so damn cool, Julia. I feel like a little asshole around you, you know that?"

I wasn't close enough to catch a blush; she said nothing for a moment. "Did they give you a bad time?"

I didn't even have any cigarettes on me; they were in the discarded workshirt I'd done the day in. I drew a deep breath. "Well, I don't know. That first group, the little boys, you know: our future rulers—they're putting together artifacts of God the Astronaut. After all they were raised on tv. Is that a hard-time? The women are just now coming out of this fantasy about cutting off kids' left feet . . . "

"The Amazons are said to have lamed their male children."

All I could do was stare at her for a second. "What if that passenger you've got turns out to be male, Julia?"

"Amazon means a little more today. It is possible to interpret the Garden of Eden as a male perception of the Matriarchy, a time when the men were happy because they were little more than beasts, and it was women who kept things going. You *could* see Adam as being handed that apple of knowledge by an exasperated Eve tired of his nagging. 'You think you can do better: fine, take a turn.' And then you might see the Amazons are just one effort of women to take back power from the beasts. The Church killed nine million witches, that's the mentality: burn women alive."

"So it's all god's fault?"

She drummed her fingers. "Anne Hutchinson asked the question that needed to be asked when Queen Mary's inquisitors had her in their charge: 'What do you mean when you say *god*?' Because if by that word is meant a male deity, a parental figure, then forget it.''

She looked like she might be getting mad and I wondered what would happen if I went over and kissed her. Then I got mad at myself, because she'd made it so clear that we were going to spend all our time talking. "What happened to Anne Hutchinson when they stopped talking, Julia?''

She bit her lip. "Is that what's happening?''

"One murder, an aggravated assault, a rape and a lot of brown powder say it is.''

I got up, which was harder to do than I thought it would be after the food and the beer, and tried not to thump the walls as I groped toward the bathroom and the pile of clothing. I needed to piss, too, and it was hard to get my fingers to work the metal zipper and belt because I kept having to grab something or the room floated sideways. It seemed strange that things wouldn't hold still, like I'd wandered into the set of a space simulation. The plastic seat was cold. I put hands on knees to bend my torso carefully perpendicular till I could ease head lower than knees, and took some extremely cautious abdominal breaths. In a minute I felt okay again, almost as if a cloud had covered the sun for a little while but now it had passed by; still there was an edge of cold to the way things bulked here and there. I thought about Florence Nightingale out in the living room; was she enough of a dyke to hold me through *this* night? I wondered who Angel picked to be the father of Julia's child—did they do it by computer, artificial insemination from some illustrious donor, or was it a local, personal, contracted alliance? The decision by two women to raise a child one of the most sensitively complex imaginable—to me, scarily honest. Was there the constancy behind Julia's generalized coquetry ne-

150

cessary for year-by-year commitment? It was a long road from believing men—and all that implied about objectivity (even male objectivity is merely subjective)—to believing women. And all that implied: about separate realities, about change. They were making a revolution in their lives doing this, did they know?

Of course. Maybe I just wanted someone to keep away the dreams one night. Something spattered the roof over my head and outside the window silver knifed tropical leaves. Suddenly the night was steaming. If anything, what I wanted was maybe excitement one-third but at least a third the rewards of contemplation and for the rest the good opinion of my sisters. All right, I thought, bending carefully to shag cigarettes where they lurked in the deep pile, be a sister, be a friend. So I pulled myself roughly back into shape, nice tabby.

But she had cleared the field; I could see shadows change through the four inches between door and jamb of her bedroom, the rain sound like brushing hair. Then I wondered if my behavior had been rude: she was as you say an intellectual and just happened to run across someone who'd gotten tired of trying to talk things to death. I must have stood outside her boudoir for ten minutes, but finally the moment was right or at least I was; speaking her name in my firmest tone I pushed through the door. Her room was pink and she was centered on the double bed like dewdrops on a rose petal. She looked up but I wouldn't say she seemed surprised. I didn't care what she thought; damn her, damn them all tampering with ideas then sending out scouts for the future like it was all some kind of big educational toy and the idea was to play a good game. Now she was not smiling at all, but she remained motionless, even when I sat next to her as she had with me, only by her hips so we almost touched, and I propped my right hand on the other side of her waist. Her arm on that side lifted almost involuntarily, then fell back to the velvet spread.

"I want to tell you a story. Then I want you to give me an answer." She nodded as if she had a choice.

"There were four or five people, and they had been together for a year. They did things together that were illegal and dangerous. They did these things because they believed they were helping to make the world better—how is another matter. There were two women and two men, or maybe three women and two men. Another person wanted to join them. Now because the things they were doing were so illegal they had to be very sure of the new person. And then the new person really muddied things by asking to bring in a 'friend.' "

I tried to watch her face, but it was a hard story for me to tell because it was true. "Now the original four were really in a bind: two possible recruits instead of just one, but at the same time twice as much trouble. So by a process which is too complicated to explain they decided that the test would be to announce an 'exercise' the new prospects would participate in. It involved terrain and communications and was set up on very simple commando tactics which they'd all discussed. There was only one problem."

She had turned her chin slightly ceilingward, and I could see the down of her throat darken into curls behind her ear. "The problem was that the recruits decided if it was just an exercise they should drop acid so as to more fully experience the trip. There was another problem."

She closed her eyes; I closed mine. "The fearless foursome really had it worked out. By making the 'exercise' real, by doing an action, they would implicate the newcomers and bind them closer. So they took real devices and real guns."

Julia wet her lips. "And?"

I took a deep breath. A jet plane seared by somewhere above us, the sound burning rain like a slow fuse. I wanted to get mad, to ask her what she wanted to hear. That they died?

"And after it was all over they could none of them be in the same room together without feeling sick. Can you understand that?"

Her eyes widened. "Yes."

"Is that like what happened with Angel and Tarleton, Julia?"

The rain noise stopped and there was a clatter of heels outside the window, and a man and a woman laughing. Inside the room not so much as a mote of dust moved and then with a tiny slap the digital clock announced 7:05 p.m.

"Is that what you think?"

My ribs began again, and my hand remembered it wanted to hold a cigarette. "Things are a lot neater in your circle, I guess. The violence is all verbal."

She had white spots in her cheeks all of a sudden, and turned her face away. I waited for tears but they didn't come; instead she pressed the three middle fingers of her left hand to the middle of her forehead.

"We don't set people up for stooges."

I sat back. "Far out. Where is Angel?"

She might have smiled her way through what she said next but she didn't and I don't know that made it any better.

"I don't know."

All I could do was grit my teeth. "I guess I'm just not allowed to know right now, in spite of the fact that I was originally hired to protect her and it is an additional fact someone is setting her up for a ringer."

She seemed to struggle with an answer, maybe a simple *yes*. Then she shook her head into fresh curls. "Right now if you could continue to conduct the classes until we find her . . ."

Maybe that's what softened my heart, that it seemed to slip out, no clear denial, finally, but a plea for help. She began to cry. I kissed her.

The rosebud Chicana with a red ribbon in her hair and a big smile for me passed off the slip of paper as she shook my hand. I went into the women's toilet and read.

> Amiga: I have had visitors. Don't go down any dark corridors.
> Huelga, si. Heroin, no.
>
> V.

. . . so much for Vincente. Or maybe a warning. Suppose the fix *was* in? When I got back outside the performance had already begun.

A girl in mauve and rose peeped from between the University Greenroom scrim and with a big smile— "Hi!"—did a graceful *enjambment* toward us. It was a very friendly smile, and her eyes were large, clear, and merry. "Hello! Good to see you, so nice you could come!" And she moved along, touching the hands of friends and stroking what seemed two petals of dark mauve velvet beginning at her arches and widening to a flare at her hips then tapering to the peak of her forehead so her face peeped like a moon in a tropical garden. Someone behind me caught on with a giggle and was rewarded with a cheerful grin from the lips of the moon as she pirouetted and swayed, humming, then voicing a tuneless song which seemed to pull her into herself for the tick of a moment; but smiling she came back. "You know it is time for all of us to learn to love ourselves . . ." And again she was indrawn, lifting her velvets to stroke more petals concealed within, these rosy and melony; langorously she stroked down their satin length. "I am . . ." more giggles which she co-quetted . . . "a cunt. Yes. And these are my—labia majora." In a clatter of applause I leaned toward Belle.

"Who did the script?"

She pointed to a woman in the shadows—tall, crop-haired—who'd permitted herself her beard and mustache.

The applause died and Cunt continued, "Now, in here, these are my labia minora. Gee, it's a good thing the spot light is strong here—you'll probably need a mirror and a good strong lamp to see me at home and it's really important because . . ." She flopped forward to grab her ankles and walked around so her face appeared between her knees. "Oh, I guess I forgot to tell you that down here is my vaginal opening." As she turned round again and pulled erect, her toes touched, yes, and lifting, the anus winked. Laughter. "Well, as I was saying it's important because masturbation is not just something to do when you don't have a lover. It's different from but-not inferior to sex for two . . . or more." Another laugh and she did a little dance and a laugh of her own. "It's a terrific way to find out what feels good and you don't have to worry about some-body else's needs and opinions, so you can learn at your own pace what makes you feel good and that makes it easier to explain to someone else what gives you pleas-ure. Now." She stood tall and her face grew stern. Part-ing her fabrics carefully in the center to reveal a lens of peach from chin to groin, its lower part pinned with numerous battle ribbons and military medals and the low-ceilinged room then rocketing with laughter that bent some of us double: "The most important part of me in terms of sexual stimulation is . . . " bringing her hands to cup her face "my clitoris. Don't I have a nice clitoris?" She preened this way and that, and a Cheshire grin appeared. "Now this is what I meant when I said you needed a good strong light to find me. I'm a small smooth rounded body which will glisten in a good light and I have numerous nerve endings which are what cause *all* female orgasms. *If* I'm properly stimulated— that means, rubbed up and down rhythmically."

Nobody was laughing now. The room was so quiet I took a deep breath just to keep myself company. Whereas before she'd been a talented beginner with a good script now her hands like flowers opening fluttered to the peak of her brow and its velvet cowl stroking all down her cheeks and her throat to breast belly loins. Her eyes were closed and her face softened. She lifted her hands again and the room seemed to whisper forward as she stroked down. And again, while the whisper grew into sounds from a tape: a woman's quick breathing like hearing yourself because it came from somewhere behind and was amplified. There was a kind of genius in the girl with her blotted eyes and elegant graceful hands writhing now over the velvets and satins as the orgasming bodiless voice around us began to rise in moans, catching and loosing, finding and letting go until the gasps began . . . I was close enough to watch her sweat and wondered whether she came.

A round-faced girl with a guitar got up to sing; it was Cabaret night. I looked around at the forty-odd women in blue jeans or cords or long skirts of patchwork and wondered whether any of them knew where Angel was.

The singer's voice was easy, as if she enjoyed her song, and when the chorus came, everybody joined in: (to the Battle Hymn of the Republic)

> Move on over or we'll move on over you
> Move on over or we'll move on over you
> Move on over or we'll move on over you
> For women's time has come.

Afterwards I congratulated the woman who'd done the cunt script (her name was Joan, she'd recently spent two years in London). "What are you working on now?"

She smiled. "I'm doing a menstruation piece."

"Are you using real blood?"

"If I can get it. Otherwise . . . " She smoothed the hairs of her chintuft. I watched her eyes slide around the room and wondered what was going on inside her head. She had the shy intelligent face of a person who'd been good at chess early. As if she could read my thoughts her gaze snapped back to mine, irises very pale, almost gray under straight brows. I wanted to ask when she'd met Angel . . .

Next night I was back at the house she and I shared, outside staring at the spaces between the stars until those spaces were stars because there'd been a rain to wash the various poisons and lungrot out of the air and this thing of relating to people little better than half my age had my brain buzzing through to places I hadn't been in a dozen years with passionate crudities. Call it looking for a place where God could come from in a spaceship and get us back on the Track, call it socialist *ennui*. It was one of those nights you leave the porch light on but stay inside. My porchlight was out and I kept forgetting to get bulbs. Call it looking at the sky and at the cars parked up and down the block, looking for (white) male faces. There's paranoia in that, but Vincente had called and we had a little conversation about the tattooed man in the parking lot and he asked, "What are you doing?"

"Where were you at the coffeeshop, hermano?"

"Did you get my note? The visit came as I left the house to get into my car to come and get you. Later I sent Eladio but you were gone."

"What did they want?"

"What else? Information."

The receiver crackled and I wondered whether anyone was listening. "They lied to you, Vincente."

"Of course. But I'm not interested in dealing with this kind of person. You don't have time for letter writing, I don't have time for drugs."

So maybe I was looking at the place between the stars and wondering whether Angel was too, and where. Yes, there was crudity and passion in this; I have my fantasies and they are not of milk and water. In a minute a car drew up and the headlights cut and a girl called Liz got out calling my name coming around the front of the car while the passenger's door opened much slower and a middle-sized person in dark clothes unbent from the small car. "This is Lady Charley, Kat. I gotta make a call, can I use your phone?"

We went inside. Behind batik curtains in the glow of the Tiffany lampshade the person was female, dark brown, and delicately boned. We sat and smoked and Liz nodded at the kitchen to ask again to use the phone, so I said okay. I wondered if she knew R. Stiller. I looked at Lady Charley. When they pulled me from the spaces in the sky—almost dazed by them or maybe it was just holding my neck back so far—I'd said, "I've been looking at the stars" and she answered, "I'm readin you, yes." Now she smiled back.

"Traveling the inland route?"

Her lips parted on small perfect teeth. "I can tell you're hip. I'm takin my time and I may even stay a day here and there but I'm tryin for Seattle. You know how it is. You have got a lovely garden here, Kat." She stood and went to look at the plants, which had survived. My neighbor of the busted color tv had jimmied the bathroom window not, he said, to see tv (for theirs was fixed) but because he "took pity on the living things dying of thirst." It had only been too late for the begonias, which were sprawling like dessicated worms from their hanging baskets that morning when Julia returned me. The coleus had lost leaves but I pinched the tops back. Neighbor's mother's name was Elena and she spoke about what was first on her mind: the difficulty of finding a new house now that this block had been condemned—money tight, few banks lending. Soon, they were looking for a house to rent but there were so few available. Finally they were thinking they might have to get an apartment, and they had always lived in a house and had a garden. She gave me cactus starts from her array, exotic things with brilliant flowers beginning to bloom as the days shortened, or moons of salmon or orange or clear citrus thrusting fat from spined green stalks. "A fine bird's nest fern," Lady Charley announced from the north window. "You have a very fine and excellent garden, Kat."

We stopped looking at each other so I tried to listen to Liz in the kitchen: something about tomorrow. *Would you work on tomorrow? I can only handle today.* Her voice had an edge which trembled between demand and supplication in a minutely frightening way, some interior mechanism ticking toward heat then easing back like a fine-tuned thermostat. She returned and picked up the guitar someone (Angel?) had hung above one of the heaps of cushions, checking the tune, then began to spin "Song of the Soul" through the room, reminding me suddenly how quiet it was.

She did not sing and she was not a particularly skilled player but her face assumed an inwardness in which it was abstractly beautiful, if such a thing is possible: flesh settling on bones as aerodynamically sound as a gull's wing. Lady Charley watched me watch Liz so I smiled at her *no hard feelings* and she said "I'm hearin what you say, Kat." Later I asked Liz how the art was going so I could see her smile while she answered, "Just right, thanks," and we both thought for a minute. What she was doing was putting up a message on supermarket walls (they get a lot of traffic) and because she wanted the message to stay up as long as possible she had designed herself some stationery and a card (A-1 Advertising—*Signs of the Times*—Bakersfield) and in her "company" truck went with job orders and set up like a pro painter, scaffolds and all. First time I saw her doing it she had gotten as far as THOMAS JEFFERSON SAID and so I went by again lunchtime to find EVERY DEMOCRACY NEEDS and at evening A REVOLUTION EVERY 200 YEARS. "I'm on my third. Blackstone and Gettysburg—nice names, huh? This is my biggest job in the series and the manager came out. I gave him the letter, which reads like: Store Manager: Your store has been selected by the People's Bicentennial Commission to receive without charge a Founding Father's Memorable Quote through a grant from the Stonewall Foundation. Your participation in this program will demonstrate to your customers—etc. He looked pretty hip, all he wanted to know was would we paint it over when the

**161**

program was through. So I told him sure. *And* gave him a voucher so he could hang it on a hook inside."

I brought out the wine when it became clear Liz was waiting for a call-back, and Lady Charley said, "Aw raaht . . . " and I caught a tone. "Where you from, Charley?" She drew herself around the A&W rootbeer mug of Zinfandel and brought her head high looking straight: "Harlem. My mother lived on welfare in Harlem and my Aunt lived on welfare in Newark and one time when we went to visit my Aunt I looked around (this was the Newark War of '63), at the time—and says to myself, 'Charley, if you stay here you will catch this disease, better move on right now.' So I came west. Been in Oakland, Seattle, and Watts, moving north presently." She drank quickly. She didn't look like she'd been on the road. Liz's voice trembled in the quiet air. "You got those bones, Charley?" So we played dominoes and listened to funeral home ads on the local classical station while we felt each other out and realized we'd been born about three-quarters of a mile apart, that I'd left New York when she was eleven and she'd been gone four years when I got back, that we'd tracked past each other any number of times. She told us what she did for a living: she worked brothels where men who wanted to be tied and whipped came after long phone calls in code—*golden rain* meant the submitter wanted to be urinated on, etc. She said when they came in the door she walked up to them and slapped them hard in the face and demanded, *Have you been bad?* and if they didn't immediately submit she refused to have anything more to do with them. She said if they submitted, she told them to take their clothes off. She used leather straps, she had numerous dildos of various sizes, she never touched their genitals but the first thing she always made them do was lick her genitals because the law read that meant they had solicited her. She could spot pigs and enjoyed tying them up and beating them. In fact that was the reason for her trip. She had to leave *suddenly*. Liz picked her up from behind an old orange-juice stand where she'd been hunkering, coming out only for old and infirm vehicles or foreign sportscars. "I hope you'll excuse these here jitters I got, I bin on the road twelve hours." That nicked: it was a long time since I'd been there. The city of San Francisco claimed sixty thousand young transients a month; they were sleeping in the doorways on Telegraph four blocks away from Catherine Hearst's Regentship. It was said the majority were undereducated young women, often with infants. Then the whole flip side: young women like Lady Charley. She was bending over a sheet of paper now, running down her method of domino notation, the pencil jerking in her fingers as if she lacked the real the proper tool for the hatchings and crosses.

Suddenly I remembered the tally marks on the up-flung palm and I said, "Lady Charley, have you ever seen anybody with a tattoo like this?" and I drew it for her. Her eyes did a little dance over it, a fast dance, the kind you wouldn't want to do long and then she looked up and smiled. "I hear what you're saying, woman. I seen guys with notches lots of times. You follow me?" "Notches? You mean like on a gun, like in Westerns?" We both smiled that one by. "Well, in somethin they carry on them all the time. Maybe it's a knife, maybe it's some little pebbles or a piece of leather with knots in it. Like Liz here—you see the bracelet she's got, it's a strip of rawhide with a knot in it and the way I see that is it stands for one of something, you follow me?" Liz put on a pained smile: "Come on, Charley, you think I'm a killer?" For the first time since they'd entered she seemed a threat. I took a couple of deep breaths. I would have laughed if I could. "I guess everybody's some kind of killer," said Lady Charley.

There was another stage just before the phone rang (in which everything turned out good vibes all around). I had to speak sternly to myself: damn Childrens' Crusades anyway. We shared what I could find in the kitchen cabinets. They took off for the next stop.

Under the Mandarins there was something called "the death of a hundred cuts" in which the alive victim was literally dismembered joint by joint; usually for treason—somebody or other, probably Uncle Ho, said that when a government has to seem all-powerful, then that is when it is weakest. Who knows? Once you have been cut it is very hard to want to be cut again; it's a unique experience, let us say. My father said before you were cut you were a fighter; if you survived you were a lover. My mother translated her mother's Spanish for us; news of the sisters left behind: *Hortensia is still sick. She released the canaries and the pair of finches, no one is able to find out why, and he was very angry. She had to stay in the house for eight days. He came over here to tell me his side of the story and I wanted to laugh in his face but what could I say?* Listening to these over a period of years I had come very gradually to understand that the method of birth control between this couple was anal intercourse, demanded by him when she refused on religious scruples to receive him in her mouth. This is the middle class, *amigas*, but there are knives everywhere: it's that brings you back because knowing what you know there's no escape. And then there was my other aunt, imprisoned under Batista . . .

Put it another way: nobody can work alone; solitude is the essence of pain. Like a whole lot of other seeming contradictions there is no problem in the U.S.A. unless you choose to remain ignorant about this. These wars we keep getting into and I'm speaking now not as the immigrant's daughter but as a true blue patriotic American we largely fight by impressing farmboys and apprentices and while they all seem to understand about working together, each war on one level a gigantic haying party, nobody thinks much about how each of us has to suffer our own pain until we are down in the mud writhing separate but equal. *Bring me* unblemished bodies . . .

The forces set in motion and called war are no more apparent to any average one of us than the swerve of the stars, and for each consciousness war is different. The most bizarre reckoning of the powers of the government wink at truth, no science fiction could ever be as portentous as real weapons. Fantasy—powerful as it is, was cool compared with its realization—which translated as atrocity. And rape, horrible as it is, was less than mutilation. Because you had to live with your mutilated body as well as your mind, bent as it might have been. There was in fact only one definition of war: when the killing started. Which made peace when the killing stopped. The rest was as they say *conditional* upon whether we were about to kill or be killed and war—especially limited, distant war—became the powerful way to control people. And if the planes which carried supplies to the front carried back (unbeknownst) heroin, that was another kind of control. For some heroin had answers and who knows otherwise what replies they might have found? It was all researched, nothing left to chance: the secret files at Fort Dietrick, the trail of dead in "unexplained" incidents connected with Army drug testing were proof they knew what they were doing. When the rapist hissed *one more chance* he was being paramilitary for someone somewhere with his finger on the trigger of a bigger gun. Looking for Angel just like the rest of us, Angel with her safe-conduct set up by Grandmother Rachel, her trips to out-of-the-way places, her boxes of manuscript, books, artifacts. If Angel had been a dupe, it looked like she wouldn't be one much longer. Looked like they were getting ready to let her in on her destiny. My healing scars itched. When I thought too long I started to shake. I couldn't think of anyone as close to me as one of those hard diamonds of light out beyond Jupiter. If I got drunk I could forget for a little while how scared I was.

# 12

The Valley received a tremendous rain: three inches in twenty-four hours. The sky opened and millions of gallons of water fell, flooding streets and sending the canals over their banks on the outskirts of the city; some of the *best streets* in town were impassable. So was ours and like a cliche, the city took its pumps to the suburbs first. I borrowed a bike and got to class just fine. It was impossible to work out at the sites until a little of the water drained; the eight-by-ten excavations resembling square duckponds or small swimming pools or large graves, depending on my mood each morning when I cycled past.

The astronauts were the best attenders in Angel's classroom: I was already having fights with two of the anglos and one of the Chicanos re: what the Bible really says about the Creation of Man (sic). One of the vets called to say he was having an attack of rot because of the rain so he wouldn't be in class for a while. There were other vet diseases, too: some of them stoned themselves all the time, and there was a blond fellow with a plate in his skull for which he got generous pain-killer scripts from his banker father's friend the physician. Vets had respect for the head-wounded, they said or showed; it was no joke to be walking around minus a part of your brain. It gave me respect, too: you couldn't mess around when your joke was somebody else's pain and one day when a word no one even really identified brought blood into the deeply sculpted forehead of this vet, the man next to him was the first to react, pulling the energy right down in the room and raising my hair— led him away from us out to the hallway.

The women called me at night. Their security was poor. They talked too much over the phone, they gossiped, they bragged. They were funky and brave and some of them treated me as if I were, too. I didn't know whether I was any more. I watched a lot of tv, the cop shows stoked my anger the most: schoolyard bullyism. My bank balance dwindled. I got itchy seeing it all melt away and with it a sense I'd had of myself as a hero. Many of my self examinations began *you're not going to make it if you keep this up.*

Then the night they finally got the water pumps to our end of town I cycled in to find a two-year-old Volvo 1800 ES, air conditioning and sunroof, parked in front of the house. In it, Mr. Andrew Stone, working a crossword puzzle with a Mont Blanc fountain pen.

He appeared like a six foot tall Dresden china statue, very fair, spots of color high on his cheeks, white hair fine and abundant. He had a nice smile, and looked me straight in the eyes as he introduced himself. Not that I was surprised: he was the man in Tarleton's film, the aging white golfer. Or maybe I should say I was very surprised, because something about the film had given me the impression the golfer was Tarleton's father, not Angel's.

"I hope I'm not interrupting your evening schedule, but I was hoping I might find Angel here." He too pronounced her name Ann *gel.* I got him a cup of coffee. He sat in the living room's only chair, which was the rocker, and I sat against a couple of small cushions. I told him I didn't know where Angel was. I wondered whether he believed me. Then he seemed to shrink a little in his fine tailored jacket and let go of something. His face loosened, he was a different person.

"Things turn out so differently than one anticipates."

I tried to help him out. "Yes?"

His eyes asked how much I knew. *Enough*, he seemed to decide. The rocker squealed as he pumped a couple times with his foot, the room got darker. "I understand there have been inquiries made about the Rachel Stone Foundation. It's a matter of public record, of course." His fingers ticked on the chrome.

"How much did you spend trying to break her will?"

He made a small smile. His eyes disappeared. "Who is your informant?"

I shrugged. "I'm guessing you spent a hundred grand."

It was almost too dark to tell, but his face seemed to suffuse solid. There was the quietest kind of menace, then, and I felt fall in the air on my cheeks. I took a couple of breaths.

"She left it to the foundation, didn't she, when the smart thing was to leave it to you and let *them* bankroll the foundation."

He stopped rocking abruptly, leaned forward. "These are areas touching national security."

"Is that what they told you when they recruited you? That it was in the national security to bring capitalism to Burma?"

He smiled again but it was broader. "Pretty soon you will be telling me about imperialism and colonialism and, thank you, I've learned the argument." He put his hand on his knees. He appeared to be about to get up.

"Do you mean to tell me you didn't know about the heroin?"

He remained poised for the count of four, then relaxed back into the rocker with a shadow of Angel's marvelous litheness in the bend of his back; yes, he was definitely her father. "I hear a lot about drugs lately. I think they are filthy and I know anyone who handles them is in a lot of trouble." He brought his hand up to his face to pinch and squeeze the bridge of his nose. His eyes were shut. Then he looked at me as if he expected somebody else—who? I wondered. Tarleton? Had Tarleton done research on the family jewels too?

"What does 'per tu amica, Angel' mean to you, Mr. Stone?"

He looked at me as if I was crazy. "I have no idea what you're talking about."

"The medallion. The gold *medaglione* her grandmother got for her."

He shook his head. "Some woman thing. Jewelry."

When I got mad I knew that was what he wanted. He wanted me to say I'd found the brown powder with Tarleton's films, he wanted me to tell him about the "Hex" box. Because he didn't know? Then he would be telling the truth when he said he thought drugs were filthy. The seconds exploded like land mines. "Mr. Stone, you know how serious this is."

He sighed deeply, rubbed one cheek. "Michael Tarleton was simply an agent of change in a disintegrating environment. I had no choice in the circumstances. When I . . . realized the seriousness of some of his . . . intentions . . . "

"How much did they give you to start the Andrew Stone Company?"

"Who is your informant?"

"It must have been a lot harder getting started than it

170

would have been if Mother had left the money the way she was supposed to."

It's a funny thing, crossing cultures. As I said this, I felt my stomach gather and I sat light, because to suggest to some men that they did not have total and unqualified control over every woman they knew might be to provoke a fight. Andrew Stone sat, sniffed short once like taking up snuff, and shook his head. "I'm not interested in talking about my mother." I thought he might gather to rise, but he sat.

"How about Michael Tarleton?" I groped for a lead. "What were his intentions? Wasn't he just some kind of little cheapshot revolutionary?"

He smiled small and his eyes buried. "Maybe. Look at it this way. You possess some information and you want to disseminate it. But the authorities tell you they do not want that, and to desist. You do not desist. Clearly then you have made a choice." He was quiet for a while then, until he gave a single low laugh.

When he hitched upward in the rocker, his clothes settled closer to his body, his face began to pull tighter. It seemed as if something, perhaps his own thoughts, had angered him. "She knows that if there is anything . . . well, she knows that." He stood, unbending tall and straight. "Tell her I take the responsibility. Tell her anything. Tell her I'm . . . an aging white man."

I watched him pull away from the curb in the almost dark, and then from the doorway I watched his tail pick him up at the corner, an anglo in a blue Chev: that was six-forty. At ten of eight the doorbell rang, and I turned the oven off on my tv dinner before I went to answer it. I was still having trouble with my knees but I thought my head was okay. I was glad I had replaced the bulb in the porch fixture: it gave me a look at them before they got one at me. I'd never seen them before: one had an

Erlichman pre-decline haircut, the other a calfskin jacket the color of cooked chicken liver and a sandy handlebar mustache. The German had his wallet out to flash in the light which also glinted from his fighting trout tietack and a gold filling in his upper right canine. Not that you could call what he was doing—when I braced open the door a crack with my foot—*smiling*, it was more a ceremonial grimace of the kind most people manage to suppress except under great strain. But crew-cut was under no strain, he just wanted to ask a few questions.

They were so polite it made me shiver. I didn't know whether I wanted them inside but mustache had a folder under one arm, a legal file four inches thick tied with brown woven tape. For all I knew his sandwiches were in it but I could also think of a lot of other things, so I was tempted and let them in. We sat in the kitchen but I didn't go so far as to offer coffee. I didn't like the way they settled into the chairs like they were comfortable.

They began by showing their Twenty Pictures of the infamous and near infamous; some of the old ones had been dropped and in their places they now had terrorist daughters of prominent families. After that, about a dozen flyers of black men wanted for Killing Federal Officer, Deserter, Malicious Attempt to Damage and Destroy Buildings by Explosives, National Firearms Act, Federal Reserve Act, Bank Robbery, Interstate Flight, Assault with Intent to Kill, Possession of Home-made Bomb, Assault With Force . . . Chicken Liver got the folders out and handed them to the German, who opened them halfway and set items in front of me. I realized that technically I was under arrest. I looked at the photographs with my eyes as far shut as possible not to say I was acting dumb; I let them see I knew the ones they knew I knew. All of this took lots of concentra-

172

tion. The German had hair in his ears and a large nose with a sharp tip, the kind you see in the anti-U.S. caricatures on the editorial page of socialist newspapers in Third World nations. There was a hint of the epicanthic fold (of some Mongol invader?) over glass blue eyes; he did not look at me, but touched his hand to some part of him every time he gave or took documents.

The deliberateness of his movements made me very nervous. It seemed to me he knew I was speeded with adrenaline and he was reining me back. I set my elbows on the table and bent over the stack of flyers and began to look at them slowly, reading the stats, the aliases, CAUTION: *R____ allegedly assaulted, robbed, and fatally wounded a deputy United States Marshal. Considered armed and extremely dangerous.* And I began to breathe deep until I could get out a good yawn. At some level in his avian being Chicken Liver didn't like that so he shifted slightly to let me see a wink of holstered metal at his belt.

Of course that gave me the paranoids about the fucked-up piece I'd bought already loaded, right now sitting beside my bed under a cushion. The older man watched the vicinity of my hands as I gave back the circulars, the other my face. I looked at the older man's scalp, which was pinky-gray, as if covered by a single enormous freckle. It was the kind of skin that made Norman Rockwell famous. As a child it had frightened me; it seemed inflamed, unhealthy, the freckles colonies of germs, the ruddy whiteness eerie. Now it just looked like whiteman city skin.

Then Chicken Liver got out a large manila envelope, the kind that closes with a string and two round tabs, with lines for an inhouse mail service printed both sides, previous addresses neatly blacked out. My mind was wrenched by the way he handled it; I felt I'd lost my concentration and something had happened I didn't know about which was very important. That's all it was, and it was thoroughly gone the instant I saw what it contained.

German handed me the eight-by-ten glossies one by one, and told me to keep my fingers off the fronts. He didn't need to. The kind of photographs they were I wouldn't touch under any other circumstances except maybe to burn them. They were perversion and the way they had been marked was perversion. The first was a head and shoulders of Angel Stone. The print stopped at the swell of her breasts; she was naked. There was a man in the photo, also naked. There was a lot more of him showing. He was black and it looked like casting picked him for size.

"Do you recognize this man?"

The man's face was in profile and he could have been just about anybody from all you could see of the dark curve of his cheek and one ear. He had an afro on the short side and a very muscular back. I found myself in the middle of a sigh and let it out slowly. He was not Tarleton. The only thing in the photo that was obvious and incontrovertible was that the woman was Angel. The scar on her lip marked her.

It was the establishing shot for a whole ugly scenario in which someone's idea of the obscenity quotient of a depicted act and hence the need to "protect" the identity of the female involved was rated on a scale beginning with a black strip over her eyes and ending with her entire head covered. It made me very angry.

"Where did you get these?"

The crew cut was brushed gently with one hand, the photographs removed, the right nostril stroked. "Apparently your girlfriend is not as fussy about who sees these as you think."

The room spins and you hold on. I held on and they made me a proposal. Their proposal was they wouldn't bring me in and charge me with Felony One for the bombing in which the father-of-two ex-Vietnam City Demolitions Officer died as he hunted for terminals— and that therefore the State of Illinois wouldn't get me on extradition charges either.

I was real tired of it. "I keep trying to treat you like human beings and you keep coming back like FBI agents."

I got the German's eyes, then. He looked at me for the count of ten and I looked at him and the polar bears padding about on the ice floes where his irises were glacier-melt green. He tilted his head, he sniffed my tv dinner, he smiled as if he had learned something. He had red cheeks, too, like Andrew Stone, but it did not seem likely he would be dispatched to show any father photographs like this. Or? Maybe he was the perfect one, his combination of Norman Rockwell and Attila the Hun the only context in which things such as these could be passed hand to hand as incriminations.

I felt deeply threatened by his smile. I was trying to decide if I had the spine to tell him to take me in and get it over with, and maybe he saw that. Maybe he figured he had me nailed and I was too dazed to do anything but masturbate until he was ready to jerk the rug. Maybe he wanted me to panic and see where I went. He left his number and said he hoped I'd call.

When they were gone I set the table and got out a beer and took the tv dinner from the oven. I sat down but I couldn't sit still. I stood and tried to eat the dinner from the counter, but the way I had to prop on my elbow reminded me of the photographs and that made me queasy again. I tried to examine the feeling: what right did I have to assume anything about the circumstances under which they had been taken. All that could be stated definitely was that they were professional photographs, the kind a photo studio would be equipped to do, and they were high contrast, as for offset publication. I'd seen a dozen under-the-counter paperbacks with photographs just like these, the lighting and backgrounds were the same, too. Except those faces were anonymous. I tried to remember the look on Angel's face but except for the first one, it had always been at least partly covered, and the first photo was a shocked void in my inner movie. It seemed she had been smiling. I tried to imagine the nude Angel of the "Dancing" film getting involved in a crude sex mag trip and it was hard so I dropped into speculations about how and why German and his groupie would lay out a scam (if it was a scam) for me. It was too bizarre to consider they manufactured the things in some underground lab the way the Chinese were said to create photos of Mao. Clearly they had been sitting in her dossier some time ready for use, and I and the father were the first civilians to see them. Even more likely they had not shown him all the photographs; the establishing shot and one other would do quite well to set him on the road aimed at me. I wondered whether they'd gotten shots of us shaking hands as I brought him inside and what it meant to them if they did.

There was another thing which was clear: this was no routine sexual slander. Supposing the photographs to be real, someone had passed them to the authorities; they were hardly the sort of thing you leave lying about. As to the circumstances surrounding their making, anyone could conjecture. From the scanty evidence it was possible to build whatever theory your paranoia patterned, from drugs to decadence. It was black-and-white which made it sinister, if those things seem sinister to you.

It was almost eight p.m. The high cold shakes had passed into adrenaline rush and I successfully resisted the temptation to dig a hole in the backyard and bury the ugly .38. I managed to stay off the phone. I had realized that I was as afraid of staying in the house as I was of the plan taking shape in my head, involving another talk with Tarleton's mother, this time without the *dueña*. How tight the Feds were on me I didn't know: they had expensive imaginations and mucho manpower for the *right projects*. The two thousand pounds of metal squatting in the carport under an increasing load of lime as migrating birds plundered the last of the grapes was completely useless to me: there was no doubt half the bozos on the beat had its make on their boards. Walking away in this city of the automobile was too conspicuous. I tried to watch tv for a while but it was one of those nights when everybody was busy acting; the scripts were bright, false, cheerful. Finally I realized I had the bike, that the alley behind the house led into dark back streets a quarter-mile-square. That it had taken me almost two hours to evolve a plan was a little scary, but it seemed sound.

With that accomplished I could make the final decision about whether to contact Julia and tell her of the visit. It was a leper's touch one did not like to reveal but there was also risk in hiding from her what she might find out about and misconstrue: into thinking I had come to terms. From my bank envelope I loaned myself four hundred dollars. Then as I was dressing I saw the gun and that was another item to run down: finally I had to take it up in my hand and feel what a cold lump of metal it was. Weapons are equalizers if you're into *kill*. I was not; I was going to talk to Mrs. Tarleton all alone, ask her about Mr. Andrew Stone among other things. I put the gun back under the pillow and let myself out of the house.

It was a beautiful night for travel: clear, with a moon going to full. The eucalyptus trees rubbed and sighed in a hard clean breeze and after I'd sat twenty minutes on the back steps I could see every dent and detail of the bike, the back fence, the bush and its rot of pomegranates, the ghosts of sweet peas against crooked stakes at the edge of the straggly lawn. I didn't even knock down any garbage cans, and as soon as I'd gotten well away, following the network of alleys until I hit a canal then using its bank to cut toward the freeway, I realized I very much did not want to tell Julia anything right then. No matter how I disarmed my statement or how modestly I asked to know Angel's whereabouts she would shrewdly gauge my mood; I would bet on her telling Angel to find another cranny in the rock garden. So what it came down to was I pedaled clear to where the long trucks fuel and found an nice secluded spot and chained up the Raleigh Sport and hung out in the coffee shop until I picked up on a gay driver who took me to the bay area turnoff where it was almost two and a half hours to get a ride with a couple of organizers going over to the Santa Cruz fields who dropped me on Interstate 5 where I got a ride straight into San Francisco with a couple and their baby. At eleven a.m. I was up the street from the Tarleton house in North Beach sitting in a rented green Stingray watching the fog roll in.

At noon I walked down to the corner Chinese grocery and bought a roll and some cheese. At five of one the couple whose Karmann Ghia was parked out front of the house went down the street to the corner grocery to return in about ten minutes carrying a paper sack of—

who knows?—maybe rolls and cheese. I recognized the woman as Mrs. Tarleton's amanuensis; the man she was with was tallish, bearded beneath mirror shades, medium brown skin. I would have liked to get a better look at him but the woman glanced at the Stingray and I got suddenly very interested in the want ads.

At quarter of two Andrew Stone arrived by cab. He went in looking agitated and stayed about twenty minutes and came out looking agitated. If he had a tail I didn't spot it or it spotted me first. I had drawn on all the margins of my paper by the time two black men in leather arrived in a white panel truck labeled ACE Electronic, and I was seeing if I could put together an extortion note using words from only one column of news when the woman of the Karmann Ghia came out, got into the car, and drove off. It sounded to me like she had a muffler problem and when she braked at the foot of the slope her left taillight didn't work. I got *person must be eliminate Early if no payment inmmediate Call* . . . I made funny mustaches on about seven world leaders including a couple of women who looked far out that way when the two leathercoats came out along with the man from the shades and beard and they all got into the white van and coasted off, popping at the foot of the hill.

By my count that left Mrs. Tarleton. There was no way of knowing who was gone for how long. I got out of the car and walked up to the door of the trim little house, trying to remember why it was so important to talk to Tarleton's mother. It wasn't until she had answered the doorbell that I realized I already knew everything I needed to know. Or perhaps not: there was one detail that was difficult to place, which I glimpsed through the open door of Mrs. Tarleton's bedroom as I came from using the toilet: two studio portraits of

Tarleton, one as a smooth-cheeked Marine recruit, the other a dozen or more years later, a showbiz shot of a mature, self-confident man, an expensive photo in an expensive frame, Tarleton the success. It was the portrait of the youth which carried the funeral rosette.

I tried to get the house on Potrero but there was no Max, no Aida, no Mickey, so I drove down to the Embarcadero, walking until I got tired of being alone in the rain building cold from Alcatraz. So I went into Alioto's for a lousy meal: too much of everything—frozen, indifferent fish. The waiter was extremely young; he was attentive in a faintly irritating way. Then after that I wandered higher into the import houses where the Christmas decorations had already gone up. I bought some little embroidered satin animals to hang on somebody's tree, thinking how the holiday always released my father's contempt: "They've had two thousand years of it and they want more!" The little decorated animals were from Poland and they had been made by women: a horse, a deer, a rabbit.

I called the house again: still nobody home. I went back to the car and cruised past the motel at the foot of Columbia which was like an enormous Italian wedding cake and finally pulled in and paid twice as much for a room as it should have cost and half again as much as I thought it would. But it was a nice room and it was interesting to catch a truly suspicious look from the bell captain. If I'd had a john they wouldn't have liked it much but they would have understood at least. I got shown how to operate the tv, tuned it to a rerun of the Marx Brothers' "Animal Crackers" and I thought I would choke laughing. There was a coke machine two doors down, free ice. When the movie was over I took a shower and turned off the lamp and opened the curtains. There used to be more lights: the city used to be dazzling, now it was more serious, with slow pulses of headlight tracking the long hill from night in Chinatown towards sleep in Marin, the headlights strobing into my dark cave. *Hi I'm a cunt. Aren't I pretty? . . . and this is my clitoris.*

There was no answer from Potrero Hill in the morning, either. It was a rainy day, and the panes streaked crooked wet cars which approached/passed like drunken insects. I wished for a change of clothes and thought of the surplus stores on Market but something buzzed my head—the name of the cemetery where Tarleton was buried. Buena Vista or Alta Vista—something like that. I remembered Angel standing in the middle of Julia's livingroom trailing a stemmed wine glass in her long fingers: "The cemetery was so *barren*." In the phonebook the listings were Buena Vista Lawn and Altamonte Woods. I decided to try the Lawn first. I looked for the bell captain on the way out, I wanted to tell him to count the towels, but there was a younger man on duty who looked too stoned to bother.

Buena Vista Lawns was south of San Jose, past Santa Rita's grim barracks and east, a forty-acre rectangle of green with a border of red and white petunias and an American Flag hanging limp. It was barren all right, but there was no Tarleton listed in the directory inside the small granite-faced mausoleum. Some of the drawers had names on them and some had a small card announcing they were sold but there were a lot of empties and when I walked out back I ran out of markers in the first hundred feet. Not that it wasn't a small town's worth of somebody's ancestors, but there wasn't a single Tarleton.

I might have gone back then, simply gotten into the

car and driven back to where they were waiting for me to turn evidence. Because there didn't seem to be any other place to go. San Jose's industry had raised thick dark clouds boiling under the overcast, everything gray and dirty. In the Valley there were at least orchards and animals. But I found myself wheeling northward instead, toward Altamonte Woods over the hill from Berkeley, past the Claremont and the homes of university professors. Altamonte Woods was a south-facing slope which might have been a vast dairy pasture a dozen years before, but there were clumps of eucalyptus higher than my head shading a winding road with two loops and a switchback where some ornamental maples blushed. Not bad for barren, I thought, and pulled in at a free-standing slab six feet through where all the drawers had names—maybe the marble was just a veneer but it didn't look it, and the plate glass over the list of "Residents" didn't have fingerprints on it.

Tarleton was in something called the Mimosa Glade a little to the right of what looked like a swimming pool on the map but turned out to be a gazebo after I'd left the car and gone on foot up two short steep hills, through a copse of paper birch and around the side of a ravine. There was no trouble finding the gravesite; as soon as I saw the bouquet of red roses I knew. In fact those red flowers on that gray day did more—they hypnotized me, they blinded me to everything else except the name Tarleton chiseled into the marker of polished basalt and underneath Michael, Andrew, Eula Bosham. No dates yet, but there the places were, waiting, and there need be no fear of the common grave.

It was as I was thinking of all the anonymous blood which had drained into the ground that I heard the click of a car door and the fire of a small engine. When I had my first library card I always figured I would be as good as Nancy Drew, but I didn't even see what color car the mystery person drove much less the color of her face. And I had to run my guts out down half a mile of birches even to catch the blush of her tailpipe. An International Orange speck, headed east.

# 13

It's not fashionable but I could write a poem about California back roads. The state is agricultural so the roads wander wherever the farmers do, slick black ribbons cresting psychedelic grasses. There's another thing: aside from detective stories hardly any ordinary person nowadays knows the roads well enough to dummy a trail, so when I saw the flash of pumpkin VW odds on she was headed home. One more thing: knowing the direction it's only a matter of velocity. Even brokewind as I was I could put my wheels at the Sierra fast enough so that only fifteen minutes lapsed before we joined. Basic algebra. So I watched the skim of grasses waving tawny sandy golden, somebody's paradise. And now and then saw them light under tilting sun so an almost sexual flash inside me traveled upward. The mountains were hard and shadowed before the orange bug glinted ahead and I drew quite near to see Angel's flash of nocolor hair next to a dark woman driving before I coasted back to a quarter-mile gap. On the other side of Sacramento they stopped for coffee and I waited in the trucker's lot. The drivers were talking about the new federal regulations on CB and they were pissed. It was four-fifteen when we turned from surface to gravel and the sun was cupped in the antlers of a ponderosa at five thousand feet. The persons—women—in the car had averaged fifty-three miles per hour on the road. Now they tracked down to ten. I waited a dozen minutes before turning off. The sign said: PRIVATE  NO TRES-PASSING  NO HUNTING  BEWARE OF DOG.

The road reminded me of other roads and I bet I would find tennis courts at the far end but the green renter sloshed grumpily through a homemade stream ford, slithering twice to the pit of my stomach on an oblique downhill run. It seemed smart to cut the engine and crawl for a while, damn the brakes. Holding for an instant on a curve I heard the crunch of tires on gravel and then the scream of a bird.

At the bottom there were three choices: Baptist Camp, unmarked, and Fire Road #107. I got out looking for tracks. It had been snowing this high, but most had melted leaving tracks dark and fresh: two sets of tires at least had gone in on the unmarked road. I was standing in the middle of the scrub oak and manzanita of a south-facing saddle in a chain of mountains stretching from the equator to the arctic circle on a road close to twenty miles from the nearest town which was itself a General Store Post Office Gas Station nodule on a vacation highway to Yosemite with night falling.

Somewhere a large bird screeched. It was close to six-thirty.

The wind pushed clouds which bubbled like molten aluminum in the cold cauldron of sky over more lodge-pole pine that I ever wanted to see and the car crawled upslope like one of the larger more cautious insects toward a lens of ponderosa announcing timberline. I drove the road and watched the metalflake green of the car hood glint darker and darker. The sun went down.

The moon was already up and full: she was in Sagittarius. Various searings of cloud raked her disk which was icy pale in the hard dusk, and the road was a nick of red earth under ponderosa rising straight from fresh snow.

About then it became a good idea to stop at the next turnout or wide spot. It was quite dark under the trees and the road had a soft unreliable wallow, as if I had moved onto a different landform. Trees thinned, the road passed along the cofferdam of a well-naturalized piece of water almost a small lake. Across it, lights. But before I got that far I encountered a gate.

The gate keeper was about five nine, very slender and dark with big friendly eyes, perfect teeth, and a holstered Ruger on her right hip. "Hi!" she said, "Can I help you out?" She bent over the side of the car, she put her elbow on the windowsill.

"I'm going to a meeting," I said. I watched her eyebrows rearrange.

"I see. And who are you meeting with?"

I really didn't feel like saying. The evening cold seemed to harden around my shoulders like a cement overcoat. I guess what it meant to the gatekeeper was a dark stare while I wondered (how many times now?) why I had gotten involved, why any of this meant a damn to me. For a blind instant I was in a teenaged nightmare trying to gain admittance to a place where older kids were laughing.

"Meeting with Angel," I gritted out.

"And your name, please?"

"Kat."

She waited a minute longer for me to say something extra and I looked at the fine dark down of her jawline and smiled at her dark eyes. She got the message and went into the hut where part of a shotgun was visible in the light of a butane lamp. I watched her lips move at a hand-held mike. She looked at the ceiling as she spoke as if she needed to unhinge her vision in order to receive sound and I wondered for a moment or two about stepping down hard on the accelerator to take out the pole barrier with the hood but the damned skinned raw pine pole was six inches through at the butt where it articulated to a tall post with steel cable brace and if it came over the hood into the windshield the cat didn't have enough lives. I watched the moon lift into mother of pearl clouds veined darkly with outer space where stars tumbled imperceptibly and you couldn't count on celestial astronauts showing up oftener than every ten thousand years Terran. Then the moon lifted from behind the veils and gauzes of the upper clouds and winked at me, so I winked back.

It must have been ten minutes before she returned and now when she bent smiling she said, "Sorry that took so long—I'm just learning how to use the walkie-talkie. My name's Haydee. They're expecting you at the lodge—follow this drive."

I hit the headlights and watched her face stop being blue and start being yellow as she passed in front to open the pole gate. The way her body moved it looked like she had had some dance, but none of the gravity-centering body arts; her stride was light, almost gangly and yet graceful. Well, she was young, and youth is beauty, they say. Was it perhaps the eyes which tweaked my cynicism, the innocence of the ceiling-ward gaze? Why a gatekeeper at all in this utterly hidden wild spot?

I expected a war council, so I was surprised when I'd parked below the "lodge"—tracking as quietly as possible through frostfilled puddles until I could get a look inside—to find only three people visible. They were strangers: a large woman in overalls who was reading on a sofa, a long-nosed skinny woman in a long skirt throwing coins in the pool of light from an Aladdin lamp with green glass shade, and the woman who opened the door at my knock, whose intelligent eyes hid behind granny glasses. She smiled to show ragged teeth making her mischievous and knowing.

"Hello, Kat. I'm Hope. Angel's still working, but you're just in time for dinner. I'll show you what's available for sleeping and get you some towels. We function as a collective, and when you are settled you can check the work sheets for what you'd like to do." She led through the large room in which the other two women sat but she did not introduce us. Off the main room was a kitchen, set up buffet style for more people than I could tell in a quick glance passing through to another large room with tables filling one end. I heard the faint tap of typewriter keys behind a door almost in the corner but Hope continued straight into the first of three large semi-attached dormitories almost as cold as outside, where here and there cots held rolled sleeping bags or backpacks or toilet kits. This time I counted twelve. Further still, a stone washhouse dribbling icy water from a brass spigot, and toilets with signs: "Our plumbing is ancient and fragile. Please be patient with it."

I didn't tell Hope that what I had was toothbrush and the clothes in which I stood. She looked like that kind of thing didn't happen to her, was probably a sign of moral inferiority. I said, "Thank you," and went to wash for dinner. She grinned again and left while I figured out that the last time I'd seen Hope was in the body of my third grade teacher, the one with freckles on her hands who played the piano during assembly.

So I washed and went back to the dining room but Angel wasn't there. The others were: just back from a hike, red-cheeked, almost raw from the wind. A tube of cocoa butter was passing along with comments and sinewy pauses: something about the map, then a hint of physical difficulties involving scrapes/bruises. Finally a problem was time, being off by an hour—"How glad I was we had the moon." We ate our stew then Hope introduced me then she gave me a tray to take to Angel, pointing to the door behind which the tapping had continued off and on through dinner.

It was a tiny room with a low ceiling and scarcely held the bed. Cold. Angel had her typewriter on a painted vanity with dotted swiss skirt and about a tenth of an acre of stage make-up—eyeshadows, pancakes in an assortment of shades, lipsticks, pencils, brushes. There were half a dozen thick candles stuck to the shelf above, behind them a length of aluminum foil had been taped—a rude reflector which did not save Angel from having to bend to within twelve inches of the keyboard. She perched on the edge of the bed wearing down-filled booties, longjohns, a down jacket, and a ski cap. The light from the open door startled her and she brought her elegant bones upward with once again the blind nuzzling stare I'd so long ago seen at the airport the time she ignored me . . . Then it passed and I liked her just fine, the dry-voiced Girl Of My Dreams.

"I wondered whether you would follow." A smile lit one cheek. I had to set down the tray before my knees went, I mean the breath had gone out of me, sucked to my head which was huge, fragile as a penny balloon. I put the tray on the bed beside her and one end went down, spilling some soup, so I had to pick it up again. She stood, got the top of her typewriter case, clicked together the paper carrier and the carriage and offered it for a table. Then she asked me questions and I answered and watched her nibble her stew.

The simplest way I can explain my feelings is so: Angel was the biggest thing that had ever happened to me. It was scary. Because I knew so much about her, maybe more on a certain level than anybody else ever had. She was this gorgeous woman walking around universally admired and yet knowing her life was as miserably accidental as anyone else's, and she was sitting next to me on the bed asking me what she should do. A couple of cheap remarks crossed my mind and I felt disgusting, dirty and dumb, knowing how much brutality had blunted my energies. I felt like a needy child and that angered me too; because she had enough of a load, she had her own needs. It helped a little to tell her what I'd found out.

"Look," I said. "Things are getting very speedy. I start out signing on for a basic security trip with all that implies about using my head as well as my back and I don't think too much of it when I wind up driving a bunch of boxes three thousand miles and sitting around a swimming pool and visiting my cousin Vincente and my aunts. Out of curiosity I ask about Rachel Stone, just because Tarleton mentions her, and I respect the man. Up to this point it's all under the heading of *Marital Dispute.* Then a funny thing happens: a punch in the nose leads to murder leads to rape and all of a sudden we're talking heroin politics and then I have to confront the fact that in some families you can't identify a single struggle because anything that happens to the ruling class happens to us all."

I watched her bend for another slow bite. Her skin blushed like the south side of an apricot, her hair shone.

"This Rachel Stone Foundation is a ringer," I went on. "I don't think you knew that, and it's even possible your father didn't at first. But Michael T. was a child of the streets and he could smell a connection. He checked on Grandmother and what he got was a front for a transportation system bringing the agricultural product of the north—Burma, Cambodia, Laos—to the south. Some of that product was opium. In the south, the opium was refined. Ethnic Chinese furnished the manpower; a tight and highly profitable operation, just right for the kind of cash dealings involved in purchasing U.S. surplus M-1's and later, M-16's. With which to fight for democracy. Entrepreneurial in the most refined degree, Ricardo would have loved it." I felt dumb again. "Excuse me, I have a big mouth and sometimes I don't think enough about what I say when I'm excited."

She looked up. "Go on." Her voice was very soft.

"Look, we're in a very competitive area when we start talking about heroin, we're into Organization which isn't on anybody's books, it's a loose confederation founded on the principle of greed . . . "

"I know. Everyone knows. Is there something else?" Her tone was flat and at the same time impatient.

"What about this, then?" I reached into my pocket and passed her the golden medallion.

Angel looked but didn't take the coin. "You think I didn't find out what this meant? I knew within a week of receiving it. What it meant was that I was a Stone, that the mother part of me was renounced. It was a warning." Her face was wild and haggard for a moment. "My father's child."

"He knows, then."

"Knows?" She seemed to wake up. "No. I don't think so."

"He thinks he's running a cover for the defense of democracy in southeast Asia?"

"I suppose so. It's a family tradition."

Afterward, I kissed her. The dialogue would probably bore you and anyway who can describe what it feels like to taste another mouth in the presence of desire? She was a great kisser: slow and slightly . . . shy, her juices sweet with cigarettes and wine, her lips soft except where the small scar ridged. I thought about the French doctor, about the smile of scar in my thigh which was youthful folly, but I did not feel alone. We looked at each other and smiled a lot and a couple of times she was quiet, her irises gray volcanoes so I asked her if things were going the way she wanted—feeling dumb but in the presence of her (imagined) greater innocence wanting to let her choose. And I asked her about Julia, because I wanted to know that, too. She came all the way: she wanted it, she said, she wanted to relate this way.

The bed was icy. I was naked and she had on longjohns, but she took them off. She was warm. She insisted on warming me and I said, "Let's just kiss." Her skicap came off and the nocolor hair spilled over my face and the thrill which comes with women quivered upward from its root. Her body had changed again, more angular, with hollows in the hip. I remembered the photographs and felt dirty and had to cling silently for a moment until it passed, and once she threw her arm over her eyes glinting in the flicker of candlewick. I touched her first and there was a little flutter of nerves along the inside of her thighs. I researched, I examined, I *investigated* Angel Stone: moles, dimples, both scars. We said maybe a dozen words, among them: Me: *What happened, Angel?* She: *I don't remember.* Her body was delicious; long legs, beautiful blond *accoutrements.* In the films she seemed finished, doll-like; but this living flesh arranged itself too briefly for any images to form, a tenuous lilac-y breath rising from her skin as she shaped herself in my arms. Over me, her face of a doomed Madonna. I didn't need, I didn't even want anything back but she gave me enough time for the candles to waver crazily so the entire room was the inner chamber of a seashell and I some spasming invertebrate. I would have to say it was not so much what she did, as the slow and thoughtful way she did it.

She fell asleep. I watched her. I fell asleep and dreamed about an owl which couldn't get its beak open so it was making strange muffled hoots but that ended when the eagle screamed. Then I was awake, rigid with heart pounding, eyes wide, lungs vised. The only sound was an almost subliminal whisper of wind in the trees and closer the tick of a clock; I turned carefully to read 2:40. Turned back. I breathed carefully until sleep began to recapture: this time the eagle barked and screamed and hooted, all very very far and only possibly from a single place. In the dream, I fought to get away . . . Then for a while blankness and again the clock, this time 4:15, fully awake. Even so I tried to let slip what I'd heard, feeling the heat of Angel's body along mine and not wanting to move all the while I lost sleep warmth and began to chill. I eased from the bed. She gave a small cry as my weight left, but she did not waken. I put on her longjohns under my levis and turtleneck. I took her down jacket and let myself quietly into the dining room.

There was light in the kitchen and the gatekeeper Haydee was frying herself some eggs. Without the pistol and heavy sweater she seemed young, bony, and correct. She smiled her friendly eyes wide. "Early riser, hunh?"

I felt the side of the coffee pot. "Had a bad dream."

"Oh?" She freed her eggs with a quick twist of the

pan, following them up and easy over. "Shall I leave this on for you?"

"Okay."

While she gathered her toast and buttered it I cracked a couple of eggs into a bowl and when the pan was empty lowered the beaten froth into a pool of melted butter, then swirled it into a plain omelet. I might have guessed the coffee would be Colombian. Then we sat and talked for a minute while I ran my eyes after a flashlight. When I asked, Haydee confirmed the moon had set at the end of her watch. I couldn't see even a kerosene lantern, not that I wanted one. It was still darker outside than in when I looked into the main room. I didn't feel like asking for a flashlight to go out wandering around somebody's back forty looking for anything that made the kind of noises that broke my sleep but it seemed unlikely I'd get any more till I tried to find the source of those desolate screams. When Haydee realized I was going out she looked from the book she was reading—Sayer's *Strong Poison*—asking, "Where are you going?" as if I had told her and she'd forgotten. "Out. To see what dawn looks like in the Sierra." She looked more puzzled than suspicious, which made me feel for a slow wingbeat as if I were so borderline on some advanced compulsion that I would leave a warm woman to go off into the snow chasing dream-sounds . . . but then she couldn't know that, could she? Unless . . . She looked up again as I was half out the door. "Don't get lost," she said with renewed cheerful smile.

I went to the green Stingray and sat for a moment to think. On KCBS San Francisco they were reading famine stats in between football recaps: I wondered how many humans had died while Angel and I danced, how many Last Cries had frozen into icicles of sound piercing my dreams? There was an ad for a resort hotel; the key words were *FEEL YOUNG EXCLUSIVE* and *SERVICE*. I cut the power, left the keys in the ignition.

The snow was like dark dunes, like sand rolling away. There was a brittle crust where yesterday's thaw refroze. I figured eight people out walking around would make a respectable set of tracks, so I did a wide circle to cross them. They headed east into higher timber. I was wearing wellingtons, not much good for walking but at least they kept most of the snow out. It seemed to me I was making enough noise to wake the dead; it was that time when the moon is down, the sun not yet up. They had not made as much of a track as I thought, or this was the wrong trail. The snow turned silver, shadows wet with darkness; the upper parts of ponderosa glowed almost green. My sounds were the only ones, my breathing, the delicate shred of ice crystals under bootsoles.

I walked for an hour and the sun rose and that at least was worth the walk. I crossed a fence. I began to wonder just how far they had gone, and remembering—far less vividly than I would have liked—a mention of time misjudged, I took an extra deep breath and began hiking a little bit faster than I really wanted to. I don't know why. If Haydee believed me she probably had me right now sitting on a large rock meditating, her innocence a large hand pushing my back.

It began as a series of hints: the trail crested and fell into a small valley deeply etched with the shadows of early morning. The trees grew thin. I don't carry a watch but it felt like I had been walking a couple of hours and the sun was in the right place for that too. I found myself stopping and listening. The woods were soundless: a fine clear day when it might go sixty on a south slope and only the chipmunks would know.

Then in the middle of the path a pile of clothes, folded as if by a chambermaid at a businessmen's hotel. That stopped me. For a heartbeat or two I had to ask myself what it was—so dark and rectangular in all this oval vastness—and then even when I had identified the clothes I had to grapple with *whose?* and *why?* A pair of service-issue low-quarters, black; navy-blue windbreaker; some kind of shirt; dacron and polyester trousers, navy. I had a feeling that if I knew who they belonged to I wouldn't want to touch them. The pockets were empty. The mystery person took a medium jacket, medium shirt, medium trousers. The shoes were men's elevens.

About ten yards further down there was blood—a lot. Blood had dripped deep holes into the blue clear snow and was spattered in arcs, there were places where it had been rubbed on and into shapes of crazy accidental mickey mice and elephants and ice cream cones. Straight ahead there was still a lot but getting less the further I went and off to the west there was more and more and more around a hummock of lodge-pole pine and suddenly the victim in a fetal position, cold and stiffening. A nude white male, not very old—say, late twenties, possibly thirty years old. Brown curly hair, a triangular jaw, high cheekbones; somebody's hotrod hero. Now he was dead of hemorrhage and it wasn't hard to see why—there'd been a knife used.

I went where I couldn't see him. His eyes bothered me the most, queerly half open and dull; in one, a speck of snow. I found a bandana in Angel's jacket and returned to put it quickly over his face, then backed off again until I felt all right for a longer look. I realized I had tracked the snow badly but there was nothing I could do. Where there was the most blood I avoided going. The more I saw, the easier it was to guess what he had done, and who he did it to.

I wondered whether Angel was up yet, and hoped not. I wondered whether the women were awake, had they been able to sleep at all. Because they had not done the castration but it had been done. Perhaps they had— the sleep of the just.

I stayed long enough to discover Mr. Medium had been a Marine or liked the jewelry—he had a signet on his right fourth—and that he was lying on a knife, nine-inches of triangular bladed French Chef suitable for turning carrots into coins, a very sharp well-balanced item found in any properly equipped kitchen. From the looks of Mr. Medium Marine it had been . . . too sharp.

So I backtracked to where the blood started in a truncated valley cut with a cliff I didn't even feel like investigating. I threw a stone and it was four seconds before it hit, then three. Gray icemelt surged a deep channel, a thick bending rope of water cold as Mr. Medium. On the bank of the watercourse a stubborn hemlock, cleared of limbs for the first eight feet. It looked like there had been an army in this place, tracks everywhere, from every kind of boot. Here and there the print of his smooth-soled service oxfords.

There was blood everywhere, too, but there was more of it under the hemlock. There was something else about the hemlock: about thirty inches off the ground was a small axed face, the kind you would make to have a flat spot to nail to. It was fresh and oozing sap into a shiny pattern of blood and resin and it had what looked like a very large fence staple—maybe two inches on a leg—pounded far enough you could almost but not quite get your thumb through the loop.

I had to go away from there for a while, too, and sit on a log where sun splashed mocking warmth. Near as I could tell this place was around the mountain from the lodge, perhaps not more than a couple of miles if you were a bird or a scream. Suppose they brought Mr. Medium Victim here yesterday around noon, stripped him and got him settled and attached to the hemlock, gave him a last cigarette and nine inches of sharp steel and his big decision: freeze to death nailed to the tree or bleed to death cutting loose? There were a lot of little decisions, too, like jump over the cliff or jump into the stream, and that last one might have worked to staunch the blood. But Mr. Marine was on the trail when he was born and he wasn't more than a dozen yards off it when he died, even though he had to castrate himself to get there.

As I was wondering what lucky feral bird had come home last night with a sackful of groceries for the kids I heard a low flicker of voices and the crackle of stepped-on twigs. I split. Didn't hang around to see who they were, or how many, though I caught three different voices at least, sound lifting as I tracked above and around. There was a clank of tools, perhaps shovels. I'd left Angel's bandana on the dead man's face but didn't care. I wondered what they would do about the blood. After a while I couldn't hear them any more and angled back to the trail. I began to notice how much my feet hurt.

By the time I got back I was carrying the down jacket, had a bad blister on my left heel and wanted a hot shower more than I had ever imagined. I got Julia. She was in the main room of the lodge and as I entered she looked, smiled her sweetest, and closed the novel she had been reading. When she got up I saw she was in a long tunic and when she led me to the bedroom at the back I could see why; a slight forward tilting of pelvis hinting pregnancy. Angel was gone; typewriter, down booties, candles. The foil had been taken down, the bed made. Julia's leather folder sat primly in the center of a chenille bedspread. She did not sit. She hung her hip on the iron bedstead and stared at the curtains, which were printed with ducks flying upside down and backwards, the sun shining through so they seemed ancient and fragile. I leaned against the bedpost and she began to ask questions in a low, almost patient voice.

"Why did you do this?"

I did not know what she meant. "What do you mean?"

"You are playing dumb. Come here. Leave the work you agreed to do."

"I saw some photographs."

She folded her arms. Nobody'd remembered to wind the clock and it sat dead on the shelf at 7:36, just about the time I found him. "I found something else."

She lifted one hand and used it to pluck her lower lip for a moment. "And?"

There was a knock at the door. Julia went out, I watched the ducks fly back where they were coming from. I thought about the bandana and my stomach asked me to move around and maybe even better far away, but Julia returned so with my gut full of all kinds of sourness and suspicion I listened to what she told me "really, actually happened" to Angel Stone.

"This is a reconstruction," she began. "I have evidence for the primary points." She paused for a long time, as if she could not decide where to begin, and then she gave a little gasp and then she did begin. "She was—for a very short time, perhaps no more than forty-eight hours—kidnapped. She was checked in on her September flight here from New York and two white men who identified themselves as Air Marshals pulled her out of the line for what they called a "routine check." She was carrying some prescription valium on her person but had lost the slip and tried to joke them out of it. They insisted. They took her down some back stairs marked *employees only,* put her in a gray van, and gave her an injection. I saw the puncture bruise."

She was going too fast for my brain. "Wait a minute. When was this?"

"September—the thirteenth, probably; she doesn't remember."

"And she was out here on the seventeenth."

"She has no memory of what happened, and when she woke up she was in the aid station at the airport. The nurse said a couple of men had brought her there after she fainted."

"And that's not possible? Lady, what are you pushing? If that's the kind of evidence you take revenge on you people are not going to be around next Thursday."

"You said you saw the photographs?"

"Yes."

"Well, don't you see, that's when they were made."

That made me shut my eyes and squeeze them tight and when I looked again the ducks still hadn't gotten anywhere. "You're saying she was kidnapped and taken some place under the influence of drugs and photographed with half a dozen assorted unidentified black men and redeposited where she was picked up and she doesn't remember any of it?"

"Scopalomine—one would of course know what was

happening but not remember on waking. Or thorazine in sufficient doses—it would blur the outlines and provide only the most vague memories. Or prelixin. There are half a dozen more you'd recognize perhaps, and a dozen none of us would. Yes, it's quite possible."

I watched her mouth: I'd never seen it tighten quite as now and wasn't sure I wanted to see it that way again.

"There's something else," she continued. "We know where she was taken." And she took another deep breath and began to tell me about a famous Army medical facility and its well-known fourth floor psychiatric facility in the West Building, which was carded *NO ADMITTANCE EXCEPT TO AUTHORIZED PERSONNEL,* where behavior mod was last week's newspaper. "You know they do this, don't you?"

"Maybe." I waited until the sick feeling passed. "What for?"

She shrugged. "Names, dates. Details. Perhaps details to build a case against Angel Stone."

"You think they mean to discredit her?"

Her eyes flamed. "She's a very effective person between them and their goal."

I felt a little queasy and the upside-down birds didn't help. "They?"

Her voice was harsh, abrupt. "I'm crazy, aren't I? A crazy pregnant woman paranoid. You want me to name names. You'd like a political definition, you'd like me to lay out a line."

I shook my head. "I have my own enemies, and they may be the same as Angel's. Have a sister who says either you're a feminist or you're a fascist. What goal?"

"Maintaining power however necessary." Her gaze was direct and clear.

I heard myself sigh. "They probably did find out

whatever they were smart enough to ask, didn't they?"

She turned and gave me a frank stare. "You know . . . the scar?" She blinked. "Not the one on her mouth—the . . . other one."

I could hear my own heart. "That's what it is."

Her lips compressed, she nodded. "Electrode." Her eyebrows winced, straightened, and winced again, like watching a cat pawing a bird. "She's strong, she's coming out of it. At first I thought they had . . . done something to her. I mean, something she would not be able to integrate."

I remembered the French doctor, her talk of cadres and scars. "But now you think she will be all right?"

"She is a little . . . detachcd. Quite often—but less as time goes on."

"The way you see it then, she was held and questioned and . . . and then set up for those photographs and released. Why?"

She gave me a dark look. "Because she was effective. Because they couldn't get ahold of Michael any other way."

My head swirled again. "And according to your recon this was just before his death?"

The ducks looked like great fat brown bees with pointed wings if you slitted your eyes; the room was warm with the sun swinging over to bake the ducks. "When she felt all right to walk they cashed some traveler's checks for her at the aid station at the airport and she went to the apartment again. She found Tarleton. He had been dead for . . . a while."

"Then she flew out here?"

"Yes."

"And you met her at the airport and I was there."

"Yes."

I slitted my eyes further and the ducks turned into

rusted twisted barbs on a wire, and some of them became fence staples with two-inch legs. "And she told you this."

I watched her blink and widen and blink but she came dry-eyed to my gaze. "I found out the same way you did."

I guess Julia wanted to detail it but didn't, her shoulders fell, she took a deep breath and they straightened. Her hand moved around behind her on the bedstead. "So you see Angel needs time."

There was so much I could verify myself I was inclined to go along with her. But: who doesn't? Who doesn't need two or three times as much time as you get? "I'm surprised to hear *mañana* from an *anglo*. What does it mean to you?"

She was back to plucking her lower lip. "I get Angel to a place where she is safe then you come and she moves out. Something about you . . . "

I said, "Look, Julia, let's cut it out, okay? We are talking about the rackets, we are talking about a whole system of control: chemicals as control, money as control, violence as control. I know it's frightening—with a baby in your belly that you want very much—to think about connections, but there's no time to space out. I need to know everything. You know I saw what's out there."

She nodded. "I'd do it for you if I could. I'd tell you what it means. If I knew. It's a process—I'm a witness. Now you know something. You keep saying you want to know what's going on and now you do."

"This? This is what is going on?"

"This is part."

I thought about that as I aimed the Stingray not toward the Valley of the San Joaquin as I had told Julia but toward the nearest East-West Interstate. Angel needed time. Julia needed time. I needed time; only Mr. Medium Marine Victim didn't need time any more, and Tarleton. I thought about it on the Nevada state line, where I made a call through information to my little brother next door who kept plants alive and I asked him how he was and he said they were moving today and I told him to get the money out of my sock and mail it c/o Lenore. I thought in Utah and Colorado in the mountains during a snowstorm when a trucker gave me a bottle of ether to start my engine when I stalled on a grade at five above in a blizzard and I thought through Kansas and Iowa. There was another thing I thought about, too: all the women in Vietnam Brazil Algeria Chile Angola Iran and other places with electrode scars on their genitals.

# 14

Iowa to the City is a run: I made it on two whites and three stops, one at a Howard Johnson's where the food tasted as dragged-out as the waitress looked. The building was ugly and durable and there was an early eight inches of snow outside so to conserve energy only half the lights were on, everything gloomy, cavernous, as if the whole place was an outpost where colonials had gone native at terrible cost to morale. I tried to locate an appetite because the speed burned pinpricks in my peripheral vision becoming rabbits chasing the fenders/hounds chasing rabbits. I stopped in the first place because driving was suddenly like being inside one of those glass globes you shake for a snowstorm and one glance upward produced a face I had to look away from before it spoke. I knew it was the hair prickling drug but a vision is a vision, this one absolutely evil and distinctively the devil. Pretty funny: nothing you learn ever deserts you so now here was my unconscious forming gestalts out of snowflakes. What if god-from-another-star was running a few performance tests on Terran forms, what if I was seeing someone somewhere because I strung my mind out like a set of busted beads and what was left was a lodestone for every alien image? Why did the devil look like Andrew Stone?

It took two hours to make the last thirty-five miles of Pennsylvania and I hit the flats of New Jersey at dawn so dazed I got sucked into traffic and became a commuter. The west side highway was closed, so I rumbled underneath, twice almost broadsided until I remembered how to drive New York. Then I was at Lenore's. It was eight twenty-five; a couple of kids were hitting each other in a doorway and at a bus stop a middle-aged woman and a short dark man were screaming names very loudly while everybody else read the paper. I found a lot and parked at hotel room prices and tried not to step on the broken glass back to Lenore's.

She answered her door in an ancient purple nylon jumpsuit. First she looked surprised then she grinned and gave me a big hug. Sitting down with a cup of coffee, I watched her finish "Tomb of King Tut, Thebes," a three-hundred-and-four-piece puzzle begun at dawn. "Some of my relatives worked for the family. Nice tomb, huh?" Osiris takes the smaller gold-robed king into his arms as Isis turns away and six baboons and many lesser gods watch. "Decadent," I muttered. She giggled. "Do you believe in decadence? Cultures are like people, are born, mature, and decay?"

So I told her what happened. Some bubbled out like a kid with a cut knee and some came arterial and dark but it all came because I'd spent a lot of time thinking those three thousand miles. It came out under the only classification system I use: animal? vegetable? or mineral? and began like this: "You know something? I swear I'm the only person involved in this whole thing who doesn't know about Tarleton . . . "

I told her about the men in the off-the-rack suits, the ones in the golf jackets, the ones with attache cases and photographs. I told about the visits we'd all paid each other including the one in the Sierra where I met Mr. Nameless Statistic and about the talks: me and Julia and Angel and me and Mrs. Tarleton and Mr. Stone and Mrs. Stone the second or third. Then I ran down the paramilitary motif while she nodded a couple of times and mentioned Congress refused to continue funds to the International Police Academy outside D.C., wasn't that good news? When I mentioned heroin Lenore tapped part of Isis's foot with a hard fingernail. "You're saying heroin is a means of controlling rebellion?" "Some say." "What else are they saying?" "That the CIA is involved; the Marines are in to their mustaches." She found part of Isis's hand. She shrugged. "Here, the Feds run their own dealing network out of federal phones. Confiscate heroin Monday, resell Wednesday; everybody in Drug Enforcement and Treasury is on some kind of take."

So I told her about notches and insignia rings and I asked her if she knew about Military Intelligence. "More than I ever wanted to," she answered. Then: "There's hardly anything nicer than a worked puzzle, don't you think? This one appears to be missing three pieces. The little girl downstairs gave it to me. But she said it was all here."

One of the missing pieces was in the tomb's ceiling, one in the gold of Tut's robe, one from the face of a baboon. "Lenore, how did Angel get the scar on her lip?"

"She was mugged. We circulated the description but it was no use, of course."

"What did he look like?"

"Forties, blond, short hair, wind breaker. Anonymous." She smiled. "It was then I realized she needed someone to look out for her. I did it until I couldn't."

"So you really did wish her on me."

Above her head was a poster: *CHARGE THE ENEMY TO THE LAST BREATH. This poster depicts a heroic fighter who, having been seriously wounded in the head in battle against the aggressors, brushes aside medical assistance and, gun in hand, charges the enemy in defense of Chairman Mao and the motherland . . .* I thought about that and Lenore thought about the missing pieces, I guess; anyway she said, "I'm sorry it turned bad on you," and I said, "If I want out what I'm supposed to do is find a replacement, is that it? The monkey's paw?"

She looked at me then began to pull the puzzle apart, piece by piece. "Every front has its guerillas defining perimeters and it's important to understand this activity because the struggle in the center is always the same." She dismantled the baboons quickly. "You know the police have begun to use silhouettes of a young woman for target practice—she is darkhaired. I learned a lot from Angel Stone, and then I didn't learn anything else so I gave her to you."

"What did you learn, Lenore?"

She lifted King Tut in a single section and crumpled him into the box. "I could never understand why her book put people so uptight; I thought everything she said was perfectly obvious. Some was a little gross: those chapter headings, like that graffiti she collected on the west coast: *rapists hang onto your balls.* Then after I was with her I began to understand why she did it and why they feared her."

"And what was that?"

She shrugged. "If I could label I could do it. I keep trying to find and use it myself. What do you call it?"

"Dangerous."

She giggled. "You think women shouldn't get involved?"

I spread my hands. "Hey, not me, Lenore. I ain't askin' for gloves."

All that remained was the left side of the puzzle with Isis smiling. Lenore sat back and looked at her for a while, then began to swing her head one way and the other, cracking her vertebrae. "I have to be at the U.N. Plaza at one."

"Leafletting?"

"No, I got promoted."

"About time. Look, I'm here for a day and I have a lot to do. I need to know a couple of things. That night I met Angel at George's place Tarleton was there with a woman. Red hair, pretty, petite."

"Ah yes, the other woman."

"Really?"

"Her mother was in the movies, married now to a chain-store exec, they have a penthouse on Riverside. I can give you the address . . . here." She handed over her E.A. Poe and I copied onto a matchcover. "You're going to see it through, aren't you. I admire you for that.

"What turned you off?"

She shut the book and placed it back on the shelf; began to dismantle Isis, feet first. "The breakup. One month they were my ideal couple and the next month they were acting . . . " She stopped at the knees.

"They were acting?"

"They acted *crazy*. They began to split apart before my eyes. He got Omega—the redhead—she was half his age and completely neurotic—no slur intended, just thinks she's a witch—and Angel went to bed and hit the bottle."

"And this was March?"

"It was just after the eighth."

"The eighth of March?"

"That's right—International Women's Day."

"You must have had some theories about why they broke up."

"That's why it shook me so. The only explanations I came up with were too strange to believe . . . "

"Oh?"

"Almost as if they'd been . . . given orders."

"Was Tarleton working on the Quantico film?"

"Started last Christmas. That's less than a year ago, right?" All that was left of Isis was her necklace of bright gold and her perfect profile. She had a headband around her brow like a fieldworker.

"So at the point he's three months into the film he and Angel go sour. Any other coincidences?"

"He was always working on some project or another—didn't seem like a coincidence. They had an amazingly settled life in spite of what they did: the first hour she got up she watered her plants, then she sat down at the typewriter: when he was home he always got up first and made breakfast."

"And then suddenly everything was changed."

"Yes."

"Did they fight?"

"Not when I was around, and I was around most of the time."

"This must have put a crimp in their social life, what with Angel on the sauce and Tarleton squiring the redhead."

"People got visits."

"From?"

"The Feds."

"And then you all realized everything was because of the Quantico Project."

"But only Angel's friends were hassled. Not Tarleton's."

"You think he could have been walking both sides of the street?"

She shrugged. "Double agentry? It is never done well, but then one seldom sees it done at all."

We both stared at Isis for a long time.

"Michael always made whatever he was doing seem so *respectable*," Lenore said.

"Maybe that was his *gift*." Lenore lifted Isis's necklace with her nailtip; it divided into two shapes and part of the chin went with. "Sounds paranoid, si?"

Lenore shrugged, propped on elbows, staring at Isis's eye. "I believe there is such a thing as evil."

"You saw the photographs?"

She shook her head, tapped the last piece with her nail, then creased a tiny x in it. "They were bad?"

"I think so."

She picked up the Isis eye and took a close look. "But Michael is dead. Why are they continuing to bother her?"

"Maybe she's part of somebody's caseload."

Her eyes flashed upward, Isis reborn, trying to avoid her Funeral Tasks.

"Was Tarleton an addict, Lenore?"

"You asked me that before."

"Tell me again."

"No. And no again."

"Then why was he working on the Quantico project? Why risk his life to find out what everybody knows already?"

She closed her eyes. The lids were shiny dark and I could see her pupils roam beneath. "He said drugs were what held imperialism together. He said opium was the most valuable cash crop around, that it was fiscal fluidity for a dozen paramilitary feudalistic regimes, that it was part of the economy of the western world, like missiles and B-1 bombers. He said a lot more."

"Yes?"

"Michael Tarleton said intelligence-gathering organizations, law enforcement, and the military contain within them parallel organizations; thus you might find a city cop involved in the interrogation of a drug informer when they're actually both dealing. Or a CIA agent listening to screams when he visits some local foreign chief of police and wondering whether it's someone whose name he put on some list. He said the cycle was based on death: from the peasant family in the hills whose only tax cash it was, to the Air America pilot for whom it was extra cash for a woman and a place to put his feet up. And the arms manufacturer from whom the feudal lord bought guns to enforce tax collection to the worker on the line who built the Mosquito biplane the Rachel Stone Foundation bought, who then went to the gate for the drugs to maintain his workerdom. More?"

"You listened a lot."

"I haven't mentioned the bad stuff."

"Isis never did."

She grinned. "He was a challenging man. He knew he was sexy, he knew about sexual power and he used . . ."

"Like a weapon?"

She drew in a breath. "Tarleton did a lot of things. He made a lot of money he spent just as fast. He was together, he was always swinging up, reaching for the brass ring. Hard to criticize anything he did because he'd run your trip down for you, stand in the middle of the room with his hands on his hips and ask in his vernacular voice, *Didn't I do this? Did I do that?* and verbally force you to your knees: macho. It was his attitude toward rape which finally drove me out into the snow: that he thought rape was only a gratuitous act of *vio-*

*lence*. Nothing personal. An aberration rather than an obsession."

"Ho hum on the revolutionary front."

"I find myself wondering whether he'd have changed if he lived."

"Of course he would—we all do."

"That's why Isis never told the bad part?"

"It's a continuum. We're all just part of the Great DNA."

She giggled. Almost a sob. "Angel's okay?"

Was Angel okay? "That's what Julia says. If she knows. But yeah, five days ago Angel was okay."

She smiled. "What do you think of Julia?"

"I think Julia's one of the sharpest women I ever met in my life, but I don't understand her."

"What don't you understand?"

"She's pregnant."

"She wanted a child. I helped with the arrangements."

"Arrangements?"

"I can't give names but the donor is cabinet rank."

The phone began to ring and when she heard who was on the line, Lenore's voice lowered to restrained enthusiasm. In a few minutes I went down to a deli on the corner for a pair of oranges to go with the bagels and cream cheese in the refrigerator. What kept running through my head was a riff about colonialism of the body: someone, say Hank Kissinger, puts four ejaculations on the market in suitably watered-down doses and suddenly thirty, a hundred, thousands of women who don't want husbands or whose husbands are sterile become host to his child. Would they be able to recognize each other in later years on the basis of the famous "K-gene" variations? Would this not condemn herds of near genius level intelligence to misery in the provinces, running film festivals in which they identified with Dr. Strangelove and the Phantom of the Opera?

In the deli were a white man, a brown man, and a black man. The white man was at the cash register. The brown man was behind the sandwich counter and the black man was lifting a box of groceries onto a little towel pad on his shoulder. So okay, I thought: the division of labor, and women haven't even made it into the shop yet. We're still in ancient Egypt, where the priest slept ceremonially with virgins, where monogamy was for the poor. I remembered the mound-builders of the Mississippi, where one grave held the bodies of ninety young women all killed at the same time, apparently to accompany the burial of a male in his forties. Suppose there never had really been a nuclear family, only a series of changing orientations: first mother, then male protector, then sexual partners, and finally children; each new trip seductive, irresistible. Driven by DNA we formed and reformed like everything else living; the future forever around the corner. There was a cat with folded paws on the back of the meat case and the oranges cost fifty cents apiece. I bought one and started walking toward Eighth.

It was almost noon of a day cut by winds massing distantly north on the oldest rock plate of the continent then lowering grimly through ancient mountain folds to the toys of Manhattan, which creaked and swung invisibly, sun glaring from all glass and clever clean-edged plastics. On Lenore's block, the urine-colored brick beloved of project designers had a snug or at least settled look and also grimy bareness. Many windows had a snake plant or cactus hibernating between glass and blinds, the effect a stilllife computer designed. But that was an illusion; the plants were there because they survived their climate and because of the longing of everyone to look at something living. It was a middle-aging neighborhood where Puerto Rican tenancy was fought block by block, hotel managers succumbing first to the temptations of welfare rents as some new economic gluttony shuddered down to digest another woman onto the rolls. At the corner a highrise was proceeding imperceptibly but the builder had provided a scaled-down painting so you knew what you were in for: twenty-four floors of urine brick. There were police sawhorses along one side of the garden which used to be The Women's House of Detention.

I took the uptown from Sheridan Square to the Bronx Botanical Gardens and walked leaf-winded streets to the apartment building of A. Hoerung, passing one *Comidas Criollas*, one Retail Clerks Local 101 picket line, a hundred mothers with carriage, stroller and/or toddlers. Four radio cruisers passed me. No A. Hoerung listed next to *Piano Lessons Given* and upstairs on the fourth floor the dim opening where an ancient spider woman had waited was locked. I rang its bell, hollow; then tried doors all down the hallway without response except at the far end, a lady just moved in, whose apartment smelt of rubber-base paint.

So I walked downstairs onto the street, where it was sunny and back toward the subway to a Bar & Grill where I ordered cognac and coffee and stared at myself in the mirror behind the bar for half an hour or so.

What if Tarleton had some leverage to use on Andrew Stone, some way to confront him on his (unwitting?) role in trafficking the brown powder . . . what if the Hoerungs were used—maybe for the first time actively—as the stateside connection in a deal arranged by

**215**

Michael T. to prove his case . . . and his mistake was to get Angel involved. Could *anybody* be that naive?

The person in the mirror stared back with an angry frown and I wondered what she was mad about . . . that one more man had dragged his woman into the battle zone . . . that victims of war were still mainly women . . . that the whole greed scenario continued unfeeling, generation after generation? Was the country corrupt, or was it simply ignorant? Trotsky said a true revolutionary must believe that a system which hinders *him* is not accidental. What if he was wrong? Did it after all get down to human nature, were there defects of character, like Shakespeare said? Andrew Stone, for instance, what hairball of guilt and emotional blackmail brought him to my doorway? Did he need fantasies or did he know enough about what really happened to want never to think too hard about it?

By three thirty-five I knew I wanted to see Tarleton's birth certificate but it was too late in the day for that. So then I thought until I remembered I knew a member of the Marines and called the American Red Cross and told them I was Thalassa Surtees, sister of Sergeant Melissa Surtees 543-46-4792, and her father was very sick. The return call clocked in at twenty-four minutes. I give them that; they have organization, even if they don't know what to do with it.

My friend Melly's voice rises when she gets excited: "Who is this—Daddy's been dead ten years." Her southern accent had thickened since we last talked; she must be stationed south.

"Kat, Melly. How the hell are you?"

"Kat—you bitch. I almost died wondering who was calling. Look, I've been saving everything with writing

**216**

on, honey, just like you told. Where you want it sent?"

"All right! Hang onto it: I'll get you an address. Meantime, sister, I have desperate need of some military medical records. Do you have any way of getting to them?"

"I don't, never tried. Maybe. How soon?"

"I wish I'd had 'em two months ago."

"That bad? Well, I'll try."

I gave her names and she gave me her number. She told me she'd just fired top with .38 in the Post competitions, and would be shooting for the Fort in the Southern Tier competitions and I said, "Right on!" I told her I'd left the newspaper and was doing a new thing on the west coast and she begged me to write and tell her, she was bored and lonely, political consciousness was in the stone age at the Fort. *To be a woman is to be a revolutionary,* I said, *Carry it on,* and she said: *Oh, I do, I do.* We got it all into three minutes, so it was economical, too.

By then it was after four so I tried my mother's number. "Where are you?" were her first words; next, "Can you spend Thanksgiving with us?" And then as I explained or tried, I heard her gasp surprise into her stout body. "You mean you're here in the city and it's two days before Thanksgiving and you can't stay *over?*"

"I'm on a job, Mama."

"Working on *holidays?* You can't give them a call?"

"No. Look—I can come up for dinner tonight, okay?"

"Well, of course, and stay here. When did you get in? Did you fly?"

There was lots more, including bad news about the job she'd had since Kennedy: teacher's aide in early learning programs, finally project supervisor. I had to promise to be at the apartment earlier than I really could. She called me by the baby name I made her stop using when I was six years old, which I won't repeat. I told her I was bringing her something and then wondered what the hell I should get—is this called trying to buy off your mother? Finally I explained if I didn't get off the phone I wouldn't be able to come to dinner and that worked. "I only want to see you" were her parting words.

Then I went back to Lenore's and found the address of Tarleton's red-haired woman and the mail: an envelope containing a scrawled message from *hermano*, ten twenties and ten tens, and a letter with no return address consisting of a newsclipping:

San Jose. November 15th: The body of an unidentified man was discovered in the back of an abandoned car by a gas station owner opening for business in downtown San Jose early this morning. The man, a white male in his forties, is described by the County Coroner's Office as having dark blond hair and blue eyes, weight approximately 185, height six feet. "An unusual tattoo on the victim's palm may aid in identification," a spokesman for the office said earlier today. Police theorized the motive for the gunshot killing may have been robbery, as the victim's wallet had been taken.

And in pen: *Tell your friends we can still work it out if they hurry.*

I turned the car in at the Columbus Circle office where the clerk did *not* like what I had done. "Look, you filled in here where it says itinerary—you put *local*. And so you were computed at a local rate. And when you have to recompute that's an additional form—oh, never mind, I'll ring it under *refund.*"

"I didn't know I'd be driving across, believe me," I said. He was a perfect pony, and his voice sounded as if he were halfway into a selling tenor.

"Well, then in that case next time just go for the flat deposit and write d.k. here, see?" He smiled. "That stands for *'don't know.'*"

Outside under the guy on the horse a mother with child accosted me, demanding money: "You're my sister, help me . . ." I wanted to fling her aside and run but I let her go through her whole ugly true rap down to and including the part about the dead baby and gave her a ten. Then I took the bus up Riverside to 96th, where sandstone castles secured vistas of fragile green to cushion the feet of racing afghans whose honey bodies mellowed crisp sunlight somehow eternally impenetrably rich while on the benches early drinkers dabbled their sundown hits at the water's edge, skimming flat pebbles on oily scud. Lenore's note said: *Omega Townend, Penthouse.* It was a building in the middle of the block and there weren't any graffiti in the lobby. There was a brand new intercom and a young woman answered, "Townend Residence" when the doorman announced me. Then he let me through the door.

The last time I pushed a brass button engraved "penthouse" I was in college and everything seemed possible. The person whose parents owned that penthouse was Sandra Shulman, who had a lisp which was almost but not quite an impediment, because nothing really, not even the long narrow skull and unfocused eyes nor the prematurely hunched shoulders nor the titlessness was enough to diminish her wealth, all these attributes being rather what made her so original. No one was surprised when she was hired out of the second half of her senior year to write continuity for a network show anymore than you were surprised a few years later to visit the house of another such friend gone Earth Mother and find her small daughter storing worms in a silver Bergdorf Goodman box. It was the way some things are which you never get because you don't want them. Later, when all desire to try left—even in the middle of cold moonless nights—you realized you could no longer get them even if you finally decided you wanted to. This passed for wisdom until the last bite of the apple, when you realized you never, even desiring, could have gotten what *Thandra Thulman* and the Bergdorf friend hinted.

The elevator whined upward with suck of air through metal walls; it deposited me in a tiny windowless space with dark red carpeting and *verd antique* walls. The door was open and a flash of paisley—the real kind, a shawl—with a brusque intent face/wisp of red hair signaled me in. The place was falling dark, view through the windows leaden, but Omega sat over a tiny cone of light revealing a tarot lay. She had distinctive gold-flecked eyes and she looked like she had grown up a long time ago, about when some of us were learning to tie our shoes. She also looked to be about six months pregnant.

I sat where she indicated in the pink icecreamparlor chair and looked at the cards on the marble tabletop. She was using the Sun as a significator; crossing was the World, above the Ace of Cups, below the nine of swords. Behind was Death, before the Lovers, and then from the bottom the Page of Wands, The Fool (reversed), the High Priestess, The Chariot. We looked for a while and I wondered whether she had drawn that way or set up for me. After we'd stared into each other's eyes and smiled a couple of times she turned the covering card: The Tower. We both stared at that for a while, too, and she reached and found a carved teak box, the kind you used to be able to get for a couple of bucks at any decent junkshop ten years ago and brought out a neatly rolled cylinder. "Thai weed," she said, lighting up and passing. I shook my head. "Makes me get all funny," I told her. She tilted her chin and raised her eyebrows and set the joint in an ashtray, where it stayed.

"You've changed since . . . that night in May at George's," she said.

"You too, Omega."

She thought that over a sec. "The police told me not to talk to anybody about him. They said if somebody would kill Michael they would kill me." She smiled. "They also said my talk might prejudice the testimony of a witness. Also they said they had enough on me to lock me up and throw away the key." She coughed several times and her stomach humped forth the foetus even more plainly. Her cough was loose, phlegmy, and in a moment she pulled out a pack of cigarettes, lighting one up. "They pulled me over at the corner in my mother's Fiat, said I made a wrong turn—shit, I've been driving this block since I was thirteen—and reached by the stickshift: 'You're under arrest and here's the evidence . . . ' He must of had it up his sleeve. Took me in, did a clap test, called me seventeen different kinds of whore."

"Jesus."

She grinned. "Yeah, some pigs. I kept thinking how the scene would all set up with a camera, angles, that sort of thing. Ghastly. I was terrified something would happen to the baby, I didn't know how strong babies

**221**

are. But all they did is question me for a couple of hours and then tell me to keep my mouth shut. Terrible dialogue, *impossible*. I barfed in the ladies' room when they let me go. What do you want to know?"

"Did you tell your . . . parents?"

"My mother? Yeah. She wanted to know what I'd done. I just said they asked me some questions. She didn't understand about Michael then, but she does now. God, that seems like centuries ago."

"When did you last see Michael Tarleton?"

She threw me a sudden look in which every golden eye-fleck flashed and dulled. "September sixth." She puffed smoke. "He was discovered on the twentieth." She coughed again, then rose and went through a doorway to the kitchen. "Want a beer?"

"Why not?"

She came back with a pair, then let them sit unopened collecting little puddles of condensation around the bottoms. "For a while I tried figuring out ways to get the newspapers to write . . . but I could never get anybody interested."

I thought over that on the way down in the elevator. I'd asked her every way I knew how/when she'd last been with Tarleton, and she stood on her story. No, he was not depressed; no, he didn't act different or especially attentive. That might have been easier: instead his death was like snipping a ribbon: one minute the satin stretches before us, the next vanishes in glitter of scissorblades. Omega had driven off to school in her mother's Fiat with the memory of his arms, so securely happy she did not feel need except to dream about him knowing he was hers if not now soon; then a bunch of active days ensued and she got a phone call. So she drove home with mad skill unbelieving: his apartment charred, the body unviewable, no funeral, at least not on the east coast. I got the message: if by some incredible subterfuge Tarleton was alive, he certainly hadn't hipped his Lady.

In the lobby the doorman smiled so nice it popped into my head he might be a good man to talk to, so I ran through my cards until I found the one which read:

Assurance Adjustments, Ltd.
London Toronto New York

. . . a favorite, done in cold type on a letterpress owned by a prof in Madison—not that he knew my friend was making them; she had said when she gave it to me, *Don't you think this promises nicely?* The doorman merely glanced; he knew rag from pasteboard. His chin was sharp and so was his nose and the peak of his cap. He was about two inches taller than me, which was pleasant; I didn't break my neck. It took about half an hour, what with tenants coming home. "This place used to be one of the top ten addresses on the West Side. Don't get me wrong: still a good address, but not the old way. Used to be everything was formal, now maybe I'll put on gloves and a boutonniere for a holiday but the rest of the time . . . maybe some of the younger ones that I've known since they was kids, I'll call 'em by their first names and they'll call me Mister." He talked to me and handled the door and the evening greetings and kept out a dog and passed a food delivery. "You never would have had a delivery through the lobby in the old days, now nobody seems to care. I'm just a guardian, I have a kind of sixth sense about who's right and who ain't, just from the way they act, and it's my job to ask 'em who they're after. I remember the black man, not that he was black, more like a kind of yellow, but he couldn't pass because of his hair was kinky. Blacks are mainly who you watch out for in a building like this; the tenants want to know you're checking all the blacks coming in. I remember him saying to me in the effect of: 'I know you're doin' your job and it's gonna be easy for you to remember me, I'm the man with the camera.' See—he had one of them tv rigs that sets on a guy's shoulder. He said, 'My name's Tarleton.' I never had any trouble recognizing him, wasn't that tragic how he died? *There* was a man who was a credit to his race.''

"Can you remember when was the last time you saw him?"

The radiators began to chime; a black woman with a Saks Fifth shopping bag appeared between the open doors of the elevator, nodded goodnight with a small smile.

"To tell you the truth I can't remember if it was the Friday or the Thursday: I was asking the wife. I was having indigestion and I called to have her make me some soup and she says she got the chicken from an ad in the shopping pages, that's Thursday. For the most part it's healthy work, but the standing gets to my stomach sometimes, y'know?''

"The week before the body was discovered?"

"Nah, this was two weeks before. He come in pretty regular from the middle of April on, then he just seemed to . . . vanish." He leaned back against the radiator. "You investigating on a insurance policy?"

"That's right. Ms. Townend's name is on a large policy, and there have been . . . suggestions that she is involved in political activity, that she is seen with blacks; it's just a check."

"Well, Tarleton was as well-behaved as any of them,

he was no street hood." He bent from the warmth. "In fact it looked to me like a marriage kind of deal—excuse me, I have to know everything that goes on around here and it's pretty plain she's expecting. Health to her."

"Any other black visitors?"

He clamped his lips and shook his head. "Never. Believe me, I would know."

I walked east to Broadway in the dark cold. The Thalia had "Love and Anarchy" back to back with the original cast Brecht-Weill "Threepenny Opera." The Midtown announced "El Ultimo Beso" and "Diablo Inamorato" and the chain had a couple of cop shows. I caught a Broadway bus and watched a youth in the stiff clothes of a Mid-East, maybe Lebanese, exchange student pick his nose and nibble what he found, then I watched the bright windows of a famous delicatessen stuffed with cheeses/sausages and then I watched addicts spectral in darkened doorways. Headlines claimed two hundred thousand workers would be laid off before Christmas and the trees were bare wires scratching the fake brilliance of neon signs: Guitars *IMPORTS-EAST-WEST* Strictly Kosher *EAT* Comidas Criollas *MODE FASHIONS.* The bus was new smelling of plastic and diesel; the ceiling lights flicked everytime the driver braked. I got out where Nedick's used to be, where you could score any hour of day and until two a.m. under fly-specked fluorescent bulbs between orange and yellow tiled walls, come back to sit out the rush with a glass of fresh orange juice or at least a cup of coffee.

It was the block I grew up on. At one time briefly probably two-thirds of the families were one kind of refugee or another from Spain, also there were Batista

**225**

refugee Cubans. Later, Puerto Ricans. Half a block away on Amsterdam the hookers were black, with blond bouffant wigs, and the produce stands sold *ruggola* and potted basil. My parents lived on the south-facing side of the street, third floor and there was a snake plant in the window, among other things.

When I was ringing I remembered I hadn't gotten anything, but then the door opened and I thought: she's getting old but she looks strong. Her hair was almost white but her brows were dark. She was wearing a red white and blue pantsuit and a pair of tennis shoes. She had on a ring I gave her when I was in tenth grade, silver, three dollars in a Greenwich Village tourist spot, and a dishtowel in one hand. She called me the baby name again and gave me a big hug; she was soft and warm. She stood back and took a look at me, turned my face to examine the faint white scar lines on my cheek, but she didn't say anything. I was afraid she was going to cry, more because this was such an awkwardly private moment than from joy or sorrow, yet we made it somehow, backing into the apartment and bumping into each other. She began to tell me the things she had cooked for dinner and how a group of young socialists had voted themselves into office in her local and now they weren't getting the work out and all the older women were disgusted and how my grandmother had a stroke and that her sister (the one in prison under Batista) now had three grandchildren. The toilet flushed in the back of the apartment and pretty soon my father came out and gave me a hug and a kiss on the cheek, apologizing for his whiskers. My father poured a good domestic sherry and sat at the kitchen table while my mother cooked and I made a salad. When my mother asked him to, he got out mats and silverware, wineglasses and napkins. She was very patient with him; she took him step by step and once in the middle of dinner he burst out against women's liberation, calling himself a male chauvinist pig so she spent ten minutes running down exactly what she meant, why it might seem confusing to him, how it wasn't really—until he nodded and said, "I see."

I watched their faces. She had deep parallel marks between her eyebrows and when he shouted she got a faintly puzzled look, as if it took her a moment to understand. Her patience was like a grindstone and I wondered why, how she did it every day. His face colored when angry; he pulled his brows so his eyes widened with uncontainable astonishment. This argument was about abortion. He said, "Fatherhood is a right; a man contributes to the conception of the child, he should have some say in whether it lives or dies." She said, "What if you're too young, don't earn enough to support an extra person, your husband leaves or you don't have a husband?"

I looked at the plants and the pictures on the walls. She had a jade plant I could remember from earliest times; trunk as thick as my bicep, it accounted for almost a quarter of the small front room. Now and then a branch broke of its own weight; these were highly prized gifts to certain women friends who rooted them in damp sand and stood them in the corner of a room to grow big. In the bathroom she started ferns, and when they got too large gave them away to the first person who complimented her on them. I thought about the antagonisms of marriage, the struggle to progress hampered by the biological difference the race manifested: sex organs and all the cultural ramifications proceeding therefrom.

My room was the other side of the bathroom sharing the airshaft but facing east, so there were dish gardens of succulents and cacti with little blownglass birds and bone china snails and interesting twigs and pebbles. My childhood bed looked the same. Corduroy covered; when I was a teenager it wasn't supposed to look like you slept in it. I sat down. I tried to think myself back in the darkness, feeling how correct all the details were: texture of cover, a certain back-of-the-building must-.iness. But there were discrepancies: a different pillow because I'd taken mine to move into the apartment with Nord—I thought about her a long time and then I was sleeping and dreaming.

It was a childhood dream, very clear because it was about my aunt, who took care of me for a month when I was a baby and my mother's health broke working double shifts four years of war and again when I was eleven and she came from Havana for six months, having to do with research into U.S. investment in Cuba. I remember her trying to explain to me the difference between portfolio and direct investment, how sugar speculation robbed the worker before the cane was even cut, how from the hooker on Vedado Beach to the teacher in the government school there was vertical integration of profits for the American businessman. Later, she came with the delegation to the Hotel Miranda but she had aged terribly, a stout gray-haired woman with the teeth at the front of her bottom jaw missing. The change was so final I was at first afraid to envision the cause; later I angrily demanded my mother tell me what she knew. She would only remind me that my aunt had been in prison, she had been interrogated and beaten, interned on the Isle of Pines for two years with bad water and little food during a time when many of the prisoners were dying of typhoid fever, malaria, and meningitis.

My dream is a long plea. I am in the house with her when they come but I'm only eleven years old and unable to speak or make them listen. There are three: a man in a Sidney Greenstreet suit with a brutal smile and two streetpunks haircutted and pressed into uniform. I try to hold them from her and pull them away and hang onto her but nothing works . . . I am waiting outside an office door, perhaps the dentist's, watching patterns in the frosted glass when the screams start to come. At first it seems all right that sounds like those should crawl into my ears as if they devolve from some clean hurt but even then they begin to burn my face so I open the door. A small room, bare dirty-white dabbled all over with color as if a crazed painter machine-gunned the walls with oilcolors . . . Men standing over a table with a bundle of dirty laundry on it, one of them slapping his palm down into screaming spaghetti sauce. While the others join pulling the laundry apart, pounding down into it grinning. The dream flows harmless: the men pull out plates and forks and tuck napkins under their chins and begin to eat from the now exposed pile of spaghetti covering the table; they lick the sauce that spatters them head to foot, they poke their forks into the writhing mass, they pick handfuls from it and pelt each other like mental defectives. One of them vomits in the corner. The floor is of octagonal tiles dirty-white and brown and the room is really a public toilet, urinals along the wall where men glance at each other as they milk the last drop. Now the room is much larger, huge in fact, an enormous floor covered with blanketed mounds or perhaps it is really a beach littered with driftwood or corpses.

I omit the silent scream which comes when I look into the faces of the dead. It differed in one detail from my childhood; the face of my aunt had become the face of Angel Stone.

In the morning my father and I rode the Broadway line together to Fourteenth and he only asked me one question: "Do you know what you're doing?" I answered, "Yes," and wondered what his words meant to him. He said, "You always were different from other girls."

Then I went down to City Hall where it took me until three p.m. to discover that at oh-eight-oh-oh (approx.) on the twentieth of December, 1933, a live male child was born to Eula Bosham, aged sixteen. The father was listed as Stone, Andrew G., aged twenty. They were not married at the time of the birth. The child weighed seven pounds four ounces and was twenty-one inches long; condition: good. Race: Negroe (sic); witnessed by attending physician, etc. etc., Seal of the State of New York. There was a note attached to refer to a court order of June 12, 1946, concerning the legal adoption by William D. Tarleton of Michael Bosham on a *nolo contendere*. I walked for a while in the marble corridors and looked at the faces of people: what familial mysteries were they searching? The older ones were more generous with emotions: tears at a wedding in the clerk's office, the mother sobbing openly onto her child's shoulder; an old man in radiant joy over a slip of green in a windowed envelope. What other incests, other deaths were being celebrated as I walked past gilt cages and catatonic clerks? I found myself outside, staring at but not seeing a line of overcoated picketers, an improvised soupkitchen—two pots, a piece of plywood, a couple of sawhorses. I wondered how it was I was still alive, as stupid as I continued to prove myself to be: and then I realized it was because I continued to find her for them, which made me feel like a death-touch. After California it was cold and the wind cut. Me they didn't have to trap and interrogate; all they had to do was go pop and see where I landed. I didn't realize I was biting my lip until something hurt and I reached up and found blood. There were two phonecalls to make so I went back inside and called Sgt. Melissa Surtees who said that Michael Tarleton was diagnosed having serum hepatitis while hospitalized for a simple fracture of the left ulna. "Somebody didn't clean a needle," Melissa giggled. Then I called Aida.

"Thanksgiving morning, hunh? You must think I own the airlines."

"Isn't there some inviolable ethic? Can't you tell them I'm a former stew for Pacific Air Transport, the Cambodia run, laid off and my mother's on her deathbed?"

"Oh, hit it, honey. Sure, I can say that. Who do you want to be? I've gone blind on names."

"Jane Doe."

"Aw, c'mon, Kat."

"Well, then—Jane Citizen."

"You political types are nuts, y'know that? Susan Owens, that's who you are. Write it on your wrist, I'll see you when you get here. Your flight number is seven ten, departing at oh-eight-five-oh from Kennedy, don't forget to check in!"

"Is this a recorded announcement?"

"Why don't you come see for yourself?"

That evening at the bar Lenore told me she was masturbating a lot and liked the freedom it gave her to be sensitive to her own rhythms but was worried a little because in all her best fantasies she was a passive victim of men with handsome soulless faces. I rode as far as seventy-second with her and talked until two a.m. with my mother about the women's movement; at six she woke me and gave me a slice of sweet roll and a cup of coffee because I wouldn't take an egg; she told me my looks would go if I didn't sleep and eat right and did, finally, cry right at the end when we stood at the door. My father walked me to the corner where I caught a cab for Kennedy.

I had almost an hour to kill after checking in so I got an early edition and ordered cognac next to coffee in the airport bar. The place was phlegmatically busy: doubleknit executives scurrying off to outfit a dozen new wars, all running more or less on their own at the moment . . . Hush Hush on the Women's Page: *Inaugural Gown Design Pondered*. I tried to remember the election, and couldn't. Yet here was the ex-Incumbent, flashing a losing smile from his mountain retreat as he thanks reporters for coming, but no, he can't comment until he has a chance to study the reports. Maybe they should call it the *olds* I was thinking as I watched a man part the doors so they came together in a hard kiss.

Because I was into one of my favorite scandals I scarcely noticed him sit down across from me except to note a dark curly beard, plaid shirt, levis, watchcap: the student uniform. Then he said, "Don't you say hello to people?" right through my paper so I dropped it to see if maybe I knew him behind the hair: he didn't look familiar at all. He had his hand out across the tiny table, a face like an angry Yorkshire pudding; he was short and muscular. What else? Something in any event flashed almost too fast inside my head: *notches*. His eyes were slightly glassy like the ones on the stuffed animals in the Museum of Natural History and I wondered: whites? and decided *reds* and had my hand halfway up to humor him—maybe he couldn't help coming on like a creep—when he tilted his fingers up

232

for the power shake as opposed to a straight clasp and that thing pushed a little circuit again somewhere in my brain, again the flash *notches* . . . Tell your friends we can still get together if they hurry. He was maybe twenty-eight, thirty, his skull seemed to be asymmetrical somehow at the temples, his eyes looked like they were operated by rubberbands and then we were gripping and I knew what was wrong: "This is how they arm-wrassle in Mexico," he said, and locked, and I thought *oh shit,* because he had twice as many muscles as I did and about half an inch and he looked like the type who practiced a lot in front of the mirror. Another part of me didn't want to believe any of it was happening in an airport cocktail lounge, but I got around that because the bastard was not friendly, he said his third thing: "I could take that bottle and cut you up." This made me very tired in my brain so I let my body do what it wanted, which was lift out of my seat and hook his chair rung with my foot and push him over backwards. This made a lot of noise rippling as others scraped chairs and turned at the commotion, but I couldn't get into that because the fucker was hanging onto my hand like he was drowning pulling me over and down with him. Then I thought *if he's got a knife*—so I let my knees catch him in the gut while somebody came close shouting and he pulled a handful of hair from over my right occipit and tried to roll on top of me while I pulled my knee back to give him one in the groin. I think he felt that thought before I had a chance to get into striking position because he let the shouting person, a black airport security guard, pull him to his booted feet.

It was nice to get the crazy off me but I was not reassured by the guard asking, "Did she cut you, man?" In fact I was up and moving out so I could miss the end of that conversation. The guard shouted, "Where you going?" while I was gone or as good as, with half a dozen people between us and my arms shaking off my body looking for a crowd to hide in. Now this was all the more scary because of the publicness, the assumption that an unprovoked attack on a woman was a man being knifed by her, the confusion, the sudden appearance of the pig: it was ripe for a bust, I could feel the potential on my neck as I blended into a phone queue, trying to think of somebody to call, maybe Lenore? watching everybody come and go, making myself a secretary-on-the-way-to-a-Puerto-Rican-Thanksgiving until I got inside the phone booth. My hands shook. I dropped the dime twice before I got it into the hole.

"Lenore? Can you talk a little?"

"Hi. What's up?" Her voice smiled through the wires. I thought about how there had been cycles of wanting her while she said she was not ready, she was directing her life-force elsewhere, and times when she wanted me and I was past desire and preferring friendship.

"I had a run-in with a creep here in the airport lounge and I don't know whether he wanted me or I was a stand-in for his perverto fantasies. I'm afraid he wanted me. Lenore, there's something else going on. Michael took it to the top, didn't he."

"Pa Bell is parked out front today; 'course a lot of people live on this block."

My head pounded.

"You okay?"

"Yeah. But I can't think. Would you help me out?"

"What did he look like?"

"Late twenties, dark beard and curly hair, student-type dress, black paratrooper's boots. Picked a fight with me and all of a sudden there's an airport guard there, blew my mind. I'm here in a phone booth. Tell me what to do, Lenore.''

"He was probably some brain-damaged vet, you know how many of those guys are walking around with plates in their heads. Are you headed west again?''

"Yes. Trying. Do you get afraid, Lenore?''

"Sometimes.''

"Are you afraid right now?''

"Right now I feel brave. Do you have a ticket?''

"Yes. Better than that.''

"Good. Can you change your appearance?''

I looked past the bored face of the next-in-line and saw a gift shop and next to it *Women's Fashions*. "Probably. Okay, that's what I need to know.''

"Watch out the other end of the line, toots.''

"Right.''

I felt lightheaded, but the shaking had stopped: pink plastic curlers in front, one of those little silk scarves tied in a tiny knot under the chin, maybe a cheap plastic raincoat, a Latin cutie.

"You okay?''

"I think so. What time is it?''

"Umm—oh eight oh five. Look—I'm sitting here reading the financial section and there's a column about family foundations—mentions Andrew Stone resigning as Chairman of the Board of Burma Foundation. Is that good news?''

I wondered where Angel was. "Maybe. I better get going. Thanks, Lenore. I love you.''

"I love you too, toots. Get yourself a replacement, okay?''

"Okay, Isis. Keep your eye open.''

"You should talk. Get anonymous, baby.''

"That's chilly.''

"Well then, here's something warm.'' She made me a

kiss which crackled inside my ear like an insect, and I laughed while the next-in-line rapped on the glass and looked mad.

The plane was half full, the air was turbulent over the Rockies and the in-flight movie was another nostalgia-piece. The earplug hurt, also it made me feel vulnerable not to be able to hear what was going on around me, so I watched only the visual and I didn't feel I lost a thing. I thought about the soup kitchen and Alpha Hoerung and incest and pain while half a dozen aging box-office greats made ninety minutes entertainment. Mainly it bored me and I worried about the tinfoil jet and how hard the stews worked to distract the passengers. When the Rockies gleamed below I listened to the red-faced man across the aisle say "O'Rourke" into a barf bag. I tried to get some sleep. L.A. International was fogged in, the pilot said; all connecting flights cancelled. In a joking voice: "There's fifty-two hundred people stranded." I tried to get some sleep.

# 15

The man who answered the door of the house in North Beach had a dusting of beard on terra-cotta cheeks between onyx eyes and lips which turned to a smile over small bright teeth. "Hello, detective-lady." He was the tall deb's boyfriend, and wore a two-tone set with suede inserts in shades of chocolate and midnight blue with a red enamel star in the middle of his beret. "Did you figure everything out yet?"

I kept on wiping my feet on the mat. There had been a bus from the airport, then another bus, a change to the closest stop, and on top of that six blocks, wetter than in New York, but warmer. "You got it, brother."

He had been standing in the doorway, one hand on the knob behind and now he pulled it shut a little, nothing you'd really notice until he pushed it open, stepping back. "Well, come on in, stranger."

There was a strong perfume of ham. One of those foil cutouts printed with a turkey and holding six small bulbs which might have been saved from the twenties was on the mantelpiece, with pine cones and silvered candles on each side, and in the dining room the debutante of my previous visits placed linen napkins.

"Honey, would you please set another place? We have a visitor."

"I don't want to disturb a family celebration," I began. He gave me a cramped smile back like that was his part of the playlet and for an instant he looked just like Tarleton. It was Mrs. T. coming with the ham who saved me: she took a clear hard look after she got the silver platter safely down. "Come in, come in, and close the door," she said. "You'll take Thanksgiving dinner with us, I hope."

She was in black except for her bib-apron, printed with swirls of chrysanthemums. "Thank you, I'd like to very much."

And for a long time we just ate: waldorf salad, ham which someone had homecured so it sliced thin and firm and with it spiced peaches, sweet potatoes, black-eyed peas, cloverleaf rolls, and honey. My feet had been wet but now they felt dry; I'd lost most of the transcontinental drift in my brain except for a ringing as if my skull was a brass bowl being worked on by an arc-welder in bedroom slippers. The deb's name was Caroline and she ate beautifully and like a horse. Everybody had seconds on everything. It was one of those meals which is so good it draws your attention away from conversation—not that we didn't talk about this and that, but there was silence peeking from every shadow and all four corners and its name was Death. Eventually we put ourselves around pecan pie and a little while after that Andrew offered me a cigar which I accepted. On the red and gold band was printed *Hecho en Cuba* and it was mild and sweet as a baby's breath. Caroline declined. Then a while after that the table was clear and we were sitting around it watching each other: there was nothing to do but begin and he did, with a question. "You say you figured it out?"

I could see myself in the mirror over the sideboard; I

could see us all, we were four different alloys of bronze, our faces four different kinds of tragic mask, which is a quality of the eyes more than anything, having to do with the way the flesh around them settles. The fiancee was the smoothest medallion, while on Mrs. Tarleton these silences gathered as the bars of a jail cell—the real kind, not the kind in the joke books—shadow the convict's reverie. Only the brother muscled his thoughts in his face, and mine was mostly tired. I said, "The government didn't kill Michael Tarleton."

"Oh, yeah?" his brother asked. "Who did?"

"I'll get to that. What counts is they think they did. C.C.I. probably thinks it was F.B.I. and *they* more than likely suspect C.I.D."

"And C.I.D.? Who do you think?"

I shook my head for answer. "What one of them did is pick up Angel Stone—probably 'for her own protection'—and work her over until she gave them everything they thought they wanted to know, and when that happened they went looking for Tarleton. Too late. You know blackmail is one of the commonest motives for murder: blackmail for concrete or emotional reasons. And ninety-six percent of homicides occur between people who are related by blood or marriage. How ironic it must have seemed to whatever buttonman they assigned the job to learn he'd come in second." I poured myself another glass of wine and drank half.

Andrew Tarleton stopped stroking his lip. "That the way you see it?"

"What's your theory?"

"She did."

"Why?"

He rubbed his cheek for a moment. "He showed her what it was to be a woman."

I didn't know whether to laugh or to cry but the deb and Mrs. T. solved the problem by letting loose with a couple of deep strong guffaws so I joined the majority. After a moment, Andrew grinned. "Okay, I'll listen."

It got quiet. "He'd been dead damn near a week when whoever-it-was jimmied his door, so all they could do was search then burn the place in case they'd missed what they were after—'cause they didn't find a thing, your brother was two or three times too smart for that. For a long time I thought Michael outsmarted us also, that maybe the dead man was some boozed and needle-weary bozo or even you, Andrew. I'm getting awful old to be such a romantic; I guess it was what I wanted to think. You didn't help much, Mrs. Tarleton, with that funeral rosette on the photo of Michael in his Marine Corps uniform; I knew Andrew had also been in. But when I saw the red roses on the grave and followed a car which led me to Angel I knew it was Michael who died."

We listened to a clock tick for a while.

"I mourn the child, Miss Guerrera. He was a beautiful bright boy. The man was—bitter." Tarleton's mother spoke quietly and we thought about that. "I know who killed my son—I have from the moment I heard. I also know there's no way whatever to do anything. Maybe I can even understand why."

This made Caroline very nervous and in the mirror I watched her long supple fingers tweak her afro as if something raised her hair: when I was a child you said, *A cat walked over my grave.* Mrs. Tarleton continued.

"I like to think he fell in love with her before he realized who her father was, I want to give him that. I was on the east coast and Michael went around with her six, eight months before there was a cause to get me in the room with . . . him. Then . . . " she lowered her head. "I recognized him immediately, of course."

"I couldn't figure that out. I couldn't imagine . . . "

Her eyes swept up. "He didn't recognize me." Her brow knotted, became the angry frown of a proud woman. "I thought, *Fine. Let my boy do what he will.*" She glanced down again. "Maybe it's emancipation for a black man to marry a white woman who is his own sister. I couldn't see it lasting."

"Angel didn't know."

"She didn't know until last March."

"March eighth to be exact. International Woman's Day."

She gave me another of her hard stares.

Andrew shifted abruptly. "It was because he put the arm on the old man, who turned around and told her. This is ancient history. I want you to tell me who hired all these expensive services. What were they after?"

"I think Michael found out so much because he presented himself as a recruit. I think he was still an undergraduate when he first tried to research Andrew Stone, and all he could find out was Stone had a business with a whole lot of foreign offices. Maybe that fact sat in his head during army duty as he watched everybody tooling up for 'Nam. Then the war itself, with all the connections laid bare by greed, and finally you, Andrew—that must have terrified Michael into action."

Andrew looked away. "It was close."

"That's when he met Angel Stone. Maybe it was an accident, maybe not."

Caroline: "It was an extremely competitive relationship."

"I can see there must have been a lot of love and a lot

of hate between them, and not enough communication." I finished the wine. "So he married Angel and suddenly he had a lot of credentials (which probably just angered him more) and so he 'volunteered' and they were forced to trust him with connections. And he just kept volunteering until he knew enough to set up his own route. To that point the whole thing was backgammon. What changed things was we lost the war in southeast Asia, and when the regulars went to Burma to set up their new routes from the Golden Triangle, where the man with the automatic is king, they found all the influence had already been peddled. They would be dealing with new people; they'd lost their vertical integration. Think of it: the capitalist's horror: from the poppy field through the refinery your people run the show, you have quality control and a good idea of output; then it's like a hole opens up and goodbye profit. The junk disappears, you haven't even got an inkling where."

"And my brother did that?" Andrew shook his head. "Come on, woman."

"He did it with the trial batch—less than twenty kilograms they sent through to check the route. Of course they pulled back immediately. It dropped out of sight after the first refining; never even made it to the Chinese ethnic chemists who do the most dangerous step."

"It was still pretty bulky."

"It was probably about seventy percent pure."

"So after they figured out what was going on why didn't they just start dealing with him?"

I gave him the count of ten to wonder why he asked. "You tell me. You're the one with one-half of whatever they were after."

242

Suddenly he and I and Caroline were guffawing. Even the mother smiled. "Film, isn't it?" I finished.

He nodded. "Seven thousand four hundred feet of one hundred twelve white individuals in uniform and civvies trans-shipping brown powder like there was no tomorrow."

"But small chance of making I.D."

"There you go."

"Angel has the names," I said.

"And there you go again! Know where?"

I took the last puff of that fine cigar and set it to die in the ashtray. "I'll need a car."

He seemed buried behind a fresh heap of thoughts. He moved his hand in a circle: "Take Caroline's."

Her eyes flashed briefly and we smiled at each other. "Is the exhaust fixed? Way it sounded last week it was asking the CHP to pull it over and hang one on."

Andrew Tarleton shrugged. "I'll drive you. Where you need to go?" He stood up. "I'm free right now."

"So'm I," said Caroline.

"I'll wash the dishes," said Mrs. T.

I said, "Hillsborough." He nodded and the ACE Electronic van wheeled smoothly inland, to where the Stones were sitting down to what looked like pheasant and wild rice. I wanted to ask who shot the bird but we all knew. They invited us in and offered us dinner and understood when we declined. They suggested brandy which we accepted, so we sat and talked with them while they ate. "Just a very simple meal," said Mrs. Stone. "We wanted our cook Susan to be able to be with her family." Everybody understood everybody else real well, maybe too well. I understood the film "Michael T." and the white-haired man with the vicious golfswing. When I heard the words I didn't even realize it was my own voice, saying to Andrew Stone, "I wish I could destroy you."

Curious, isn't it—the Andrew Stone Company was the penthouse on the whole cardboard edifice of power. Tarleton knew what he had was enough evidence to pull down the Incumbent like that worthy was feet up on a second-floor balcony. He knew, and he tried to tell the world. Quantico was the focal point.

Imagine his surprise when media wouldn't touch it. He—the always and forever before successful "new" black—told to cease and desist. So he goes to Angel, tells her at least some thing about his big discovery . . . or he confronts the aging white man.

Even if Tarleton was not that careless, the AWM had found out—rumor? gossip? the German?—and Somebody whispered into an assassin's ear.

Too late. The rumor was out in the corridors of government, they were saying *here's what Watergate was the tip of, this is the real scandal.* The house of cards fell with the Incumbent still feet up on the balcony with a smile on his face . . .

I kept thinking about Michael and how he must have come to talk with his natural father, every smile and wink seeming a threat—having the film, the birth certificate, the testimony of the mother herself to gig him with.

"You have destroyed me, my dear. I've resigned from the Foundation and am closing all offices of the Company . . . except the Nassau. We are closing our home of twelve years here."

I imagined father sitting across from daughter that day—perhaps only hours before she taxied to Tarleton's place—probably at one of those small French

244

restaurants near Rockefeller's museum, they had *paté* and *coq au vin* while the urgency swelled his brain. What if she said she didn't care? I watched Andrew Stone take apart his pheasant like a drunken surgeon, the knife blade flashing, and saw the flash of that other weapon: a Tarleton exhausted, shaken, wracked by what he'd found and how to deal with it, nodding away a brain-deadening hit while his father lifted and swung. Viciously. In everyone's eyes we all knew: the blue and the brown—even now when he stopped staring at the silver and the wood and the candles—in young Andrew's eyes. His mother had, after all, made him a namesake. Revenge? We all knew, and we understood, I suppose, that anything like this was a blot on one's family: first to abandon a woman and child, then murder . . . His face must have twisted horribly; the mouth which fitted succulent shreds of pheasant and rice between firm lips at *this* celebration was then the mask of a monster Procrustes, fitting us all to his iron whim. The mouth a cruel gash which might crookedly smile or squeeze thin, eyes wise as a bird's.

Dessert was macaroons: "I had this little bit of egg white and I never know what to do with egg white except to throw it out or make macaroons," the man's third or was it fourth wife said. Now he had lost his daughter, at least for a while. While she crept into Julia's warm arms he bit macaroons with carefully tended teeth, while she kissed a woman he sucked coconut shreds from between those teeth, he neatly poked a pinkie to nudge debris, nibbled and swallowed.

My stomach turned. I saw that Andrew Stone would take his lady to Nassau, to a big house overlooking the ocean. I saw him starting an association for retired intelligence officers, to argue their side: commie menace, kooks and queers, junglebunny blacks, lazy panchos; the crazy, deluded, the chiselers, spoiled rich kids—a word for every "deviance." Like a man who knows all will be right, though he may not survive he'd set it straight, by his lights. No one he knew was brave enough to betray him, and ordinary death visits the poor before the rich.

The sun was sliding into the ocean like a sackful of pus when Andrew Tarleton pulled over the hump. It was one of those rides when you don't say anything and worry a lot. The engine had a backfire that scared me sick and something else scared me too, so much I heard my mouth say, "Can you pile on a little more, brother, can you move a little harder?" And feeling bad when he eased the needle higher because of that backfire when the engine choked. Scared because now I knew what Angel had and where it was and that made me the only one. But they thought she knew in spite of the fact that she didn't and all I could hope was that they didn't know where she was. I heard my mouth again: "On the way into town, make a stop, I'll direct you, to pick up this shot-out piece of shit I have; at least it packs a .38." I think he would have argued except there was nothing wrong with him for smarts: looked like most of the brains in the family came from Eula's side. On the radio a woman DJ with a soft bright voice told us it was beautiful in the foothills of the Sierra, sunny and warm under cloudless skies with one of the most spectacular sunsets she'd ever seen . . .

. . . so I thought about that because the other was too ugly and there was nothing to do but get armed and start at Julia's place. I guess we also had a kind of a fight, between the dark dead odor of Ripon's bouillion factory and the savaged vineyards of Fresno: a strange ugly fight which brought us close . . . while the DJ told us motorists were being turned away from the California State University campus until a bomb threat phoned in just after midnight, Thanksgiving morning, had been investigated. He said, "You fell for her just the way he did."

I said, "Oh yeah?"

He said, "That's right. *She's* the connection."

I laughed. "No, my friend. She *broke* the connection. She transcended. Tarleton put it back together."

"And that's *black*mail?" He took the exit braking like melting butter, lights blooming hard large and tired on either side: WELCOME TO THE AGRIBUSINESS CAPITAL OF THE WORLD * TOURIST BUREAU AHEAD.

"He did what he did."

"And I do what I do. I have three prints of that film out, L.A., Detroit, D.C."

"Can I have odds you're infiltrated?"

He was quiet, then grinned. "And you?"

"As you say, first one has to do something."

He laughed then. "That so?"

There were other moments. "Is your mother ready to lose you, too?"

"My mother told me to survive. She also said we were the generation she wanted to raise."

I thought about my mother, her job, plants, her mother, sisters, husband. Sometimes she said to me, "I look at you and I think *I didn't do too bad.*" There was a lemony moonslice tumbling in cotton wool over hard cold mountains beyond the city and a couple of hundred car-crazed juveniles gunning rpms in the shadowed hulks of abandoned gas chances littering the main drag like the teeth of a corpse. There was a black and white every other block, there were crowds at the Bobs and the Wienerschnitzel and the MacDonalds, it was Thanksgiving night. I wondered what my parents had to eat for their dinner, was it turkey?

"What did you find out so far?"

"About agents? That they pick the ugly ones, the ones who don't got what it takes, maybe they're a little slow or they got some kind of hangup in their background, and they turn them into agents."

"Just like that."

"No, no, first they catch'm doing something and then they say 'If you cooperate we won't tell your mama.' And if the punk cooperates pretty soon they say 'We got a job we think you can work on, pays more money,' and sooner or later 'how about you try to crack this one for us, it's got a bonus, if you carry this from A to B, if you plant this on X we can get him, otherwise the bastard's too smart for us, he knows the law.' You follow me?"

"I hear you."

"Eventually they got a baby agent, somebody they know his strengths and weaknesses, and then they can start on bigger setups. Guns, explosives. Somebody to provide the evidence, you see."

"I'm hip."

"I believe you are. Some of the 'evidence' is damn near wore out from being checked in and out of inventory, that's what it amounts to."

Turning onto the dark street of the little house Angel and I occupied among vacant condemned bungalows waiting for the dozer blade, he asked suddenly, "If Michael was your brother and you were me, would you kill that old man?"

"No." Only three of the houses still had lights soft behind curtains.

I turned to the tall soft woman beside me, Caroline. "Would you?"

"No," she admitted.

"Why not?"

"I'm not a killer."

I could see that the front door of our house was open. My gut seized. "Let me out at the corner and go around the block. Looks like we had visitors."

Andrew nodded.

I asked him, "Why didn't you?"

"He was my mother's husband."

I looked for a smile as I slid from the high seat, but there was none.

I skirted the house, coming in through the back yard where the tarantula had its nest under the pomegranate bush. Somewhere about a block away somebody's stereo played Santana, then I heard the ACE van backfire softly. The kitchen door was open, too. All I could think of for a weapon was the tire iron from the bird-limed wagon under the grape arbor, the metal so cold it seemed to stick to my skin, or maybe I was just holding too tight. Strobing in and out was the pointed nose, the upflung chin of the man in the parking lot, and once again I counted his notches *one two three four* slash *six seven eight nine.* Inside the door I listened for about a century to numb silence, then I did the same thing at the living-room arch and the bedrooms. Then I switched on the lights.

Whoever did it had wanted to for a long time, maybe since he was a little boy. What could be broken was, and the plants sat lopsided in puddles of drying earth lik  bombed defoliated jungles. Animal? Vegetable?

Mineral? Is it smaller than a breadbox? I walked through piles of clothing and bedlinens while feathers from the ripped down sleeping bag and pillows lifted like sparrows in front of a hunting housecat. My piece was gone from its hidey-hole. I went to the phone and dialed Julia's number and waited twelve rings before somebody picked it up. I didn't say anything and neither did they. My scalp ticked like a bomb when I set the receiver back.

Then I went back outside and started the big gold wagon and checked the gas and cleaned the windshield like a tourist getting ready for a weekend in the country. I backed out of the drive tapping the brake pedal for the ACE van to follow, and laid rubber toward Julia's garden apartment. On the way I learned a preliminary search had failed to turn up a bomb on campus, the search was continuing.

It was not dark and the door was not open. It looked like everybody else in the place had taken off for the weekend. I said, "Look, friends, we got a door and a window. Which do you want?" He said, "'I better take the door 'cause I don't know the layout." I found a cement frog under an oleander and when I gave him the sign he started pounding on the door "Open up! This is the police!" and I shotput twenty pounds of hard cold concrete through the window of Julia's room and followed holding the tire iron. The room was dark with the door outlined yellow from the hall light and I can't even remember going through but I was in the living room where a couple of very surprised bozos had stopped playing with their knives to try and figure out what the hell . . . ? that looked to take longer than I wanted, and I dropped the one over by Julia—bringing the tire iron down as hard as I could on the hand with the blade in it, hearing the snap of bones and a little squeak, which was all he said as he sagged toward the wall. Then I turned bu Andrew had his boy down, stripping the belt from his trousers with one hand as he held the chump's neck.

"Here." I threw him the roll of electrical tape that was on the table along with a candle, my .38, a pliers, and about forty cigarette butts. "It's what the pros use." I checked them both for guns and wondered why they didn't have any.

Caroline had cut Julia loose.

Her eyes were so big I could have crawled inside but nobody would want to go where she'd just been. At some point her nose had bled; tracks of dark and dirty blood on her upper lip, chin, throat, breasts, and down the front of what had been a rose-colored velvet robe. Now it was a tangle of bad colors against blue-white and lavender. Her nipples were prominent and dark, her abdomen beginning to swell. There were small rais-ed spots like measles or burns on her breasts, also tiny vees swollen purple-dark and a few lines which looked like they'd been inked by somebody with a very steady hand. I closed her robe. She closed her eyes, took a deep breath, and began to cry. Andrew was taping the feet of the one I'd dropped with the tire iron. I said, "I don't want to hear what they sound like, either." When An-drew nodded that one said, "But I won't be able to breathe," and I said: "Too bad."

I went to the bathroom for a washcloth. There was a long-dead butt burned into the top of the wash basin, and somebody who put the toilet seat up hadn't both-ered to flush. I got a clean cloth, rinsed it warm, and went back to wipe Julia's face. She was still on the floor, shuddering and crying silently, tears appearing like transparent beads sliding and dropping; then new

**251**

tears, all utterly silent. I went and looked up Genevieve Perigot and called and got her in; yes, she would come right away.

"I can't believe nobody heard that," said Andrew.

"I screamed," Julia said. "I screamed and nobody came."

"People hear what they want to hear," said Caroline.

The broken-wristed punk with a bear tooth on a thong around his neck was moaning through the tape over his mouth so I walked over, pulled my foot back about six inches, and smiled and he shut up while his forehead beaded. The other one was a few years older, dark straight hair and the vacant lustful gaze of the hyena at the zoo. He squinted his eyes as if he meant to look mean but the tape over his mouth just made him look dumb and I laughed while his face got redder and redder. "Go ahead—have a heart attack. I won't mind."

He started to twist dangerously on the thick carpeting so I left him alone to wear himself out. "Andrew, how come these brass hotdogs have no artillery?"

"Dogfaces, m'am. Spec Three's. Somebody's cheap muscle."

"Or else somebody's slowing down, getting cautious . . ."

"Or the trail is getting too long."

"Help me get them out of here," I said. "Before they make me vomit."

We undid their feet and walked them out to the wagon where he showed me a way to fasten the belt around their ankles and I showed him how to tape their thumbs together and both of us covered them with the blanket in the back seat. From outside the car you could think they were a couple without shame but that was only if you happened to be one of those people who stares into parked cars.

When we got back inside, the doctor was there and Julia was in bed. Andrew slumped into the silver velour and put his hand over his eyes. I went to talk with Julia.

"Where's Angel?"

"At the lodge."

"Who knows that?"

"They made a phonecall . . . I tried not . . . but nobody came . . . " She began to cry again. Dr. Perigot made little sounds and she calmed, closed her eyes, caught her breath like a small child.

"The baby is fine, we have a fine heartbeat," the French woman said.

I thought okay and I called Vincente's mother's house, yes they were in, Thanksgiving evening. I breathed carefully the whole time the neighbor went to call him, ten long lungfuls into my body and my head stopped pounding.

"Vincente."

"Salud! I know who this is."

"Good. I'd like you to open something up for me."

At Vincente's, music began to play, a long slow song about dying. In Julia's living room Andrew sat, rubbed his face, and went to the kitchen. Then there was the sound of water running.

"I need this, Vincente."

"You ask a great deal."

Andrew returned, set the glass on the silver-veined table. The song about dying ended, one about the love of an outlaw for his lady began.

"Dispénseme, ¿ estoy hablando verdaderamente con Vincente, hijo de Emilio y Felicia, mi prima?"

Tarleton followed me toward the university and when we were under the peach trees on the east side of the campus I hit the brake twice and we peeled into a 7-11 store. Behind the window a yonsei tended cash-register while half a dozen students purchased six-packs and wandered off into darkness around the university. I went inside and said my four friendliest words of Japanese to the clerk, and she gave me the key to the pump. Tarleton followed me like I was going to self-destruct . . . into the store, back for the five gallon ration which hardly moved the gastank needle past the halfway mark, again into the store to pay. No Vincente. "Look," I told Andrew. "What you're after is in there: try HERSTORY and the film box first. And if you get so much as two pages out of order . . . "

"I got lots of confidence in you, too, baby," he replied. "Thanks for the loan of the muscle," I said. "You move pretty good," he replied, and that made me grin. "For a woman?" And then we laughed. "Do me a favor," I said. "Get your girl friend's muffler fixed." He stopped laughing and stared. "You're a bitch, you know that?" "You watch who you call bitch, nigger." We laughed but not so hard. We passed a smoke. "Is it true you don't like men?" he asked. "What's it to you?" I said. He raised his eyebrows. "Did you ever . . . " "Yeah. Did you?" His face settled. "What's it to you?"

So we watched the searchlights over the campus while I wondered what Andrew Tarleton would do with the list of names, the film which proved the connections— and was glad I wasn't him, even while I also feared for him in a way I hadn't for his big brother.

"Wait a minute," I said. I could see a pulse strobe over the place you're supposed to have a third eye.

**254**

"Are you attempting to convey a message of importance to me, woman?"

"When they tell you they have a percentage for you, when they say they know you're hip, are you gonna be ready for it?"

His eyelids drooped and the pulse beat and for an instant I thought he was going to gather the front of my jacket and slam me against the door of the wagon until whatever he didn't like shook loose and fell out on the asphalt and then he grinned. "Git 'em, tiger."

Vincente arrived. He was wearing his good clothes. He nodded at Andrew, he nodded at me. He did not say his four friendliest words of any language, he said, "Talk a minute, cousin? *Algunas veces creo que hay demasiado de la ciudad en tu alma; no sabes nada de nuestras cortesías del campo. ¿Dónde estabas cuando pedimos ayuda con nuestras cartas? Pides ayuda y te la dan; pedimos y nos rehusan. También, lo que pides es arriesgado, peligroso . . . Ponga en peligro la comunidad entera si me equivoco. Tu estás envejeciendo en dar tu energía a los anglos. Esta compañía con que tratas va a mascarte como un aperitivo y vas a desaparecer en un trago.*"

"*Vincente, ¿es verdad que todos hombres son hermanos? Este es un hombre con que debes hablar. ¿Esas cartas? Se salieron, ¿no? Sí, me falta ayuda. No para pensar y hacer decisiones . . . pero para llevarlas a cabo, yo no soy diferente que los otros. No me digas a quien debo dar mi energía—tu lo has tenido por tres mil años. No es realístico odiar a los anglos . . . es realístico llevarles presión para que cambien. Esta gente . . . e han tratado exactamente en la manera he sido tratado siempre, y por largo tiempo no comprendi que eso fue lo que supo Tarleton: Que meramente ser una persona*"

*del tercer mundo en el misterio seria bastante de re-
solverlo. Haz tu esto: abre la puerta a este hombre. Voy
a volver.''*

I watched ideas chase themselves around inside
Vincente's Aztec eyes and then he shrugged. "We will
leave the vehicles here." He smiled at Andrew. "You
afraid of loud noises, amigo?"

For a long time after they faded into the orchard toward where the lights of the university blazed, now, and
headlights tracked their nervous searches, I asked
myself questions. Just about the only thing I didn't
know was who hung the paper on the wagon: three warrants totalling eighty-seven bucks. Well, maybe I never
would know the answer to that one. Or maybe I could
get to where Angel was, fast, and find out before somebody else did.

When I had the wagon well out of town I pulled over
and checked my cargo; bear tooth seemed smart enough
to be frightened and he had somehow managed to convey it to his prehensile partner; when I asked if they
wanted to look out the window they shook their heads
and closed their eyes. I left the blanket off anyway.
Then I read the map, the gas tank, and did eighty miles
in seventy minutes, and then ten miles in thirty. The
moon was a remnant sliver going into Pisces and the
birds probably screamed but it was too windy to hear
them—fine with me. There were a lot of things I didn't
want to hear.

Also there were things I didn't want to see, but I did:
at the gate the body of friendly Haydee, ripped almost
in half by the slugs which warned the women in the
lodge they had visitors. There was goose-down and
blood everywhere, even sticking to the completely dead
blue lips. About a hundred yards closer to the stone

lodge on the other side of the cofferdam I met Hope with the schoolteacher's eyes; she'd heard the car. Hope pointed her glasses into the gathering dark around the lodge. "They can stay in there for a month, far as I'm concerned. They're going to get awful damn cold, though. We've got the firewood and the white gas. They've got four walls and a couple cans of tuna."

We listened to the night for a while. "Two of their kennelmates are in the back of the wagon."

"Did yours have a radio?"

"They didn't even have guns. These?"

"Just the cutest little tommy gun. You saw Haydee. And a .45."

We stood around in the snow and got cold. "I don't think they have radios."

Hope grunted. "I wish. Alice is listening on the Zenith, so far nothing."

"These creeps have connections, but they're all unofficial."

Then I worried about Angel and spent a dozen minutes walking around under the hard cold moon, heart pumping, scalp tight until I found her bent over a snow bank. At first I thought she was sculpting a snow man. My skin crawled at what I'd find when I looked into her eyes—had the men gotten to her? And then I saw she was making snowballs, so I asked myself how I would handle her craziness, knowing I meant to stay with her until she was mended new again. Crouched in the snow, Angel clawed handfuls of icy stuff. The breath went out of me at the sounds of her nails shredding icecrystals, then lifting, rubbing her face, her throat, her hands, reaching fresh ice, washing, scouring her wrists, her neck, eyes. I went to her. I touched her shoulder.

The eyes which swiveled up at me were empty enough

to disappear into and never be found again, big enough to contain a whole city of lost souls. "Kat?" she began to shake. "Get me out of here."

The rise, I thought, and the fall of the Staple Gang. Had they but staples enough and time . . .

Other things happened. I wound up driving Angel to a place in the north, where snow was deep and blue white and people laughed as we threw handfuls of powder at each other under a warm yellow sun. In the night I told her, "If you would live with me I would take care of you and you could do your work and never be afraid again." She kissed me. She said things to me: "There is a curse on my house. Mea culpa—there was a day when I thought a choker handmade by the Boston Strangler in his rehab group was an original prize for a charity raffle." And later, "How can you bother? You have your own struggle." Much later: "You frighten me because you make me feel what I know and relive what I have survived. Detectives are genital, clients are cerebral. I must believe that I am free." So I knew it was time to go and I tried to make a joke for us both to remember but all I could think to ask was, "What did George whisper that evening in May?" and she couldn't even remember for a moment but finally she did: "That? He said, *Not bad for a welterweight blond.*" So we did have our laugh together anyway. When she had been welcomed at the place she wanted to go I shook her hand and told her I loved her and asked if she needed Vincente, he was a good head and calm in an emergency and she thanked me *no*. The Angel smile, scar streaking from white teeth creasing tan cheek: "I know they are always out there. I understand that I will die." I wanted to say they had moved on, everything would be okay, *but* the truth was *la luta continua* so I said that and she brought her fist to her heart. That was the last time I saw Angel Stone in the flesh.